Intentional Grounding

An Opposites-Attract Sports Romance

Ella Haines

LIBRA LIBROS LLC

Warning: This book contains content such as explicit language, sexy times, and PTSD. *If you have triggers – please see the Author's Note page or Content Warning at the end for more details.*

This is a work of fiction. Names, characters, places, and incidents are the product of the author's imagination. Any resemblance to actual persons, living or dead, events, or locales is entirely coincidental. It warrants repeating: this is a work of fiction. Made up. Fabricated. Not real. Suspend your disbelief and just enjoy the ride. Some things may be inaccurate. Police procedurals. Medical processes. The mental wanderings of a fictional character. I try to be as accurate as I can during the time of writing: I research, I collaborate, and reach out to professionals. But at the end of the day, this is fiction, so sometimes I need to draw a line and keep getting words on a page. Go with it and just enjoy the story in the spirit it was intended.

www.EllaHaines.com

First edition November 2023

Cover designed by Get Covers

Edited by Des Holton and Imagination Pen Editorial and Markups by Mackenzie

ISBN 978-1-956865-43-1(paperback)

ISBN 978-1-956865-42-4 (eBook)

Published by Libra Libros LLC

Contents

Author's Note About Content Warnings

See list of content/trigger warnings here on my site at www.EllaHaines.com/Triggers

The list is also found at the end of the book through the table of contents

WARNING: will possibly contain plot spoilers by nature of disclosing – proceed as you are comfortable

Blurb

An introverted artist. A renowned athlete and ladies' man. A life-changing plane crash and a nude sketch that reveals a relationship-shifting truth.

*

Mia Garcia would rather deal with paintbrushes than people and is on her way to a life-changing art residency on the East Coast. But when her flight plummets from the sky, it's not just the plane that's sent into a tailspin; her artistic muse disappears as well. In the heart-pounding chaos of the emergency rescue, she shares a life-altering moment with a captivating stranger, leaving her forever haunted by the "what if."

*

Super Bowl MVP, Michael Dillon, never expected a second encounter with the angel from the plane—the one he was told died in the accident. Their reunion unearths not just the shared ordeal of the accident, but the emotional scars they both bear. Michael is torn between the haunting past he longs to leave behind and the present she embodies. In this delicate dance, sparks fly, igniting a connection that defies all logic. After all, what's an introverted artist who hates violent sports doing with an outgoing running back...

*

In the face of their painful histories, will they summon the courage to confront their pasts and unlock the potential of love, or are some wounds truly too deep to heal?

Intentional Grounding is the fourth full-length novel in the
Springfield Spartans series of steamy interconnected (happy
ending) standalones featuring the football players of Springfield,
Massachusetts—a friends-to-lovers, shared-trauma, opposites
attract, professional football romance with plenty of heat and angst.

CHAPTER ONE

August 25, Thursday
Mia

Why hadn't teleportation been invented yet?

Mia's heart fluttered as she sat on the plane to the East Coast, clutching her sketchbook in a death grip. Her leg bounced rapidly as she stared out the small oval window into the inky blackness where the lights of Seattle glittered on the horizon.

The final passengers shouldered through the closing cabin doors and rushed down the narrow aisle, their bags clanging along behind them.

The flight attendants finally sealed the cabin doors.

Mia closed her eyes and rested back against the headrest.

This was it. In just a few hours she'd be starting her new life.

Someone lowered themselves into the first-class seat next to her. By the smell of musk and sawdust and the way he took up the whole seat, including the armrest, it was a dude. A big...nice-smelling dude.

Was he as sexy as he smelled?

Trying to be discreet, Mia raised her head and lifted one eyelid in a squint.

Gods above. The man was a stud.

He was captivating – tall, muscular, with a strong, faintly stubbled jawline. His bald fade haircut was expertly manicured, the edges of his dark hair cut into crisp, straight lines.

How often did he have to go to a barber to maintain that?

No matter – the guy was *fine*.

You don't leave scratches on a Ferrari, you buff those puppies out, and that man was designed to be styled and primped every day of his life.

He smiled as he read something on his phone before tucking it away into his jacket pocket. As if sensing her gaze, the man turned to her with an eyebrow raised under his huge retro-frame sunglasses.

Shit! She was totally staring.

Mia dropped her gaze to her notebook and ran her finger over the embossed amethyst and black tourmaline crystals on the cover. It wasn't as good as the real thing, but maybe the image of those energizing stones would help transfer some calm into her anxious heart.

The roar of the engines vibrated up through her seat and automatically, her hand whipped out to grab onto the armrest, knocking inelegantly against the man's strong fingers.

She grimaced and looked up at him from the side. He was staring at her with a concerned – albeit curious – expression on his handsome face. He slid those sunglasses up, resting them on the top of his head while never breaking eye contact.

"I'm sorry, I'm a nervous flier," Mia blurted out. "My parents died in a plane crash when I was a kid. Something happened on their way back from visiting our family in the Philippines and that was it. Boom. Over."

He gave her a kind, understanding nod. "It's okay. Flying is very safe these days." His voice was deep and soothing.

"That's what everyone says. But I can't help picturing the plane going down in flames."

He smiled and shook his head. "What's your name?"

"Mia. What's yours?"

"Michael."

They shook hands briefly and Mia's skin tingled with the warmth of his touch. She then fidgeted with her seatbelt as the attendants started going over the safety protocols.

Michael clearly didn't need the refresher and kept his attention on her.

"What takes you to Philly?" he asked.

She didn't correct his assumption that philadelphia was her final destination. He didn't want to hear about her connecting flight to Hartford only to end up in Springfield.

Mia pulled her eyes from the safety manual that she had grabbed and was frantically trying to absorb. "There's a chance at an art residency with an amazing mentor. I was accepted to participate in his expo in two months if I meet with him in a couple of days and hand deliver my signed letter of acceptance." Mia rolled her eyes, playfully. "He wants a display of commitment and proof that I'll be there working towards his expo pieces, so," she gave finger quotes, "no out-of-towners."

The flight attendants continued their demonstrations in the aisle and Mia tried, vainly, to focus on them.

However, she could practically feel Michael's warm brown eyes fixed to her face.

Mia turned to look at him and cocked her brow, expectantly. "Yes?"

A bright, white smile bloomed around his dark lips, and Mia's already racing heart gave a stutter.

The plane taxied down the runway and Mia threw her head back against the seat, blindly moving her hand down to check her seatbelt one more time. Two small children across the aisle from Michael started fussing and their mom made shushing noises as the cabin lights dimmed.

Mia squeezed her eyes shut, forcing herself to envision a smooth take-off and landing. If she thought about it hard enough, she might be able to manifest it into existence.

Nothing was going to go wrong.

She could do this.

In just under six hours, she'd be back on land.

Totally safe.

The engine revved louder as they taxied to the edge of the runway.

Holy shit. It was almost happening.

A bubble of hysteria welled up and she was hit with the sudden vision of standing up, yelling that there was no *phalange,* and that she needed to get off the plane. Mia let out a quiet chuckle, which sounded more like a whimper, and tried to stop her leg from nervously bouncing.

Once again, Mia felt Michael's eyes on her.

"I'm sorry. I took something for my nerves and I think it's making me more jittery than anything," she admitted.

Michael chuckled. "No need to apologize. We all have our things."

Yeah, right. Like he was afraid of anything.

But, his calm demeanor helped settle her racing thoughts.

"I'm like the heroine in a romantic comedy. Watch me start oversharing my deepest secrets, only for you to end up being my future boss or something later." Mia flashed him a suspicious look. "You're not Asher Wielde in disguise, right?"

He laughed, his white teeth flashing. She studied his features – strong, almost clean-shaven jaw, deep brown eyes, and muscular frame hiding under that fitted suit.

"Ah, the infamous Asher. I've seen him before. I don't think I could pull that look off," he grinned.

She laughed, her nerves fried. "No, Asher is short, skinny, and has killer locs. Not tall and built like a Greek statue."

Michael's eyebrows shot up in amusement. "Is that your professional artistic opinion?"

"Absolutely. I know these things," she quipped.

Mia tilted her head, studying him with an artist's eye. "So, what do you do, if not secretly run an art empire?"

"I don't know if I should tell you. It's more fun to keep the mystery a bit longer." Sure enough, the man was flashing another blinding smile her way. In fact, the man was all smiles for anyone he looked at. He did, however, lower his sunglasses again.

Mia smiled. He was a bit of a diva. An adorable one, but still.

She noted the way his muscular shoulders filled out his tailored suit.

"Hmm, a bodybuilder," she guessed.

He chuckled. "I do spend a lot of time in the gym."

Mia took a moment to further survey him and noticed faint bruises on his hands. "The suit says business and the muscles say sports. Are you a trainer of some kind?"

He grinned. "Getting warmer."

The guy absolutely peacocked under her needling attention. She had it!

"Oh my gods. You're an influencer, aren't you? Some personal trainer who has a crazy social media following – the next Tony Horton!"

She was giddy with figuring it out. That, or these drugs had her amped.

Not what they were supposed to do, Doc.

He looked surprised and a little confused, then he smiled slowly. "Something like that." His expression held a touch of glee, like her guess wasn't quite right, but he wasn't going to correct her.

The plane started moving again and Mia pressed her head back once more, closing her eyes tight. One arm squeezed the armrest while the other clutched her notebook to her chest.

As the ground dropped out from under them, Mia clenched her jaw, willing her pounding heart to slow. Right on cue, the toddler and baby began wailing. Just when Mia thought she might start screaming too, a large hand covered hers.

Michael. She clung to his fingers for dear life until the plane leveled out in the air. Mia's heart hammered against her ribs with enough force that she thought they might splinter.

"It's okay. I've been on hundreds of flights and never once crashed," he whispered.

Duh.

Even so, it was nice of him to try to calm her down. Somehow, hearing that silly reassurance from him – this kind, solid presence beside her – made Mia feel just a tiny bit calmer. She kept holding his hand, drawing comfort from his strength as the plane continued its bumpy course through the dark, starry sky.

Holy shit, she was flying.

After a few minutes of deep breathing through the panic and trying to drown out the fussing children across from them, Mia felt a gentle tap on her arm.

She opened her eyes to see the flight attendant leaning over Michael with a sympathetic smile. "Can I get you a drink to help calm your nerves, miss?"

Before Mia could respond, the flight attendant's gaze drifted to Michael, her eyes widening slightly.

"Oh! I'm so sorry, I didn't realize...um, hi." Her cheeks flushed as she fumbled over her words. "Can I get you something as well? Warm blanket? A drink? A cover for your eyes?"

Michael gave her a friendly smile, but steered her back toward Mia. "Let's get Mia a glass of water if we can, I think she probably needs it more than me. She's looking a little...no offense...pale." He shot her a wry look and Mia couldn't help but imagine just how awful she actually looked.

She could feel the sweat beading on her forehead.

The flight attendant gave Michael an eager smile, "Please let me know if you need anything at all during the flight."

Michael gave her a polite smile, back. "Thank you, but I'm all set. After Mia's water, maybe you could check on that mother across the aisle, though? I'm sure she could use a hand."

The flight attendant nodded, looking slightly disappointed that she was course-corrected.

Mia looked at him curiously, as the flight attendant walked away. "You know her?"

"Ah, you could say I'm a...familiar face around the airline," he said evasively. "So, tell me more about your art. What kind of project are you thinking of submitting to the expo?"

Oh, art. She should talk about art. Then she wouldn't focus on her ears still feeling so full.

"Um, I've moved into a bit of a sketching phase recently." Mia puffed out a small chuckle, "I actually just came out of a painting chapter." The flight attendant came back and handed her a chilled bottle of water before turning to assist the mother across the way.

Mia smiled her thanks and opened the water as Michael asked, "Sketching? What made you choose that over...something else?"

"I'm not sure. It just felt right. Who knows, maybe I'll be on to pottery next."

"And what does that mean for your art submission piece?"

Mia snickered quietly and banged her notebook against her forehead. "I have no freaking clue. None. Nada. Zip. I have no idea what I'm going to submit." She peeked around the book at the gloriousness of him. "Don't suppose you'd let me sketch you naked and submit that, would you?"

He looked better than the models she had in art school and she was nearly drooling at the thought of portraying all of his sculpted deliciousness in full glory.

Michael tossed his head back in a booming laugh, completely oblivious to the squinted eyes he was drawing throughout the cabin.

A disembodied 'shh' volleyed over the seats.

Whoops.

Michael sobered and cast a warm, jovial look her way. "Somehow, I don't think a naked sketch of some dude on a plane is going to win you a spot with Asher Wielde."

Mia snorted. "You either...one, haven't looked in a mirror. Or two, are insulting my skills. Both of which seem unlikely."

Michael's laugh was much quieter this time, but it still caused their joined seats to rock.

"I'd love to see some of your work," Michael said. "I dabbled in art back in college. These days I find woodworking relaxing, though…" he leaned in, lowering his voice, "that's our little secret." And gave a playful wink.

Mia grinned, intrigued, and handed him the notebook. "Take a look. And feel free to mention me on your platforms."

He chuckled once more and started flipping through the pages. Mia couldn't help herself; she leaned over his shoulder and pointed out various aspects of her sketches – where she messed up, where she perfected a technique, what she hated to sketch, and most importantly, what she loved. As the plane cruised steadily onward, Mia found their conversation pleasantly distracting. Michael's warm presence and curiosity kept Mia's nerves at bay.

She found herself hoping that they could stay in touch after they landed – he really was quite beautiful and she could already see a sculpture of him carving itself in her mind. She was imagining the swell of his muscles and the contours of his dark skin. The longer she looked at him, the more her fingers ached to *create*.

Sketch, paint, sculpt, carve, craft. Whatever. So long as she could continue to stare at him and do so.

She was sharing more than usual about herself as they talked; perhaps it was the dimmed cabin lighting or the inherent intimacy of sharing such close quarters at thirty thousand feet.

"Because Asher is pretty…eccentric, he requires that all of his applicants be living and breathing the New England air," she explained. "Though it doesn't hurt that the art scene in Boston, New York, and DC are thriving. My roommate, Sean, is driving our stuff out now. He's meeting me there."

Michael had poised his sunglasses on his head again as they flipped through her book and now he turned to her with a crease between his brows. "Big risk given that you might not be accepted."

Ouch.

But not wrong.

"Yeah. The first and only true risk of my life." She gave a self-deprecating snort. "Trust me, it wasn't my decision. If it was up to me, I would have played it safe at home and not risk everything just to move across the country and possibly still get denied mentorship. But Sean said I *needed* to. He literally requested a transfer to the Springfield office for work and arranged for a new apartment and everything. I didn't stand a chance." Mia paused, wetting her lips. "My aunt and uncle have never been...warm. Sean's been my only constant."

That was a way to put it.

Michael paused his flipping of the pages to level her with an amused gaze.

Mia, who was now leaning over his shoulder, her upper body in full contact with his, pulled away and felt the burn in her cheeks.

Guess she was inching a little *close*. She could smell the mint in his gum, after all.

"Boyfriend?"

Mia wheezed out a laugh, nudging him with her shoulder. "Oh gods, no. We've been friends forever, that's all."

Michael's forehead wrinkled. "If you say so."

Why did everyone always doubt her when she said that?

"I do," she insisted. "Anyway, as much as I want to vomit being up here in a flying tin can...I'm excited for a fresh start. Maybe I'll even get a pet once I'm settled. I've always wanted a dog."

"I have two dogs back home," Michael said in a tone, warm like crushed velvet. "I worry about them when I'm traveling for work. They're part of the family."

"Life of a jet-setting influencer? What are some of the places you go?"

Michael hesitated. "All over, really. Even Europe sometimes."

A sharp cry pierced through the quiet of the cabin. Mia glanced over to see the toddler across the aisle fussing in her mother's lap.

Michael turned and leaned over the aisle. "Everything okay? Anything we can do to help?"

The flustered mom looked up apologetically. "Oh gosh, I'm so sorry. We're still working on using our inside voices. And I think her ears are bothering her," she said, bouncing the squirming toddler on her knee. Her other baby was asleep in a travel car seat in the chair next to her.

"Don't worry about it," Michael assured her. "Just let me know if you need an extra set of hands. I'm Michael, by the way." He reached across the aisle and offered his hand.

"Mindy. Thank you, I really appreciate that," the woman replied, relief washing over her face. "Isla," she nodded toward the fussing toddler. "And Charles," she nodded at the baby.

As Michael settled back into his seat, Mia blurted out, "It was a bit of the nerves and the prescriptions talking earlier, but I really would love to sketch you."

Heat flooded her cheeks. Apparently, she still had a bit of the nerves and narcotics in her system.

Michael merely tilted his head, as if considering her proposition. "I don't pose much, but if you think it'll help calm your nerves, I'm game. Though, I think I'd be tossed off the plane right now, if I started stripping," he said with an encouraging smile.

No way. They wouldn't throw him off the plane. They'd cheer and give her a standing ovation for inciting such an incident.

Free flights for life...not that she wanted them.

Mia fumbled for her sketchpad, embarrassment mingling with inspiration. As her pencil moved over the page, Michael watched with an intensive curiosity.

She continued sketching him as they talked, comforted by his presence amidst the uneasy rumble of the plane. She'd sketch his face, focusing on the lines of his ear and then turn the page and start detailing his perfect nose. His thick, glorious lips...

Mia didn't realize she was favoring his side of the seat until their shoulders touched...and stayed connected. His presence was the only thing steadying her nerves as the plane drove headlong into another pocket of rough air.

She gasped, her graphite pencil tip skidding in a bold slash across the page.

Was there normally this much turbulence on flights?

Mia leaned back in her seat and tried to steady her breathing, but the plane shuddered again, more violently this time. Her sketchbook slipped from her lap and clattered to the floor as she seized Michael's hand in both of hers.

She grit her teeth as fresh tears sprung to her eyes.

This was a mistake. No job...or chance at a job, was worth this.

Hell, she could get there, prepare shit pieces for the expo and be sent packing.

All for what?

When she pulled The Tower card that morning, she knew there was going to be upheaval in her life. She didn't want to believe it meant it literally!

Michael turned toward her, his handsome features etched with concern. "Hey, look at me," he murmured.

He wrapped his free arm around Mia's shoulders and pulled her against his chest. "We're going to be okay. I promise."

And she felt like she could believe him. Mia pressed her face into his shirt, inhaling his clean, woodsy scent. His rhythmic heartbeat and the heath of his embrace made her feel protected, if only for a moment.

The plane continued to lurch and dip erratically as other passengers began to whisper and groan. The seatbelt sign dinged on. Mia couldn't stop the frightened sobs that began escaping her throat.

Michael held her tighter, whispering reassurances into the silky black of her hair. His composure kept Mia tethered to reality.

"Ladies and gentlemen, we've just turned on the fasten your seatbelt sign. Please return to your seats and ensure your seatbelts are securely fastened. Thank you." The flight attendants were buckling themselves into the seats as well.

Holy shit.

As the turbulence eased, Mia became acutely aware of how closely she was curled into this handsome stranger's arms. She pulled back only slightly, wiping her tear-streaked cheeks.

"I'm so sorry," she said shakily. "Thank you for...for that. Only a few more hours and I'm out of your hair."

Michael offered her a gentle smile. "Don't worry about it. I'm glad I could help."

Mia's heart fluttered unexpectedly as she shyly returned his smile. She settled back into her seat, her body still tingling everywhere they'd touched.

Mia took a few deep breaths to calm her racing heart. Though the worst of the turbulence had passed, she still felt unsettled.

Michael studied her, concern in his dark brown eyes. "Hey. Talk to me," he gently urged. "You're not bothering me. That was sketchy, even for me." Michael bent to retrieve her sketchbook and pencil from the floor, then sat back up, handing them to her.

Mia avoided eye contact and fiddled with them in her lap.

Sure, he didn't think she was annoying now. Several more hours of this and he was going to be begging for coach just to get away from her.

"I just...I feel stupid, freaking out like that. I was acting worse than little Isla over there." Mia looked over to where Mindy was softly cooing to the kids.

"Don't be so hard on yourself," Michael replied. "Fear isn't logical. You have nothing to be embarrassed about."

His sincerity made Mia's cheeks flush. She tentatively met his gaze again.

Michael shrugged, "Plus, what can I say, I'm a sucker for a damsel in distress."

Mia laughed softly, his lighthearted joke easing the tension in her shoulders. She studied the intricate lines of Michael's face, wanting to capture them on paper.

"So, woodworking, huh?" she said, recalling their conversation from earlier. "That's an unusual hobby for a fitness nut."

Michael laughed. "I find it relaxing. I also try sketching, some metalworking...I don't know. Anything really. Working with my hands helps me...process things, I guess."

Mia nodded thoughtfully. "I feel the same way about my art. And swimming. It's like therapy."

"I feel that. I was just in Seattle for a woodworking expo and it was incredible. Soul cleansing for me. Some of the things that people can do nowadays...it's incredible. I enjoy my own version of art, but I'm not art-exhibition-candidate caliber." He tipped an imaginary hat to her. "I get by but just from looking at your work here on the bumpy plane...I'm peanuts compared to your skill level."

Mia felt the blush burn her cheeks and she looked down at her sketchbook, wiping some imaginary dust away from the page.

Mia's nerves began to settle as she chatted with Michael. His solid presence and dry humor made her feel at ease.

Sure, it was a red eye flight and they *technically* should be sleeping.

But what was the saying?

They could sleep when they're dead.

For now...she had a god to memorialize in her sketch pad.

Or she might wake up one day and wonder if he had even existed.

CHAPTER TWO

August 25, Thursday
Mia

Another bumpy hour later, Michael begged to break his pose "Okay, I give. I need something to do. You've been silent for twenty minutes and I need something to do other than stare at the seat in front of me or make silly faces at Isla across the way. Just let me grab a magazine or something. I promise I'll go right back to letting you sketch my oh-so-gorgeous hand."

Stifling a laugh into the back of her hand, Mia lowered her pencil and leveled him with a mocking, but oh so serious look. "You have twelve seconds. Find something to read, *fast*."

"Thanks, Angel." Chuckling deeply, he slid his arm from the armrest, where Mia had positioned it for a closer look, and bent down to pull a magazine out from his backpack. Its cover was painted with a logo that resembled a helmet from some Persian warrior movie, or something along those lines. Mia avoided anything with violence like the plague – violence made her nauseous.

What didn't make her nauseous?

Come to think of it? Being called *Angel*, in that deep, sexy voice of his.

That made her feel something else entirely.

And those sexy as sin smiles? She'd bet anything he was a Gemini. A charming, dual-natured, Gemini. Classic.

As Micheal worked on getting comfortable, Mia stole a quick glance out the window, swallowing hard at the dark night beyond the glare of the window. Her pale and ghostly form reflected back at her in the dimly lit cabin. A sudden drop in temperature and the hair on her arms stretched tight. Goosebumps tickled her skin.

Ohh, maybe there was a spirit here. The tantalizing thought pulled her away from the window and back to Michael eager to ask about his hometown, Massachusetts, lore.

He was resting back in his seat, reading an article with one hand while letting his other resume its position on the armrest where Mia and positioned him earlier while trying to get his wrist contouring just right.

"Have you been on any of the ghost tours in Salem? One of my friends back home said that the tours there are phenomenal and that I," she utilized her air quotes again, "'can't *not* go' once I'm there. She actually bought me my first tarot card set years ago. And she got me hooked on improv dancing..."

Mia's voice faltered as Michael swung towards her, his eyebrows shooting up in stark disbelief. His eyes bore into her with a mix of humor and incredulousness.

She froze under his scrutiny. She jolted when he started laughing loudly, only quieting when a bald businessman down a row or two turned his head in Michael's direction and glared while peeking out from under his eye mask.

Mia shrunk in her seat to avoid the man's scowl.

"You've been dead-ass silent for twenty minutes and the second I find something to do, *now* you want to pick up a conversation again?"

Well, when he put it like that. Mia felt heat bloom in her cheeks.

Michael was consumed by another wave of laughter, though at least this time he had the decency to cackle into his palm. Luckily, Michael looked absolutely delighted by her awkwardness rather than irritated at her ill-timed inspiration for conversation.

"Uh, yeah. Sorry about that."

What else could she say?

Michael moved his art inspiration arm to rub at his face. He then cast her an adorably entertained look.

"I've never been into ghost stories or anything to do with the occult – but I can ask a friend and see if they have any suggestions on the best tours to go on." After she nodded her approval, Michael dug into his pocket, pulled out his phone, and shot off a text message. "I'll let you know what she says."

"Oh, thank you. That's...thank you."

He shrugged his thick shoulders and the nice suit jacket looked like it was ready to rip. Even expertly tailored suits could only handle so much muscle and the guy was packing.

"She's always trying to tell me to burn sage because she senses a darkness around me but she's kind of a nut. I try not to take her too seriously... Well, we all try, but Lexie can be...challenging."

Lexie. A girlfriend? Could she ask?

Scratch that, there were more pressing matters.

"A darkness? Are you okay?" Mia adjusted in her seat to better face him so that she could try to get a sense of his aura. Maybe that was the presence she felt a second ago. "I might have some selenite in my backpack if you want some." She kept looking at him to see if something felt off. Michael gave her a funny look but otherwise didn't seem concerned with what he shared.

"What? Yeah, no. I'm fine. No selenite is necessary."

He said the word slowly like he'd never heard of it before. Amateur.

Though his facial expressions were adorable. She was tempted to suggest some other methods just to see his reaction.

"I just figured she'd have the drop on some good tours for you to go on. Hopefully, she'll get back to me soon and I can let you know."

The plane jerked and Mia pressed back into the seat, eyes squeezed shut.

Deep breaths. In and out.

Faintly, she heard the seatbelt sign ding on again in reminder, and baby Charles across the row started fussing once more, too.

"Hey, stick with me here. No panic attacks allowed in tin cans thousands of miles in the air, okay? How about you keep sketching and we keep talking?"

Mia slowly opened her eyes and forced herself to reopen her sketchbook. She took some deep breaths before repositioning her pencil on the page. Mia focused on capturing the striking features of his face – his strong jawline, his full lips, and those piercing dark eyes that seemed to hold a hundred stories. He was like Derek Morgan come to life...what she wouldn't give to hear him call her 'baby girl' just one time.

"So, you're into art, rocks, ghosts, and apparently tarot. Your friend got you your first set? You have more than one? Is it like pokémon and you can just collect them? I clearly know nothing about this." He grinned mischievously at her and she immediately wished she had a canvas so she could paint him.

The way he repeated her words back to her in his slow, controlled way slowed her racing heart and allowed her to focus a bit more.

Ah, her tarot cards. Her lovely little decks.

It was obvious he didn't put any stock in it, but it was sweet he was asking to try to center her.

"You don't need more than one, but I like looking at pretty things. And my current favorite is a set that has a colorful pastel dreamscape vibe with a holographic background. It has gold foil illustrations on each card and it. is. gorgeous." She sighed, dreamily. "It brings me joy."

Michael gave a low chuckle. "Sounds pretty." He paused and then added, as he watched her pencil rub over the sketchpad, "I also have something that is shiny and pretty at home. It doesn't do much for me, but it does bring me joy to look at it."

"A picture?" She asked as she chewed on her lip and tried to get the scar on his left pointer finger *just right.*

Michael fidgeted and cleared his throat quietly. "Nah, a ring. Gaudy thing. I don't like wearing it. But it reminds me of...happiness, I guess."

Mia paused, going draft-paper pale as mortification washed through her and Michael's face grew concerned.

"Oh...oh, gods. I'm sorry. I...I should have figured you were married.I'm so sorry.

Michael's lips turned up in a failed attempt at hiding a smile. He cocked his head and looked like he was going to say something so she rushed to finish her apology.

"And here I was...flirting with you like some...some trollop!" Mia leaned away, horrified at her behavior. She was basically hanging all over the guy. And giving him compliments like they were candy!

Michael cocked his head and pulled his sunglasses off his head to slide them in his jacket pocket, all the while, not breaking eye contact. "*That* was you *flirting*?"

He didn't need to sound so surprised.

Mia pursed her lips and narrowed her eyes on him.

"Well, not really? I don't really...*flirt*." She felt like she was going to have a stroke. Right then and there. She heard once when people die on planes, the attendants just put eye masks on the person and cover them with a blanket so as not to disturb the other passengers until they landed.

That was going to be her. Dead in the seat from a heart attack. Her embarrassment causing her body to give out. Boom. Dead as a doornail.

"So...you weren't flirting?" Michael gave her an amused look as he watched her bumble through her explanation.

"I, uh...."

The plane jerked again and the combined wails of the children across the way saved her from having to answer.

"Well," Michael began, turning away from the kids who had grabbed his attention for a moment and back to Mia, grinning mischievously, "If it was flirting...it was certainly subtle and not as forward as most of the girls I meet. If it was just you being friendly...then that's good, too. Either way, I feel like I should clarify...I'm not married." When Mia opened her mouth, he spoke faster. "Also not engaged. And also not otherwise committed. Okay, Angel?"

"Why are you calling me that?"

He nodded down to the wing tattoos on her wrists. "You have wings, plus you're gorgeous and sweet—hence...Angel. Though, I've never heard of an angel who was afraid of flying." He cocked a dark eyebrow at her and she curled her toes.

"That's me. The unicorn of angels. One of a kind."

Michael didn't react to her self-deprecating tease. Instead, he just stared at her, taking her in.

Time for a topic change. His undivided attention wasn't helping her nerves, and she was already a hot mess.

"Any tips for surviving the winters over on the East Coast?" she inquired as she turned back to her sketch and furiously shaded the contours of his face, striving to capture his charm.

"Bundle up and embrace the snow," Michael advised, winking at her. "Oh, and find someone who knows how to shovel."

"Good to know," Mia chuckled, her heart fluttering at their easy banter. "Thanks for trying to keep me distracted, Michael," she murmured, her voice filled with genuine gratitude.

"Always happy to help a fellow traveler," he replied softly, his eyes meeting hers with a tender gaze that sent shivers down her spine.

Time seemed to lose all meaning as Mia and Michael chatted intermittently between her sketching sessions. Her earlier drawings had been tentative, but now she was hard at work on a new piece, fighting a yawn as she experimented with colored pencils to find the perfect combination of hues to match his dark skin.

"You really should get some sleep," Michael teased her, clearly amused by her dedication to her art and obvious sleepiness.

"Are you sleeping?" she countered playfully.

"Touché," he chuckled, his deep voice resonating in her chest. "I'm not tired."

Just as Mia's hands were deftly applying the finishing touches to her latest portrait, the aircraft jolted abruptly. Overhead compartments rattled and fellow passengers were startled awake as turbulence gripped the plane. Panic surged through her, and she clutched at the armrests, her knuckles turning white.

"Hey, it's going to be okay," Michael reassured her, his calm demeanor standing out against the mounting unease of the other passengers. "Turbulence is normal and the pilots know what they're doing."

Mia nodded, trying to draw courage from his words, though her heart continued to race. She forced herself to take slow, deep breaths, focusing her thoughts on the comforting weight of Michael's presence beside her.

"Here, why don't you hold onto this?" he suggested, gently prying the colored pencil from her trembling fingers, and placing it in her other hand. "Sometimes having something familiar to focus on can help. And now you can use this hand," he grabbed the hand closest to him. "To hold onto me."

"Thank you," she whispered, her eyes brimming with gratitude as she clutched the pencil, and then his hand like a lifeline. As the aircraft continued to shudder, Mia fought to keep her panic at bay, reminding herself that if Michael had faith in their safety, then perhaps she could too.

The turbulence intensified, shaking the plane violently and sending Mia's heart into overdrive. With a sudden, gut-wrenching jolt, unsecured objects and passengers were bumped around the cabin. Overhead lights flickered and dimmed, casting eerie shadows on the faces of the terrified passengers.

"Please remain seated with your seatbelts fastened," the flight attendant announced through the overhead speakers, her voice barely audible over the frightened murmurs and sobbing children. "If you have any personal items out, please stow them in the overhead compartments or under the seat in front of you."

"Shit," muttered Michael, his brow furrowing as he gripped the armrests tightly. He turned suddenly to Mindy across the way and started asking her what she needed. He loosened his belt enough to reach out and throw up the tray that Isla had been coloring on. The girl was already crying, so the loss of her coloring table didn't register.

As panic spread like wildfire through the cabin, oxygen masks dropped from above, swaying gently in contrast to the tumultuous bouncing of the plane.

"Ladies and gentlemen, we have a change in cabin pressure. Oxygen masks have been released from the overhead compartments. Pull the mask down to start the flow of oxygen. Place the mask over your nose and mouth, secure it with the elastic band, and breathe normally. Be sure to put your mask on first before helping others. Please remain seated and keep your seatbelt fastened until further notice. Thank you for your attention."

Mia's breath hitched, coming rapidly and shallow, as she stared at the mask dangling before her. Her sketchbook had slipped from her lap and was forgotten as her chest tightened with fear.

Michael turned to Mia, whose hands were shaking so violently that she couldn't manage to put on her own mask. He tenderly pushed her trembling fingers away and slid the mask over her face, making sure it was secure. "Breathe," he instructed as he stared deep into her panicked eyes.

"Uhm, okay," she stammered. The thin elastic band pressed against her cheeks, a strange reassurance amidst the chaos.

"Good girl," Michael said softly, donning his own mask and taking deep breaths.

He helped her first. He didn't listen to instructions very well.

As the plane continued to be tossed around, Mia closed her eyes tight.

Was this really the end?

Was she destined to meet the same fate as her parents, perishing in a plane?

She glanced over at Michael, who somehow still managed to exude confidence even in the face of danger.

She wished they had met under different circumstances – ones where they could explore the magnetic attraction between them, instead of being brought together by disaster.

Ah, who was she kidding? She'd never have connected with someone like Michael if she hadn't been seated next to him for hours on a plane. She never would have had the courage to strike up a conversation. Fate had given her a chance to bask in the genial glow that followed him and she should be thankful for that – otherwise, she never would have met him.

"You're doing great," he reassured her, his voice muffled behind his mask but still clear enough to convey warmth and support. "Just keep breathing." He turned to check on Mindy and the kids again.

"Thanks," Mia managed to choke out to his back, her thoughts a whirlwind of fear and gratitude. She felt as if her very survival was tethered to his presence, drawing strength from him in a way she never imagined possible.

As turbulence continued to batter the aircraft, Mia clung desperately to Michael's hand and the hope that somehow, they would make it through this nightmare alive.

The captain's voice crackled over the intercom, slicing through the chaos. "Ladies and gentlemen, we are experiencing an unexpected failure of some of our mechanical and electrical components. We'll be making an emergency landing as soon as possible. Given our location above Lake Michigan, it will be a water landing. Please remain calm and follow the instructions provided by the cabin crew."

Mia's heart pounded in her chest, the blood roaring in her ears. In one hand, she gripped her right armrest, nails digging into the upholstery, as fear threatened to swallow her whole.

"Stay with me, Mia," Michael said, his steady gaze never leaving hers. He reached for the emergency exit instructions attached to the seat in front of him, his movements deliberate and focused. There was something about his unwavering composure that kept her from spiraling into a full-blown panic. The flight attendants started talking on the speakers, barely audible over the roar of the passengers.

After he studied the instructions intently, Michael reached under their seats and pulled out two uninflated life jackets. He handed one to Mia, quickly pulling off her mask and guiding it over her head with delicate but firm hands. When he slid her mask back on, she tried to take a deep breath, but her lungs refused to cooperate.

"Thank you," she whispered, her voice barely audible.

With a reassuring nod, Michael removed his mask, donned his own vest and then unbuckled his seatbelt. As he stood and stabilized himself on the seat backs with his arms outstretched, Mia felt as if the oxygen had been sucked out of the cabin, her lungs constricting in terror. But as she watched him reach under Mindy's seat across the aisle and retrieve life jackets for her and her squirming toddler, a wave of awe washed over her.

Wow.

This guy.

Was he military? Was that why he seemed so entertained at her guesses? He really wasn't a personal trainer at all but really some branch of the military?

The bucking of the cabin didn't make it easy for Michael. Mia held her breath, hoping he wouldn't be tossed against the ceiling to break his foolish, hero-complex neck.

Distantly, Mia was aware of the flight attendants shouting over the clatter, ordering Michael back into his seat.

Michael secured the life jackets around the mother and toddler. Mindy was starting to panic, trying to keep both the toddler and the baby in her arms as the plane started a rapid descent.

"I can take one." Michael's deep voice traveled to Mia under the screams, cries, and prayers bouncing around the cabin. "Trust me, please. I'll take one."

Mia leaned over and watched Mindy make the hardest decision of her life.

Mia's heart broke from watching the devastation in the mother's eyes as she hesitated and then pushed her toddler toward Michael's waiting arms. The little girl's screams rioted over the chaos and Mindy had tears streaming down her face as she pried her daughter's fingers off her arms. Mindy closed her eyes tight as she pushed her daughter into the arms of a stranger.

Gods.

Michael didn't waste any time in returning to his own seat and buckling up once more, this time with a frantic toddler in his lap. He lowered his mask over the little girl's face and held her close, rocking her tightly against his chest.

As Michael turned to Mia, she found herself caught in the intensity of his gaze, her fingers itching to capture on paper the tenderness and strength she saw there. How could a stranger come to mean so much to her in the brief time they'd known each other?

He took in Mia's tear-stained face. "Okay?"

Not even a little bit.

Swallowing hard, she managed a shaky nod. "I'm okay," she lied.

"Good," Michael replied, his voice a balm against her frayed nerves. "We're going to get through this. Just take it one breath at a time."

As the plane began a steeper, more violent descent, Mia clung to Michael's words like a lifeline. And while she knew there were no guarantees in a situation like this, somehow, having him by her side made everything feel a little less terrifying.

She'd never felt more inspired and couldn't help but find humor in the fact that her desire for art was calming her even as their plane was, quite literally, crashing.

"Hey," Michael said softly, his eyes catching hers. "Just breathe, okay? We're gonna get through this."

Mia nodded, forcing a shaky smile. "Yeah. Breathing. I can do that." She tried to steady her nerves, focusing instead on the planes of his face, the angle of his jaw, the curve of his lips. She knew she would remember him...her angel...forever.

As the pilot came on the speaker and prepared them for impact, they all leaned forward in their seats, just as the instructions told them to. Mia was able to hug her knees, while Michael leaned into the seat in front of him, Isla now holding him tight, her little eyes squeezed shut.

"Everyone, brace for impact!" the captain's voice squealed through the intercom and then it felt like the entire Universe was holding its breath.

With a deafening boom, the plane dive-bombed into the dark waters of an endless lake, sending shockwaves through every bone in Mia's body. The once-luxurious cabin became a cacophony of screams and splintering metal, while the sheer intensity of the impact stole Mia's breath away.

CHAPTER THREE

August 26, Friday
Mia

As the initial shock of the rough landing began to subside, Mia fought to regain her bearings, her ears still ringing from the violence of the impact.

Her mind raced back to the map that had been displayed on the TV screen in front of her – she vaguely remembered seeing a great lake, but she couldn't recall which one and the captain's words weren't exactly registering when he announced it. She peeked out the window and swallowed her terror.

The water outside seemed to stretch on forever, swallowing the plane and everyone in it.

Everything was still and silent, like the world was holding its breath.

Then the screaming started, as passengers panicked when water started drifting around on the floor. Mia's heart hammered against her ribs, her hand clamping down on Michael's in a vice grip. Adrenaline flooded her veins. Michael's other arm cradled Isla, while the little girl's wails rose over the chaos.

The plane groaned as it tilted to the side, sending Mia's stomach into her throat. This was it. This was how she would die – drowning, not flying. She squeezed her eyes shut, willing herself not to vomit.

Michael pried his fingers from hers, snapping open their seatbelts with trembling hands. "We gotta move."

Mia gulped down her nausea and nodded, unbuckling her seatbelt as Michael leaned across the now-busy aisle to help the mother to her feet. They stumbled into the teeming aisle, the stench of jet fuel burning Mia's nostrils.

In the economy section of the plane, passengers clamored toward the emergency exits, their shouting echoing in Mia's ears. Her heart stuttered at the sight of water swirling around their feet, soaking her converse sneakers.

Gods, it was rising swiftly.

And holy crap, it was freezing.

This couldn't be happening.

She flinched as Michael's hand found the small of her back, guiding her forward. "It's okay," he said, voice wavering. "I got you."

Despite everything, his touch anchored her, keeping her nightmares at bay. She followed in his wake as he pushed through the stagnant line, the cries and sloshing water receding to a dull roar in her mind. As long as Michael was here, she could face this.

Why wasn't the line moving?

Mia's feet splashed through the frigid water as they pushed through the crowded aisle. Up ahead, passengers shoved desperately at the emergency exit, their panic rising as the door refused to budge.

Mia could hear shouting at the other end of the plane as they struggled to open another exit as well.

"Help us!" a woman screamed, throwing her shoulder against it.

Michael surged forward, pulling Mia with him as he pushed through the bodies. "Stay close," he said firmly. Michael handed Isla to Mia and forced his way to the door.

The darkness and dimly flashing emergency lights only increased the panic..

She huddled close to Mindy as Michael added his strength to the efforts, bellowing for everyone to coordinate their shoves against the door. It burst open with a screech of metal and plastic, unleashing a wave of black water onto their shins.

Was the plane supposed to be higher up in the water than this? What kind of damage did it take during the landing?

Behind her she could hear the flight attendants shrieking that the rafts weren't working.

Oh, gods.

The toddler sobbed, face scrunching as the shoving began.

Michael and one other man at the door were being pushed by panicking passengers.

Oh jeeze, were they going to push him out in their attempt to escape the sinking plane? Would he drown if they jumped down and landed on him?

Mia fought for breath, and she was jostled around and squeezed from all sides.

"It's okay, sweetie," Mia soothed into the toddler's hair as she tried to use her body to shield her.

"Hey! Back the fuck off!" Michael's roar and resulting shove had a ruddy man in a business suit stumbling back into the people behind him. The emergency exit door on the opposite port side was already opened up into the dark sky and people were madly escaping through it.

"Stay calm and listen to where I tell you to go." Michael's voice rumbled over the clamor.

One by one, Michael, with the help of the other man who pried open the door, started helping people out on the starboard side of the plane.

Mia felt a bubble of hysteria come up as she remembered how she studied what a port and starboard side was, thinking it was going to prove useless. And now here she was, thinking about the people entering the water on the port and starboard sides.

She clutched Isla tighter. Once she got up to Michael, she realized why their line was going so much slower, the exit was placed right next to the wing, but part of the wing had been...ripped off.

Michael was directing people where to go...

Some he was instructing in the water...some he was helping onto the wing.

There wasn't enough room for everyone on the wing, and he was...

Mia looked at him in horror.

He had to *choose*.

He was stuck having to *choose* who went in the frigid water and who went on the dry wing.

Oh, gods.

Michael looked back and realized she was next and he froze as he took Isla and her in. He looked behind her at the increasingly nervous passengers and he looked back at Mia with hopelessness in his eyes.

She reached out and rested her palm against his cheek, already knowing what he was torn up about.

"I was a high school swimmer. All state. I swam in college too. You think those pools were heated? Ha." She tried to make light of it as she rubbed lightly at the bristles on his cheek. "A little water doesn't scare me. I can show Isla my swim tricks." Mia pulled her shaking hands away and tried to hand Isla to Michael.

He hesitated. "Mia...Angel...the water is freezing. I don't know how long we'll be in it..." He practically whispered it, so that the others behind her couldn't hear. Even so, she was able to hear his nerves finally breaking through.

He thought she was going to freeze to death.

Mia looked up at him and stepped close, all too aware of the increasingly less patient attitudes behind her. "I can't take a spot from a kid...or a mom...or a dad...or..." Mia swallowed hard. "I can't take a dry spot from someone who really needs it. It's okay. I've seen Titanic. Maybe I'll track down the door you guys popped off and get comfy on there. Come find me when you're done here. I promise *I'll* make room for you." Before she could rethink it, she rocked up onto the balls of her feet and pressed a tender kiss on the corner of his lips. She dragged herself away from him and before she could dwell on it, she jumped into the cold, awaiting darkness.

CHAPTER FOUR

August 26, Friday
Mia

The emergency lights flickered across the black surface of the water, casting an eerie glow on the nightmare come to life. Bodies bobbed in the water around her and trembling figures huddled on the wing of the plane. Once everyone was out, Mia glanced up to the open port where Michael was standing, taking a deep breath at the door.

Was he afraid of the water or was he just processing everything that had happened so far?

Despite the fact that he had been overseeing the exit of the other passengers, it was almost like he had been keeping track of her in the faint light, because when Michael finally jumped into the lake, he swam directly over to Mia. His powerful arms cut through the water with astonishing ease.

Shouts and splashing erupted behind them as passengers began to fight over the limited space on a part of the wing that had been ripped off and was floating nearby. Others tried to squeeze onto a small flotation device that a flight attendant had pushed out of the emergency exit doorway.

A device that was not nearly big enough for all of the people that were marooned in the water.

Michael frowned; tension etched on his face as he continued treading next to her, his life jacket doing most of the work.

Was he reliving his decisions? Regretting them?

How long would these vests stay inflated for...

"This is madness," Mia said, through chattering teeth.

They couldn't even see a hint of a shoreline. Thankfully, even though the plane was taking on water, it didn't look like it was sinking too fast, so the people on the wing had a chance to stay drier longer.

Michael's jaw tightened. "I know. But, we'll get through this. Rescue teams are probably only minutes away. We'll all be fine."

She hadn't known him long, but as she watched him scan the darkness, his eyes peering into the unknown, she knew...he was lying.

And Mia sensed he wasn't a guy who lied a lot.

Still, his calm determination steadied Mia despite the anarchy around them. Michael had steered the elderly and anyone with children onto the wing, while directing other able-bodied adults into the water. His firm direction had brought order to the chaos. However, Mia could hear screams and shouts echoing from the other side – the port side she thought, with a humorless correction. That side hadn't benefited from Michael's order and direction. Their side was calmer; there were quiet sobs but no fighting...at least not yet.

Floating beside him, Mia marveled at how this near-stranger had become such a rock for her in this storm.

Fate was funny like that.

Michael and Mia hovered in front of Mindy and her children, who were huddled together on the perilous wing. Mia sang softly up to the trembling children on the wing, trying to entertain them, despite her own violent shivers. Michael stayed as close to her in the water as possible, rubbing his hands along her arms in a vain effort to keep her warm.

Around them, the stranded passengers grew quiet, their energies depleted by cold and fear. The wing sank lower as the plane continued to slowly descend into the dark water. Michael met Mia's worried gaze but said nothing, not wanting to voice their shared concerns.

A commotion erupted as a husky man tried muscling his way onto the crowded wing, knocking an elderly woman into the water in his haste. There were gasps and shouts as the frail woman was assisted by those floating near the wing.

"Fucking dick," Michael hissed. He swam swiftly over, fury etched on his face. When he arrived at the wing, Michael's strong arm shot up and out of the water, grabbing the man's ankle and ripping him off the wing.

Mia winced at the screams of the easily excited spectators and the colorful swears the blustering man had for Michael. Once the man was done splashing about like a fool, Mia watched Michael pin him up against the edge of the wing. Their side of the plane fell quiet as everyone watched the scene unfold. For better or worse, Michael was their default captain, now everyone was listening intently, despite the non-stop clamor coming from the other side of the plane.

"Stay in the water or I'll drown you myself," Michael growled, his stern face barely illuminated by the faint, flashing emergency lights.

The man scowled but wisely took a minute to assess the tone of the other passengers surrounding him, watching. When no one jumped to his defense. Reluctantly, it seemed, the man complied, by pushing away from Michael and swimming toward a huddled group of water-bound survivors.

Michael helped the elderly woman back onto the wing before returning to Mia's side.

"I hope no one else pulls a shit stunt like that," he muttered.

Mia squeezed his arm, drawing comfort from his presence and trying to inject a bit of solace with her own.

After a long, freezing hour of bobbing in the endless expanse, silence reigned on both sides of the plane. Michael had made rumblings at one point about swimming over to check on the other side, but Mia couldn't hide her panic. What if that douchebag tried to get back on the wing – and what if this time, it was Mindy, Isla and Charles who were tossed into the water? An infant couldn't wear a life vest and he'd absolutely freeze to death if submerged in the chilly water.

Thus, Michael had reluctantly agreed to stay on their side of the plane.

Mia's teeth chattered uncontrollably as she floated numbly in the water. Beside her, Michael looked just as miserable, his muscular frame wracked by tremors as he tried to hold her close.

Desperate to take the frown from the face of the man who had made the most valiant attempt to keep them safe, Mia said the first thing she could think of. "Why am I just now realizing that there could be...things...below us in the water?"

Michael cracked a stiff smile, some tension leaving his face.

"Why do you think I'm cuddled so close? I don't need to swim the fastest, I just need to swim faster than you." He joked from between chattering teeth. "Distract me so I don't climb up on the wing, myself. Tell me a secret."

Her skin was pale, lips almost blue, but Mia felt her cheeks heat as she blushed, then found herself admitting, "Well, besides this being my first, and only, plane ride? Ever." She stressed the last part. "I'm pretty much an open book. Well, not open, so much as closed – until opened...Someone needs to open me." The cold was messing with her head. She wasn't even making sense anymore.

"Yeah, I get you," Michael said, starting to rub at her arms a little firmer. "To be fair, I really have been on hundreds of flights, and this is my first crash – if you can believe it. I wasn't lying."

Mia barked out a somewhat hysterical laugh and rested her forehead on his shoulder, her heart fluttering.

"Here I was, assuming you've been in loads of crashes."

"Nope, just this one."

Mia chuckled weakly and shut her eyes.

At long last, the distant whir of helicopters could be heard in the distance. Soon, they arrived overhead, with giant spotlights illuminating the scene and the Coast Guard dropping from the choppers. The rescue workers began to swim through the huddled passengers, performing triage while they floated weakly in the water.

Shortly after, rescue boats appeared with more spotlights to cut through the darkness. Michael and Mia clung to each other, their numb hands entwined, as the various engines roared in the quiet night.

"Never let go, Jack," Mia mumbled weakly, not even drumming up the strength to smile at her pathetic joke. They were a far cry from the North Atlantic where the icebergs were, but the massive lake was still somewhere in the sixties for temperature – not exactly Maui-warm.

"Mia?"

Gods, she was just so tired. Now that the rescuers were here, she just wanted to close her eyes and sleep. Forever.

"Mia!"

Mia pried open an eye and peeked up at him. "Leave me alone. I'm trying to sleep. Finally. You were the one that said I should sleep."

Michael gave her a little shake. "Yeah, three hours ago. When we were warm on a plane. Not now. Now? Now, you should stay awake. Especially because we need to climb up into a boat in a minute. Hang in there, Angel."

"Yeah, yeah," she mumbled, not bothering to open her eyes.

A rescue boat puttered up before Michael could reply, its bright lights shattering the surface of the dark water surrounding them. Taking orders from the floating coast guard team in the water, the boat crew quickly scooped up the people in the most need. Another boat replaced the now full one, and they did it all over again, until they finally got to Mindy and the kids on the somewhat submerged wing. Mindy had to resort to standing with the kids about thirty minutes prior to reserve space. She'd been able to keep Charles in his car seat, but it had to be getting heavy.

More rescue vehicles arrived, and Mia and Michael continued to cling together as passengers were plucked from the water. Some were immediately raised into the helicopters while others were loaded into boats.

"Okay, guys. Your turn. We're going to help you up." The rescuer leaned over the small boat and tried to grab for Michael.

Michael actively avoided his hands. There was clearly no way Michael was letting himself be pulled to safety before Mia.

"Buddy, you got to let her go so we can get her up here. Same for you, hun. You got to let him go. We have space for one. The other boat is right behind us and will grab the other. I promise. You guys are safe."

"I'll find you," Michael promised as he pushed Mia up into the waiting arms of the rescue worker.

Mia blinked sleepily back at him, unable to form words. Mia's heart ached, but she trusted him. He'd find her. He'd promised.

Mia shivered violently as she was hauled aboard the rescue boat, the cold water combined with the chilly wind against her damp flesh made her even colder. She huddled under a foil blanket as the medics handed out heated packs and water bottles.

"What's your name, hun?" one kindly asked as the boat sped away back toward a larger rescue vessel.

"M-Mia," she stammered, through chattering teeth.

The medic nodded, consulting a passenger manifest. "We'll get you warmed up soon, Mia. Just hang in there."

Mia closed her eyes. She was exhausted and the day's trauma was sinking in. She couldn't help but overhear the rescue team discussing the deceased, which included both pilots.

"Mechanical failure," someone said, grimly.

As horrible as it all was, Mia could only think of Michael, hoping he was safe. They'd only just met, yet she felt connected to him now in a profound way.

They transferred her into one of the larger rescue boats where doctors and other medical personnel were hard at work. As the boat motored toward shore, Mia made a silent vow – no matter what, she would find Michael again. She needed to find her guardian, her savior, both to make sure he was okay and to thank him.

For now, she took comfort in knowing he was out there, probably in the process of being plucked from the water and being brought to the nearest hospital, just like her. They would meet again soon. She had to believe that.

Once they got to shore, the passengers were loaded into waiting ambulances, the bright lights making Mia squint.

She was exhausted, freezing and just wanted to cry.

Unceremoniously, they plopped her onto a gurney and loaded her into an ambulance, replacing the damp blanket with another warmed, dry one. Mia winced as the ambulance doors slammed shut, the sound jarring her senses. The ambulance took off right after Mia was poked and prodded as the paramedics assessed her condition.

"Are you experiencing any pain or difficulty breathing?"

Mia shook her head. "Just cold. And worried about..." She hesitated. He'd never told her his full name; there were probably a dozen 'Michael's on that plane. "About one of the other passengers," she finished. But then she thought that she might as well try. "His name is Michael. We were in the water together. I just want to know he's okay."

The paramedic gave her a sympathetic look. "I'm afraid I can't share any information about other patients. But I'm sure he's being cared for, just like you are."

It was a hollow assurance. Mia needed to see Michael with her own eyes, to hear his voice. She tried to remain alert as they treated her for mild hypothermia, dehydration, and shock, but her thoughts kept drifting back to him.

At the hospital, when she was finally settled in a private room, exhaustion finally took over, and Mia fell into a fitful sleep. Her dreams were filled with the plane crash, this time with dark water closing in over her head. Each time she awoke, Michael's face swam in her mind's eye. Her heart ached, not knowing if he was okay. She resolved to keep searching for him, no matter what it took. He was her angel she couldn't lose him now.

CHAPTER FIVE

August 26, Friday
Michael

The blinding flash of ambulance lights cut through the haze of shock that had engulfed Michael since the crash. He blinked hard, trying to shake off the numbness and focus. All around him, rescue workers swarmed the rocky shoreline, pulling shivering passengers from boats and loading them onto stretchers.

"Mia!" Michael called hoarsely, his voice all but lost amid the chaos and the open expanse of the lake. He strained to catch a glimpse of her dark hair, those angel wing tattoos on her slender wrists. But the workers kept shuffling him about, loading him into the back of an ambulance before he could spot her in among the crowd.

Michael leaned forward, wincing at the ache in his exhausted muscles. "Wait, I need to find someone! A woman, she was sitting next to me on the plane."

A paramedic shone a light in Michael's eyes. "Everyone's being taken care of, sir. Just try to relax." Michael had an IV brusquely inserted, was piled high with warm blankets, then they were off to the nearest hospital.

As the ambulance sped away, Michael collapsed against the gurney, while fear crept into his gut. Where was she? Was she hurt...or worse? Guilt and helplessness washed over him. He should've kept her closer or insisted that he stay with her. Instead, he'd let the rescue teams tear them apart.

But...if he'd kept her with him, she would have been stuck in the chilly water even longer.

The entire way he warred with himself about the decision.

Once at the hospital, Michael fought to keep his eyes open as he was ushered into an exam room. Though his body shook with cold, his mind burned with a singular focus: Find Mia. The doctor spoke to him but Michael barely registered the words. Hypothermia. Shock. Dehydration. He needed rest. Michael nodded absently as another IV was inserted into his arm.

"Is there a Mia here too?" he blurted out, interrupting the doctor from updating his chart. "From the plane crash, dark hair, tattoos—"

The doctor frowned, while the nurse concentrated on taping up the IV. "I'm not sure. We have multiple patients coming in. But I could check – is she your wife?"

"No, no…just…just a friend. But a good friend." He amended his statement hoping it would help his cause. "A great friend actually. We were traveling together. I need to know she's okay." It wasn't quite a lie. His stomach clenched as the doctor leveled him with a disappointed look.

Fuck.

"Oh. Well, I'm sorry, sir, but we can't share patient information unless you're a relative."

As the medical team shut the door behind them Michael leaned back onto the stacked pillows, exhaustion seeping through his limbs.

But he couldn't rest yet. Not until he knew Mia was safe.

Until then, the image of her soft smile, her hand clutching his in the cold water, and her quiet laugh, would remain etched in his mind. He had to find his angel again.

Michael's eyelids grew heavy as the medication flowed into his veins. He fought against the drowsiness, anxious for the doctor to return.

Minutes ticked by. He glanced repeatedly at the door, willing it to open. Where was the doctor?

Frustration mounted. He should've asked for Mia's last name on the plane. He didn't think he'd need it. He thought they'd have time…

Michael's fists clenched.

Damnit.

He was used to getting what he wanted, when he wanted it.

He blinked, rested his head back and fought the drowsiness of the medication flooding his system.

Should he pull some strings, use his celebrity status to get answers? They were in a hospital in the Midwest, but the flyover states loved football. Hell, he was a Wolverine and played at The Big House in Michigan – surely, he had to have a fan or two here...

No. He discarded the thought quickly. This was already about to become a media nightmare and drawing attention to it would make it more of a fuckin' nightmare than it already was.

After what they'd just endured, the right thing was to go through proper channels and respect the hospital's protocol.

Still, not knowing if Mia was safe ate away at him.

The curtain finally clanged open and a nurse entered, flipping through notes on a clipboard. Michael sat up straighter, hope and fear swirling inside.

"Sorry for the delay," the nurse said. "The doctor said you were looking for someone? Your wife? We're still cataloging all the patients between here and our sister hospital—what was her name?"

Michael squirmed, "Uh, not quite. Not my wife. Just a woman who was in first class with me."

The nurse looked behind her and frowned. Clearly, the doc didn't disclose that this wasn't exactly a kosher request.

The nurse then turned and met Michael's gaze. "I'm very sorry but I'm not allowed to share that type of information."

"Just...just, is she here? Is she okay? I can walk about, find her myself."

The woman pursed her lips and looked down at the sheet quickly, debating. "What was her name?"

Hope erupted.

"Mia. I didn't get her last name."

"There's no one by that name here."

Michael's breath caught. No Mia? Then where was she?

The nurse gripped Michael's shoulder reassuringly. "Don't panic. We have new patients arriving continuously. I'll keep checking for you. For now, just try and rest."

Michael exhaled shakily. He had to trust she was safe and being cared for somewhere. He could do nothing more...for now. With his eyes burning, he laid back and the image of Mia's smiling face followed him into his dreams.

Michael tossed and turned, sleep eluding him as his mind replayed those terrifying moments on the plane. He could still feel the bone-chilling cold of the water as they huddled together. Mia had been so brave, keeping him focused while keeping the kids distracted.

He reached for his waterlogged phone that sat, dead as a brick on the bedside table. He wished he could call his buddy and teammate, Danny. He had texted Michael yesterday afternoon about meeting an intriguing CPA, but hadn't mentioned anything after their mysterious text. Michael had returned the favor and sent him a text mid-flight about being partnered up with his own adorably, awkward angel.

A wave of sadness washed over Michael as he realized he may never see Mia again after...everything. Fate had brought them together and now, just as inexplicably, their paths had been diverged.

Michael squeezed his eyes shut, overcome with guilt. If only he'd been more forceful about squeezing her onto the wing or going with her in the boat. If only...

A soft knock interrupted his spiraling thoughts. The same nurse entered, her gaze gentle. "Sorry to bother you, but we have an update on Mia."

Michael bolted upright, wincing at the pain fatigued muscles. "You found her?"

The nurse hesitated. "There was a woman by that name who arrived in grave condition at our sister hospital. Hypothermia. I'm ...afraid she didn't make it."

Michael's stomach dropped. His angel – gone?

After everything?

He could only stare at the nurse in stunned disbelief as tears stung his eyes.

She was fine when they loaded her into the boat.

She was fine! She was joking with him!

Michael shook his head, unable to accept the news. "There must be some mistake. Can you check again?"

The nurse gave him a sympathetic look. "I'm very sorry, but I confirmed it with one of my colleagues over there in the ER."

Michael's breath caught in his throat. After the whirlwind of their time together, the connection he'd felt with this stranger, the thought of losing Mia so senselessly was so...

"She was terrified of flying, you know," he said quietly. "I promised her she'd be fine..."

He trailed off as a fresh wave of guilt hit him.

"I'm so sorry," the nurse said again. "I'll give you some time."

The nurse gave him a small smile and let herself back out through the curtain.

Michael thought back to Mia's sketchbook falling to the ground during turbulence, how she had so carefully attempted to get his skin color exactly right. The way she'd kissed him before jumping into the cold abyss – not even giving him a hint of blame for sending her into the water, versus joining the others on the dry wing.

Brave, selfless Mia.

Michael wiped his eyes roughly, fighting the burn of tears threatening to overwhelm him.

Fuck, he hardly even knew her.

Somehow though, in their fleeting time together, Mia had left a stubborn mark on his heart. He would carry her memory with him always, a bittersweet reminder of how fragile and delicate life could be. And a stark reminder of how he failed her by not putting her on the wing of that plane...

Michael lay back down, utterly spent. He closed his eyes, picturing Mia's face once more.

"I'm sorry, Angel," he whispered.

And now she was gone, before he could even learn her last name.

He laid there in solemn silence as memories of their brief time together flashed in his mind. The way Mia had made him chuckle, despite the dire circumstances. The sincerity in her voice when she'd thanked him for keeping her calm. The jolt of electricity he'd felt when their hands had touched again and again as she positioned him for her sketches.

Mia had been a light in the darkness that often hovered around him. And now that light had been tragically extinguished, leaving Michael with a grief that felt almost unbearable.

A single tear slipped down his cheek and as he wiped it away, he noticed his hands were trembling.

How many others had perished out there in the icy water because of decisions he'd made? He kept replaying each moment, questioning if he could've done more.

Michael knew such thoughts served no purpose except to deepen the anguish and guilt churning inside. But he couldn't seem to stop them from invading his mind.

He had to keep perspective: as much as he wanted to save everyone, the reality of their situation had made that impossible. All he could do was make the best choice, based on the information available.

Still, the weight of the self-imposed leadership bore down heavily. Michael despised this feeling of helplessness – in knowing that, ultimately, lives had been in his hands. It was a burden he'd never wanted, yet fate had seen it his responsibility to shoulder. And he'd failed them. He'd failed Mia.

With a heavy sigh, Michael pushed the button to lower his hospital bed.

She was too good for him anyway...he should have known the universe wouldn't let him keep her. Not after what he'd done.

Chapter Six

September 12, Monday
Mia

Mia stared at the mountain of cardboard boxes stacked haphazardly around the sparsely furnished living room. Sean had detoured on his way to Springfield, Massachusetts, to come pick her up from the hospital, and in the weeks since, she just hadn't been able to work up the energy to unpack.

Thank Fate she had Sean's number memorized and not just stored in her phone – or she would have been stuck at that hospital for an eternity.

After only hours of rest, fluids, monitoring, and a 'standard' psych eval, the hospital discharged her.

One would have thought being a plane crash survivor would warrant a longer stay...but apparently, beds were in *short supply*.

Once Sean arrived, Mia had ranted to him the entire ten-hour drive to their new home.

Why wouldn't the hospital staff just tell her where Michael was? She hadn't asked for medical specifics!

Mia just wanted to be pointed in a direction, so she could wander around herself until she found him.

Even the psych doctor hadn't budged. However, he did say she had some sort of hero worship complex that he wanted to explore further.

Screw him!

She just wanted to find Michael.

After circling the hospital one too many times, and being escorted by security to the front lobby to wait for Sean to pick her up, Mia finally broke.

She was never going to find him.

The tears and the reality of the situation finally sunk in and it just...overwhelmed her.

And that was how Sean found her.

In a pathetic mess on the hospital lobby floor, being chaperoned by a retired police officer-turned-security guard.

And now, here she was, sidestepping around the stacked boxes and dragging her feet through the foreign room, dodging empty tissue boxes.

Maybe she'd start unpacking today; throw away the tear-stained tissues that were covering every surface...

She looked over at the high stacks of all her other worldly possessions...

Maybe not.

Motivation and energy weren't her friends lately.

She moved robotically through the space, tidying the few things that were already tidy, just for something to do. Her hands shook as she lined up the remotes on the coffee table for a third time that morning.

Nightmares plagued her sleep. Flashes of the emergency landing, the screams of passengers, the feeling of her seat dropping out from under her as the plane's wing partially sheared off. She'd wake drenched in sweat, heart racing. Sometimes she wouldn't sleep again for the rest of the night.

Showers were another new terror. The spraying water triggered memories of the bobbing waves as she floated in the dark water. She could only bathe with the door open and with Sean sitting in the doorway – to be there, in case she started to drown.

Keys jangling outside the wood front door made Mia jump.

Sean came in and froze when he saw her standing in the living room. He winced as he took her in. Still in her Disney pajamas, despite it being three in the afternoon.

"Hey, how'd it go today?" he asked, his voice on tip toe.

He didn't need to ask. He knew.

"Same old, same old. Cry for a bit, have the shakes, scream into the pillow, cry again. You know."

Sean stepped inside, sat some grocery bags on the counter, and approached Mia. He put a comforting hand on her shoulder and peered down into her eyes. "Baby steps. You've been through a lot. It's going to take time." At 6'3", Sean towered above her moderate 5'4" frame, so he had to bend his knees a little to bring them eye to eye.

Mia nodded, wishing she could believe him. Some days the trauma felt like it would never release its grip on her.

Sean led her to the second-hand leather couch and sat down, flipping on the TV. He said he liked the distraction, but Mia knew it wasn't for his benefit. It was for her. Her and her broken mind.

As he channel surfed, Mia's thoughts drifted back to the crash.

The screaming, the smoke, the water closing in over her head...

And him. Michael. The one who'd made her feel safe, even as the plane plunged toward the sea. She wished she'd gotten his last name. She wished she could thank him for saving her life.

Then again, it wasn't like he was chasing her down.

Maybe he didn't want anything to do with her.

That would be fitting.

Just like everyone else in her life, he left her. Her only constant was Sean.

She should just be happy with Sean.

Mia turned and gave Sean a small, grateful smile. He glanced away from a sports newscaster to meet her gaze and offer his own affirming smile back. She curled up on the couch next to him and grabbed her purple aluminum crochet hooks off the battered brown coffee table.

Maybe she could finally turn this tangle of yarn into something other than one giant mess...

Then again, her creativity was completely absent lately, so probably not.

Her muse left her somewhere in the clouds or had sunk to the bottom of the Great Lakes.

The sports channel caught her eye, and she turned to see a familiar face in a football uniform, giving an interview. Her mouth fell open and her crochet hooks dropped from her fingers.

"Oh my gods, Sean!" she gasped, "That's him!"

Sean gave a confused glance between the player being interviewed and Mia. "Who?"

"Michael! From the plane!"

Mia tried to slow her racing heart as she lowered her feet to the floor and leaned forward, mouth agape.

Sean studied the TV skeptically. "Wait, you're telling me that *Michael Dillon* was on your flight and you didn't recognize him?"

"Dude. You know I don't do sports!" She was standing now, staring in awe at Michael's face on the screen.

It was really him.

But...Michael looked...haunted.

His eyes, once bright and lively, now appeared dulled as he stared at the camera. Sure, he just had a game, but his face was etched with lines of a deeper exhaustion. A tribute to repeated sleepless nights.

Mia's heart squeezed.

"You don't do *violent* sports. There's a difference. Also, he's Michael-fucking-Dillon. Running back of the Springfield Spartans. Everyone knows him. Hell, he was even on the cover of People for being one of the sexiest men alive. He's dated everyone from pop stars to heiresses to foreign princesses. The guy's a legend." Sean turned to look at where Mia was standing, her eyes glued to the TV. "You're telling me he's your seatmate from the plane?" His voice went high and tight at the end and Mia pulled her eyes from the screen.

"Yes."

"You said you sat next to a guy who saved your life."

Why did he sound so accusatory?

"Yeah. And?"

"You said he was a fitness influencer."

Mia cocked her head, still trying to piece together why Sean was looking increasingly upset.

"Yeah, and clearly he fibbed." She turned back to the television and muttered, mostly to herself, "I guessed mostly correct."

Sean stood and stepped in front of her. "You failed to mention you were sitting next to People's Sexiest Man Alive."

What did that have to do with the price of tea in China?

"He didn't exactly give me a resume—"

"You have eyes, don't you?"

Woah. Easy, bud.

Mia popped out a hip and crossed her arms. "What the heck is your problem?"

"You sat, sketched, and flirted with an attractive stranger for hours and didn't for one minute ask him his name?"

"I did get his name! Just...not his full one." Mia shook her head. "Anyway, dude, slow down. I'm confused. Are you mad at me for sitting next to a sexy guy? For sketching him? For not asking for his resume? Like...I don't get where you're going with this?"

Sean's pretty hazel eyes were wild as he just stood there, looking at her. After a tense beat, he threw up his hands. "I don't know where I'm going with this either! It's just...Mia, hun. You sat next to Michael fucking Dillon and didn't even realize..."

"You play soccer! I don't get why you're getting so worked up-"

"Yes, I play soccer! But that doesn't mean I live under a rock! I play fantasy football just like most guys! *Dillon's on my fucking team* for Christ's sake! You just...you just..." Sean rubbed at his face in frustration before his hands dripped away and he stared at her in disbelief. "I thought you sat next to a nice, fifty-year-old man who was flying back home to see his kid's homecoming game. Not...Michael Dillon."

Oh.

Warmth hit her cheeks and she looked down at her feet.

Maybe Michael had been onto something. Maybe...

No. One moment of jealousy did not an unrequited love-match make.

Mia's pulse pounded as she turned back to the TV, where they were now showing game highlights from the previous days' game. "How is he even playing?"

"How has the media not gotten wind that he was on the plane, barking out orders about who lives and who dies?" Sean mumbled back.

Mia winced, just before her body locked up. She could feel the first rush of cold water over her toes. The vast empty darkness of the open sky. The flashing lights bouncing off the black waves. The airplane wing sinking lower, and lower, and–

Sean had her shoulders in his hands and he was giving her small shakes.

They were on the ground, together, in front of the couch and her cheeks were soaking wet.

Crap.

Embarrassed, she wiped at her cheeks and pulled away, looking anywhere but at Sean, who was now trying to apologize for his callous, and incorrect, view of events.

"No one from our side of the plane died..."

"I know, Mia. I know, I'm sorry–"

"The deaths happened from people on the other side. The side that didn't have someone like Michael to direct traffic and help those that needed it..." Her voice, raspy and quiet.

Sean reached out to her again, "I know, I'm so sorry, Mia. I shouldn't have said–"

"I need to go lay down," Mia recoiled from his touch, and he flinched. She clumsily stood and wiped her sweaty palms on her PJ bottoms.

She glanced back at the TV and caught a headshot of Michael in the top left corner. A swirl of emotions washed over her – shock, regret – and an undeniable longing.

Maybe he could help her make sense of it all. But, did she have the courage to reach out across the void that had separated them? Clearly the guy had more than enough means to figure out where Mia was and hadn't tried contacting her. Maybe he wanted that chapter closed up tight, despite the promise he'd made to look for her.

Maybe he did 'look' for her, found her, and then considered his promise fulfilled.

She didn't think he was that type of guy...but how much did she even really know him?

Mia didn't even know he was a famous football player, for Pete's sake.

Mia wrung her hands, torn between yearning and fear.

Sean watched her, brows drawn together in concern. "Hey, it's ok. We'll figure this out," he said gently.

Mia nodded, but her thoughts raced on. Michael was real. He was out there, carrying on after the crash had shattered her world. And maybe, just maybe, he held the key to putting the broken pieces of her life back together. All she had to do was find the strength to turn the key.

Ever since the accident, creating art had become almost impossible. The wellspring inside her felt dry, choked by debris from the wreckage. But seeing Michael's face stirred something within. Inspiration, small but stubborn, took root.

Mia was hit with a wave of emotion. Her hands trembled slightly as her muse snuck up on her. The temperamental bitch had been absent since the crash, and now here she was, coming out on the tail end of a panic attack?

Fickle bitch.

The image in her mind came slowly, tentatively. Bold splashes of brown for his kind eyes that had anchored her during the descent. Strong lines, capturing the steadiness of his hands as he helped guide the passengers to safety. And a streak of violent red to showcase the strong determination he'd shown, as he forced the emergency exit door open when it was stuck.

Seeing him again was like a second chance.

Maybe Fate was *giving* her another chance.

Mia dithered, biting her lip. "Maybe I should try to contact him? I never properly thanked him for what he did. But what if that's weird or he doesn't want to hear from some random girl he met on a plane?"

Sean considered this, a frown on his handsome face. "I don't think it would be weird, especially with what you two went through. Could be healing for the both of you." He hesitated. "I could probably find out the name of his publicist from one of the guys on my soccer team. Then, maybe you could write him a letter – if you think it'll bring you closure?"

Mia nodded slowly. "Maybe that would be...good." She felt a new sense of resolve. Michael deserved to know the depths of her gratitude.

Who knew – maybe they could help each other process the trauma of that harrowing flight.

She just had to be brave enough to reach out.

But what if he didn't remember her? What if she was just one in a lengthy line of women and he was just being friendly with her to pass the time? Or worse, what if he was offended by her intrusion into his life?

Her stomach knotted with unease.

"You okay?" Sean said, eyeing her with concern.

Mia nibbled relentlessly on her lip. "Just overthinking..."

"Don't stress," he tried to reassure. "Take some time and just think about it."

Mia cast one last look at the TV before retreating to her bedroom for another night of fitful sleep.

Yeah...time.

Something she never used to think about, but now her time on Earth felt altogether too long...and far too short.

CHAPTER SEVEN

September 14, Wednesday
Michael

The sun blazed down on the Springfield Spartans' practice field as Michael Dillon sprinted through his drills, sweat dripping from his brow. The exertion was nothing new for him, but lately, it felt like he was carrying a heavier burden than ever before. It wasn't just the physical strain of pushing his body to its limits; it was the weight of the memories that threatened to devour him.

His mind was consumed with thoughts of the plane and the split-second decisions he'd been forced to make.

It all haunted him, relentlessly.

He couldn't shake the image of Mia's tear-streaked face, her eyes wide with fear as she clung to his hand as he *promised* her it would be all right. He remembered the panic that had gripped him, the overwhelming need to protect her, even as he made an impossible choice between who would be cast into the freezing water and who would remain perched precariously on the wing.

He should have protected her.

He should have found a way.

"Did you guys hear the latest news report about the freak plane crash?" One of Michael's teammates, who he wasn't particularly close with, asked as they wrapped up their drill. "Turns out one of the pilots had alcohol in his system. And the other was boinking the mechanic who signed off on the mechanical check."

"Damn, seriously?" another teammate chimed in.

"Yeah, it's all over the news. Can't escape it. It's fucking crazy. And each time they bring up all the dead and their families too. It's fucking painful. Like...let it rest already. Their ghosts need peace, ya know?"

As he had done for weeks, Michael tuned them out. He didn't need to see or hear what the media or anyone else had to say about the crash.

He lived it. Every night in his dreams...he relived it.

A chill danced on Michael's bare, sweat-soaked skin. His heart raced as he pretended not to listen, focusing instead on wiping the moisture from his forehead with the back of his hand.

Only Danny and upper management knew he'd been on that plane, and he wanted to keep it that way.

"Hey, Dillon!" Liam Polowski, one of Michael's best friends and one of the Spartan's tight ends, called out as he came jogging up beside him. "You killed it out there today, man. You were an absolute truck." He gave Michael a slap on the shoulder pads.

"Thanks, Liam," Michael replied, forcing what he hoped was a convincing smile.

Danny Parker, wide receiver, and Kyle Justice, their fullback, joined them. His friends' expressions showed they were equally impressed at his performance.

Danny's face, however, had a hint of concern as he began to overhear what the linemen were discussing just a few feet away.

"Yo, anyone catch the Sox last night?" Danny asked loudly, attempting to steer the linemen's conversation away from the accident that he knew had so seriously affected Michael's psyche. "Walk off to win it!"

"Right? Love a good comeback," Kyle agreed, not realizing he was joining in on the distraction effort.

The linemen quickly took the bait, and the chatter turned to baseball instead of the accident.

Michael sighed in relief, grateful for his friend's intervention. But he knew it wouldn't be enough to erase the constant reminders of the accident that plagued him every day.

He took a few steps away from the group and heaved in a breath, trying to stuff down the heaviness that was invading his chest. Danny stepped up behind him and gave him a tentative smile.

"Man, you've gotta stop beating yourself up," Danny said, reading his friend's troubled expression. "You did the best you could under the circumstances. No one could have done more."

"I don't know about that," Michael murmured, his gaze focused on the ground beneath his feet. "I just...I can't help but wonder if there was something else I could have done. Some other way that wouldn't have left me feeling like this."

"Hey, MVPs!" another teammate shouted, interrupting their conversation. "This is for being the stars of the game last weekend!"

Before Michael knew what was happening, a torrent of icy water cascaded over his head, drenching him from head to toe. The sudden shock of the cold sent him spiraling back into the past, his heart pounding in his chest as vivid memories of the crash flooded his senses.

Instantly he was back in the water...trying to keep track of bodies...

"Michael. It's cool. You're here, man. You're here," Danny whispered, grabbing Michael's arm and pulling him back to the present. "You're okay."

Michael was unable to move as his breath came in ragged gasps. "I'm fine. It just...caught me off guard, that's all."

The guys continued to laugh around them – unaware of their triggering actions.

"Michael, you deserve it, after that game-winning touchdown last weekend!" one of his teammates jested, face plastered with a huge grin. The other players chimed in with light-hearted banter, oblivious to the panic attack lurking beneath Michael's motionless exterior. The rest of the team chimed in their two cents as they elbowed one another, jovially.

Danny spoke under his breath, careful not to draw attention. "You're fine, man. Breathe through it."

The presence of his best friend somehow seemed to steady the ground beneath his feet, making it much easier to catch his breath.

Danny continued the distraction efforts, starting an easygoing conversation about their upcoming game, providing a welcome distraction from the whirlwind of panic threatening to consume Michael.

"Come on, time to head in," Danny suggested, draping an arm around Michael's shoulders and guiding him toward the locker room. "And next time, give a guy some warning before you dump a bucket of ice over his head, will you?" he shouted over his shoulder at their oblivious teammates.

Michael managed a weak chuckle for appearances, grateful for the attempt at humor despite the lingering tremors that wracked his body.

He needed to confront the ghosts of the past if he ever wanted to move forward, but every time he tried, the crushing weight of guilt and self-doubt threatened to consume him entirely. It was okay...probably. Healing wasn't linear...right?

He'd be okay...he just needed to stay focus and not get sucked into thinking about it.

"Hey," Danny said quietly, his voice laced with concern as he guided Michael down the field. "We'll help you through this, all right? Whatever it takes."

A shiver raced down Michael's spine as the last of the icy water dripped from his head onto his neck. He forced a shaky laugh, trying to conceal the anxiety that clenched his chest like a vice. The world around him blurred as he focused on some breathing exercises: inhale deeply, exhale slowly, repeat.

"Think you can break your record for rushing yards this weekend?" Danny teased, nudging Michael with his shoulder.

"Only if Butch eases up on the screen passes to you," Michael retorted, forcing himself to respond, despite the lingering quake in his limbs.

Butch, their offensive coordinator, had found a knockout quarterback-to-wide receiver combination in Ryan and Danny. And he was using it to the team's full advantage. Eventually, though, the other teams' defenses were going to figure out a way to stop the one-two punch.

"Seriously. The man is going to serve up a hospital pass for me if he doesn't stop being so predictable. It's like he's forgotten Kenny, Liam, and Kyle even exist..." Danny frowned, his eyes narrowing as he considered the dilemma and the possible solutions.

The sun dipped low in the sky as Michael and his teammates made their way back to the tunnels leading to the locker rooms, casting a warm golden glow behind them over the football field. The scent of freshly mowed grass left the air, replaced by cleaning products and rubber. Without the benefit of a fall breeze, their various sweat odors started to swirl together as well. With each step into the tunnel, Michael's cleats clacked on the pavement, the sound grounding him as he tried to keep the lingering shakes in his hands at bay.

As the group reached the locker room, relief swarmed him.

Soon he'd find peace in a hot shower.

He could momentarily escape the relentless pressure that seemed to bear down on him from all sides. He could burn it all out of him...for a little while at least.

"Hey, Mikey," Danny said, leaning in close to Michael as they began to unstrap their pads at their lockers. "You know we're here for you, right? With what you're going through, we've got your back."

Michael stiffened but tried to make it appear like he hadn't as he nodded and forced a smile.

He knew his friend meant well and he was grateful for his support, but only *he* could face the demons that lurked in the shadows of his mind. It was a battle Michael would have to fight alone, even if it threatened to tear him apart in the process.

As he scrubbed at his drenched hair with the towel, Michael worked through the various coping mechanisms he'd learned to stave off his panic attacks. They were far from perfect, but they allowed him to regain some semblance of control in the wake of the accident.

"You're doing great, you know that?" Danny said softly, giving Michael a gentle nudge with his elbow. "You got this."

Michael tried to turn his grimace into a smile of gratitude. Based on Danny's deepening frown...he failed.

If Danny even knew half of it...

When Kyle and Liam approached the personal alcoves next to their and Danny pulled away from where he was whispering assurances in Michael's ear.

"How's that woodworking project coming along?" Danny asked Michael. "The one you were telling me about a few weeks ago?"

"Woodworking?" Liam chimed in, looking over with a mischievous smile as he grabbed a towel from his open bag. "I should have known you'd be into something so...medieval." He winked at Michael.

"Watch it, Polowski," Danny teased. "Or he might just make you a nice wooden headboard to knock some sense into that thick skull of yours."

"Ooh, you promise? It sounds kinky," Liam retorted with a devilish grin, nudging Michael's shoulder as the others laughed. "Just leave a notch for the handcuffs to go through."

"You guys are idiots," Kyle said, grabbing his own towel and shaking his head with a tired yet affectionate smile.

"Hey!" Michael interjected. "Don't lump me in with these two clowns."

Danny turned to Michael, his face sobering as he pushed for more details about the project. "But really, how's it going?"

Michael hesitated, rubbing the back of his neck as he considered how to respond. Truthfully, he hadn't set foot in his woodworking shop since returning home from the crash. The thought of creating beautiful art reminded him too much of the angelic artist he'd met.

The woman he was responsible for killing.

"Uh, it's coming along," he lied, hoping his friend wouldn't notice the tremble in his voice. "Just taking my time with it, you know?"

Danny clapped him on the shoulder. "Can't wait to see it when it's finished."

Michael nodded, forcing another smile.

As Michael continued to chat with Danny and the rest of his friends, the weight of his guilt pressed down on him.

Lately, it seemed to seep into every aspect of his life, tainting his relationships with his friends and family. He found himself retreating from them, consumed by anxiety, guilt, and an overwhelming desire to be left alone.

But that wasn't possible in his line of work.

"Yo, have you seen that gorgeous, news reporter that's been hanging around practice?" Ryan, their quarterback, asked before rat-tailing Michael playfully with a towel. "I heard she's doing a piece on the team's winning streak. Bet you already got an interview scheduled, don't you, Romeo?"

Great, just what he needed.

Michael snickered with the other guys, but his heart wasn't it.

The media was a constant presence in his life, from intrusive paparazzi to exhaustive interview requests. It was impossible to escape the scrutiny that came with being a star athlete, especially when he tended to attract the cameras.

A curse of the pretty face.

No one saw what lay beneath it.

Except Mia.

A hint of a real smile tugged at his lips as he remembered Mia teasing him about being gorgeous. She was so convinced he was a fitness influencer; it was adorable. But as she spoke with him, sketched him, he could feel that she saw him differently than that. Her art...it *showed* him. Just in the two hours of sketching him, she *drew* the real him. The sketches were beautiful, and not just because they were of a classically pretty person. But because of the feeling she'd injected into every line.

The tugging at his lips faded as he thought of her and her too-short life.

"Come on, man, lighten up." Kyle interrupted Michael's painful reminiscing. "She's not that bad. It's not like you haven't dealt with reporters before."

Michael blinked and was brought back to reality. Right. The reporter.

Peyton Knowles.

Knock-out. Kickass reporter. And certified ball-buster.

"I don't need anyone digging into my personal life right now," Michael mumbled, his jaw clenching at the prospect of yet another invasion of privacy.

Kyle shot him a curious look but otherwise didn't pry.

Good man. Great friend.

As the banter continued, Michael let himself be swept up in the laughter and conversation, buoying his spirits like a life raft in a stormy sea.

A raft he wished he could have magically manifested for Mia.

CHAPTER EIGHT

September 17, Saturday
Mia

That Saturday, Mia settled into a folding chair on the sidelines, her sketchbook balanced on her lap. Sean's soccer game was in full swing, but she couldn't focus on the action. Athletics had never been her thing, and thankfully, Sean appreciated that. He knew she'd rather be reading or creating. However, she was there to support him, even as her soft-spoken nature tended to make her feel out of place amongst the boisterous crowds.

Her fingers fluttered over a blank page, pencil poised, as she watched Sean dart around the field. Try as she might, she couldn't bring herself to sketch him.

She'd never been able to sketch Sean. It was the weirdest thing. They were probably just too close.

Luckily, Sean never pushed the issue or seemed insulted.

Mia sighed, feeling a sudden longing for the strong hand that had once held hers. She closed her eyes and imagined a musk smell with a hint of sawdust. A wistful smile crossed her lips, and she tried to draw Michael from memory, the memory of Michael's touch guiding her tentative first strokes.

"Seriously, what is even happening right now?" a voice called out, pulling Mia from her reverie. She looked up to see a trio of girls sitting in captain's chairs twenty feet away, their faces a mixture of confusion and amusement as they tried to understand the game. They were an eclectic bunch, with various expressions of bewilderment and curiosity etched in their eyes..

A petite woman with jet-black hair tied up in ridiculously high pigtails was frowning as she watched the men run past. One made eye contact with her and she threw him a wink, then blew a saucy kiss. When she turned back to the other girls, Mia saw the ghost of autumn colors present in her black hair. Thick strips of red, orange, and yellow were woven through the woman's strands.

Absolutely dope.

The other two women were beautiful too, just more subtle in flaunting it.

"Okay, so he just...threw the ball? I thought soccer players couldn't touch the ball with their hands?" The pigtailed one asked, gesturing wildly at the players.

"We told you, the goalie can. Yeesh, look at those muscles," another chimed in, fanning herself dramatically. "Dios mío. I'd love to get my hands on him. I bet he'd lose that limp within three weeks."

Hands on him? Lose his limp? What was she – a witch?

Their laughter filled the air, and Mia found herself smiling along with them, making sure to keep her head tipped down to her notebook so she didn't look like she was eavesdropping.

She was.

She just didn't need *them* to know that.

These women were loud and endearing, the complete opposite of her.

"Hey, you!" the colorful-haired one called out. Assuming the woman was talking to a player, Mia looked up to see what was happening and then froze when she looked eyes with the ringleader. "You look like you could use some company. Come join us."

It was not a request.

Mia hesitated for a moment, her heart racing at the thought of engaging in conversation with these women. What was she even going to talk about?

But she had a feeling that Queen Punk Bee was not going to take no for an answer. So Mia took a deep breath, closed her mostly blank sketchbook, and made her way over to their little gathering, dragging her own pop-up chair behind her.

"Uh, hi," she said softly, clutching her sketchbook to her side. "I'm Mia."

"Nice to meet you, Mia," they returned, inspecting her lowkey black jeggings and oversized tan sweater.

"Pop a squat, girlie. You're ours now," The woman who had waved her over said, her voice fuzed with warmth and spunk. She gave a friendly wave. "I'm Lexie."

"Jen," the next woman introduced herself, her voice sultry and smooth. Her amber eyes sparkled with mischief.

"And I'm Megan," the last woman added, the only one to reach out to shake her hand. "Pleased to meet you."

"Same," Mia replied.

What the hell was she supposed to say...

Her anxiety was ratcheting up a notch as she sat there in the silence.

"Oh, I thought you were here to watch the soccer game..." Jen asked, arching a brow as she noticed Mia settle her sketchbook onto her lap. "Sorry about dragging you over here..."

Oh, crap. She didn't want them to think they bothered her.

"Uh, well, kind of. I have a friend playing," Mia explained, feeling her cheeks heat up under the curiosity of their gazes. "But I don't really get into it, so I was just sketching. Or...trying to."

"Ah, an artist. That's neat." Megan said, her head cocking to the side as she looked down at the blank pages. "What do you like to sketch?"

"Anything...usually. My muse is being a little...bitchy right now and not letting me access my creative spark."

"Oh, I *love* that."

Her friends looked at Lexie, aghast, and she waved them off.

"Oh, shut up." She laughed. "Not the muse being a bitch part. But the personification of it. It's so...fascinating," Lexie said with an air of sophistication. "I've always admired people who can create art. I didn't inherit the creative gene."

"Oh. Um, yeah," Mia said, smiling at the women, unsure of what to say to that.

"Anyway," Jen continued, her eyes still chastising Lexie for her superiority, "we're here for a couple different reasons. But the main thing is, we all love a good sports game – even if *some of us* don't always understand what's happening." She gave Lexie a heavy look that implied that Lexie was the only one who didn't know what was happening.

"Bitch. Soccer is new to me. I'll get it. Give me more than one game and I'll kick your ass in trivia."

Jen leaned close to Mia and stage-whispered. "Her dad came to all my college soccer games. But did she? No. She was always nowhere to be found."

Mia chuckled softly, her nerves dissipating as she found herself drawn into the lively debate that ensued. Their teasing was infectious, filling the air around them with warmth and an aura of camaraderie. Mia found herself relaxing around these women in a way she never thought possible.

As the game progressed and Mia became more comfortable with her new friends, she couldn't help but think about Michael. Her short time with him brought a similar spark to her life. He'd probably get a kick out of these crazy ladies.

"All right, here's the deal," Lexie announced, her voice booming and authoritative. She leaned in, her eyes twinkling with excitement. "Secretly, I'm a zillionaire."

Her friends rolled their eyes and they couldn't stop their smiles.

Unsure of the joke, Mia smiled along, though it felt more like a strained grin.

"Anyway, I've got some extra cash and I'm thinking about buying a soccer team because, well, have you seen these guys?" She gestured toward the field with a wicked grin. "Hella sexy."

"Ah, to have spare cash to just buy a team, no problem." Megan rolled her eyes good-naturedly.

"Oh, shut it. But before I approach the owner of the local MLS team, i need to know a little more about soccer. Hence, why I'm here at this men's league game. Plus...they're gorgeous."

They were indeed.

But not quite Michael levels of gorgeous.

"Well, I'm not a zillionaire. I just needed a break from the kids, so I left them with my friend's mom."

"Sure. He's just a 'friend,'" Jen gave her finger quotes and an eyebrow raise. "We'll pretend to believe you." She looked to Mia. "And I'm a prehab therapist and I'm trying to expand my client base. Plus, it doesn't hurt to watch these men in action."

These women couldn't be more different.

Mia *loved* it.

They were loud and animated, but endearing all the same. As a quiet person herself, she found the conversation hilariously one-sided as the women took turns vying for her attention, asking her questions and making jokes.

"So, which one is your *friend*?" Jen arched a bro high and gave Mia sassy finger quotes.

Megan snickered and rolled her eyes.

Mia scanned the field where the men were shouting and calling for the ball. "Um, that one." She pointed at Sean across the field.

The girls stared at him, slack jawed as he dominated the field and rifled off a killer shot on net that was saved...barely.

"You're joking." Jen whipped around to stare at her. "You're here with Sean Becks?"

Mia rolled her angle as watched Jen's eyes get impossibly huge. "Uh, yes?"

"Holy shit." Jen breathed, her eyes going back to the game.

Megan watched Jen get lost in the game and turned to Mia with an amused look on her face. "So...I take it Sean's got a following."

Jen whipped around again. "A following? He's like soccer royalty! He was a darling of the MLS and then he just...quit. Boom. No notice." Jen inspected Mia, trying to figure out if she was the one to cause his soccer drop out.

Mia shrugged. Sean's personal business was his own, and not for her to share with these ladies, no matter how much she liked them.

"Wait, so how do you not know anything about sports if you're *friends* with Hottie Mchottie over there?" Lexie asked, her face skeptical.

"Uh, well..." Mia hesitated, suddenly feeling self-conscious. "I guess art has always been my passion, not athletics."

"Fair enough," Megan said, grinning widely. "But I think you'll find that there's an artistic to the way these guys move on the field, too. Give it a chance – who knows, maybe you'll find inspiration in their athleticism."

"Maybe," Mia hedged, not really buying it.

Then again, Michael's muscles had been inspiring. And apparently he was a professional athlete, so maybe Megan wasn't too far off.

"All right, ladies," Jen declared. "Let's focus on the game, shall we? I think our team is about to score!"

As the three women turned their attention back to the action on the field, Mia found herself grateful for their company. They were so different from her – boisterous, outgoing and unapologetically themselves – but they had welcomed her with open arms, making her feel like she belonged.

Despite their insistence on watching the game, the conversation continued in earnest, with Lexie, Jen, and Megan firing off questions and observations about everything from the players' physiques to the finer points of their game strategy. Mia listened, occasionally offering a comment or observation, but mostly she just basked in the warmth of their company. It was a nice change of pace – not being home alone, in her PJs.

"Okay, Mia," Lexie said, leaning forward in her captain's chair with a sly grin. "So, Megan's not going to spill about what's going on with her and her man-meat. So what about you and Sean? Give us the deets. I need juice in my life."

Mia felt her cheeks grow warm as she waved her off. "Sean and I are just friends."

The three women exchanged dubious glances, causing Mia to squirm in her seat. Yeah, all her friends in high school and college had the same doubt in their faces too.

Their disbelief brought Michael and his own question about Sean to the forefront of her mind. An ache settled in her chest. She wished she had a way to contact him – none of Sean's leads had been able to secure his contact info.

Apparently, the man had a lot of fan mail and his publicist had sort of...cut it off.

The sky finally delivered on its gray and dreary promise as cold droplets started to come down. The weather app said that the rain was supposed to hold off until this evening.

She shouldn't be surprised the forecasters were wrong. At this rate, she should just believe the opposite of whatever they said.

As the cold raindrops sprinkled down on her face, unwanted memories of the plane crash began to surface and Mia's hands started to tremble. Her breathing grew shallow as the sights and sounds of the soccer match began to fade into the background while the sensations of the terrifying ordeal took over.

"Mia?" Jen asked softly, her voice cutting tender through the fog of Mia's memories. "Are you okay, honey? You look a little pale."

"Is everything all right?" Megan asked gently, placing a reassuring hand on Mia's arm.

Mia took a deep breath, her trembling hands betraying the fear that gripped her heart. "A month ago, I was in a plane crash," she admitted, her voice barely audible. The girls gasped in shock, their eyes filling with concern. Mia hesitated for a moment more before, surprising even herself, she opened up to them. Her words came out in a rush, like a dam breaking, releasing all the pent-up thoughts and emotions she'd been holding back since the crash. It wasn't until she finished speaking that she realized she'd shared more than she'd ever intended, but the warmth and sympathy in her new friends' eyes told her she hadn't bored them with her PTSD woes.

"Thank you," Mia whispered, her voice shaky but sincere. "For listening and for being here. It means more than I can say. People seem to always just tell me to 'get over it' when I talk about it. I try not to bore people with it..."

"Bore? Girl, you were in a plane crash. It's not up to anyone else to tell you how you should feel about that."

"One hundred percent," Megan nodded with Jen's assessment. "You heal when you heal. And if someone tells you that you're 'boring' them with trying to talk it out, then—"

"Fuck 'em. Lose 'em. You don't need those kinds of assholes in your life." Lexie declared, not even batting an eye. "You need to talk shit through? No problem. You got us. We love to talk."

Mia gave her a watery smile. "I don't usually love to talk..."

"Even better," Lexie winked. "We love people who listen even more than we love people who like to talk."

Megan leaned forward and whispered conspiratorially. "Balances out the crazy."

"She's not that far off. You'll see," Jen promised, compassion in her light eyes.

What the heck did that mean?

The sprinkle shower had blown over and the clouds dissipated enough to reveal that that sun was beginning to dipped below the horizon, casting a warm glow over the field. And now, comforted by both the dim evening light and the support of these women, Mia felt the desire to share just a tiny bit more.

"The whole thing was my worst nightmare come to life..." Mia continued, "but...there was this guy on the flight...he...he was amazing. He helped me when I was terrified and he saved so many lives during the emergency landing." Her thoughts drifted to Michael's strong arms and the way they had held her so protectively as they bobbed in the endless expanse of dark water. "I've been trying to find him ever since, but I didn't even know his last name. Earlier this week I found out who he was…but now I don't know if I should reach out. He promised he'd come find me, but he never did, even though I think he has more than enough means to…" Mia couldn't help how pitiful the last part sounded.

It sounded pitiful because she *was* pitiful.

A pathetic little hanger-on that didn't know how to catch a hint.

She shouldn't even have brought him up. What was wrong with her?

"Wait," Lexie interjected, her imperial demeanor reemerging as she leaned forward, not one to shy away from prying. "You can't just drop a bomb like that and not tell us more about your mystery hero."

"Yeah, who is he?" Megan asked, curiosity gleaming in her eyes.

Mia hesitated, suddenly reluctant to reveal too much. She glanced at Megan and Jen, who seemed torn between wanting to know and respecting her privacy. "His name is Michael," she finally said, feeling an inexplicable urge to share her secret with these newfound friends. "He plays for the local football team."

"Oh, like one of the men's leagues?"

"Not quite…" Mia bit her lip. Was she supposed to say he was on the flight? In the five days since discovering his last name, she'd spent *a lot* of time researching Michael Dillon. And one thing that was noticeably absent on every single page about him? The fact that he was on the plane that went down in one of the Great Lakes. Maybe he pulled strings to shush information he didn't want spread…and maybe she shouldn't have shared his name; after all, they were basically strangers.

"Mia?"

"Yeah, uh…"

Think, think, think. Find a way to back track!

Her mind was spinning but going nowhere.

"Dude, don't tell me he plays for the Spartans…" Megan drawled out as she inspected Mia's guilty face. "Dude!" she shouted after she read the look there. "Holy shit." She ended on a soft exhale, looking at the other women with wide eyes.

Crap. Crap, crap, crap.

"Wow," Jen breathed, her energy momentarily quieted by the revelation. "That's definitely a twist we didn't see coming."

"Michael?" Lexie repeated, her eyes ballooning in surprise as she finally processed who Mia must be referencing. "As in Michael *Dillon*?" Mia winced and nodded, feeling a sudden shyness wash over her as she regretted the enormity of what she had just revealed. The women exchanged glances, their expressions a mixture of shock and intrigue.

"So, small world, but we actually know him!" Jen eagerly exclaimed as she leaned forward, her feisty nature now back on in full force. "How did we have no idea he was in a plane crash! Lexie Lou?" Her voice got stern at the end as she turned a frown onto her best friend.

Lexie scowled at her. "I obviously would have told you if I knew. We would have set up a care train or something." Lexie turned her attention away from her friend and looked back to Mia, "I kinda…own the team. With my dad."

At Mia's confused look, Lexie grimaced. "Michael's team. The Spartans…"

Mia might not *do* sports, but the significance was not lost on her.

Oh, fucking shit. Did she just get Michael in trouble for not telling his boss about the plane crash?

Oh gods. What if he was interviewing with another team and that's why he was in Seattle?

Was that how athletes worked? Interviews and stuff? Like a real job?

Was there even a football team in Seattle?

He saved her and here she was, destroying his life.

Oh, shit, she was going to be sick.

Mia wrapped her arms tight around her middle and closed her eyes, rocking a little to music in her head.

Megan was looking up at the sky like it was the biggest factor here, not like Mia's secret sharing was going to get Michael fired.

Could Michael get fired for not telling his boss about that?

Shit, she really should have paid more attention whenever Sean spoke about sports!

Jen's fingers flew across her phone screen, her gaze intent on finding something to show Mia. When she finally found what she was looking for, she held up the device, revealing a picture of herself and Michael with their arms around each other. He was wearing sweaty football gear and had a big grin on his face. "This Michael?" Jen asked gently, a soft smile gracing her lips.

Mia looked at the photo and her heart skipped a beat as she saw the huge plastered smile on his face. He looked so...happy. Her stomach knotted as her mind began to race with the possibility that Michael and Jen were a couple. Her disappointment was palpable as she looked down at the picture, feeling as though the small glimmer of hope she had been holding onto was slipping through her fingers.

Jen's slow smile pulled Mia from her thoughts, and she looked up to find the other woman studying her carefully. "John, my *husband*, is great friends with Michael," Jen explained, her voice gentle. "He was a groomsman in our wedding."

Whoops.

Mia gave her a shy smile filled with embarrassment for being so transparent.

"Wow, this is amazing," Megan mused. "What are the odds?"

Okay...so they weren't going to talk about Michael being in trouble for not telling anyone about the crash?

"I think we should run to the store and buy some scratch-offs because it is Mia's lucky fucking day," Lexie quipped.

Mia could only stare at the women in wonder, marveling at how quickly they had embraced her story and offered their support.

"Do you want us to connect you two?" Megan asked, watching her closely, confirming Mia's buy-in.

Mia bit her lip, contemplating their offer. The idea of reconnecting with Michael both exhilarated and terrified her. What if he didn't remember her? Or worse, what if he did, but had no interest in seeing her again?

She had learned that lesson time and time again: people always leave. Sometimes when you need them the most.

Then again, sometimes people pulled through, even when you didn't ask them to.

"All right, ladies," Lexie declared, taking Mia's silent contemplation as agreement, her voice filled with determination as she clapped her hands together. "I think it's time we put our heads together and come up with a plan to reunite Mia with her hero."

CHAPTER NINE

September 20, Tuesday
Michael

Oh, my fucking God.

Michael sat in the middle of the practice stadium's cafeteria, his plastic tray before him, laden with food he barely tasted.

The loud voices and clattering utensils faded into a sepia background as his gaze locked onto a hauntingly familiar figure standing across the room.

Mia?

His heart pounded fiercely, threatening to break free from his chest, and for a moment, time seemed to stand still.

Was this even real, or did he have a concussion?

He'd passed the protocol last weekend after a savage hit...but here she was.

His angel had returned.

Rather than tell his friends to call 911 for him, Michael just stared.

If he looked away...she might disappear on him, again.

However, Michael was jerked to reality when Jen grabbed Mia's elbow to escort her along the edge of the cafeteria. Mia's eyes scanned over the massive amounts of people who had assembled there for lunch.

Michael's own eyes darted to follow her as he struggled to process the impossible.

She was alive?

She was *here*?

Breathing?

His hands shook.

"Hey. Mikey, you okay?" Danny asked, brow crinkled with concern as he nudged Michael with his elbow. "You look like you've seen a ghost."

"Maybe I have," Michael muttered, unwilling to take his eyes off Mia. Slowly, he pushed up from the bench and without much cognizance of the room around him, made his way around the lunch table.

Their eyes locked as she watched his towering frame come to its full height and Michael's heart thundered in his chest.

Sluggishly, he approached her, with excitement and apprehension coursing through his veins.

"Angel?" he asked, terrified that she'd dissolve away like a mirage.

Instead, she looked up at him, her brown eyes wide and warm as she examined his face. He noticed tears begin to pool at her lash line and her lower lip started to tremble.

He let out a shaky breath. "Angel, baby."

With a whimper, she threw herself into him. Michael was more than ready, and he caught her in a hold so tight before he pulled her somehow closer while pushing his face into her impossible softness of her inky hair.

Distantly, he registered the noise of a hush falling over the room but he refused to move as Mia sobbed into his chest.

After several minutes, Mia lifted her tear-streaked face to look up at him. She was only about six inches shorter than him, so it wasn't like he was awkwardly taller than her. In fact, she fit...*just right*...against him.

"Michael?" Mia blinked, her voice barely above a whisper. "I can't believe it's you." She gaped at him, her expression a mixture of shock and relief. "I mean, I knew it was you. But I just...can't believe I'm really here..."

"Is it really you?" he asked hesitantly, still unable to shake the feeling that this was all some strange dream. "I thought..." He swallowed hard. "They told me you were dead..."

Mia shook her head, tears still tracking down her cheeks. "No. I'm very much alive. Just..." She hesitated, glancing away before returning her gaze to Michael. "Still just me."

"Me too," he admitted, his voice hollow. Memories of their time together on the plane flooded his mind; the connection they shared as they clung to each other during the emergency landing.

"Can we talk?" Michael asked, gesturing to a quieter corner of the cafeteria. Mia nodded and they walked side by side, leaving Jen and the rest of the world behind.

As they settled side by side onto a commemorative bench that was pressed against the wall, Michael couldn't help but notice the way Mia's hand trembled when she rested her purse on the seat beside her. It reminded him of their hands clasped together on the plane, offering each other comfort amid the terror. He wondered if she remembered it too, and what that meant for them now.

In the dim corner of the cafeteria, Michael studied Mia's face more intently. Time had left its mark on her since their last encounter – the lines around her eyes, the dark circles beneath them and there was a certain frailty in her posture. Despite these changes, he thought she looked just as beautiful, if not more so, with this fractured aura which hinted at the very depths of her soul.

"Hi," he said so softly, that he could barely hear even himself over the clatter of lunch trays and boisterous conversations which had returned to the space.

"Hi." Mia's response was equally cautious, her eyes wide as they searched his face for...something.

"It's been a while."

She just stared at him.

"Angel," Michael whispered.

Mia's eyes were glistening and wet , and she let out a choked sob before leaping into his arms again. The world seemed to fall away as Michael held her close, feeling the warmth of her body pressed against his and the beat of her heart against his chest. It was as if time itself had stood still, allowing them this one perfect moment of reconnection.

"Michael," Mia murmured, her voice muffled by his shirt. "I can't believe I found you."

"Me neither," he admitted, pulling back ever so slightly to look down at her tear-streaked face. "I thought I'd lost you forever."

"Guess fate had other plans," she said with a shaky laugh, wiping her eyes with the back of her hand.

"Seems that way." Michael smiled, his heart swelling with equal parts relief and awe. He knew they still had much to say, questions to ask and stories to share. But for now, all that mattered was the undeniable connection that had brought them together once more.

"Where do we even start?" Mia asked, her eyes shining with a mixture of sadness and hope.

"From the beginning," Michael replied, his voice filled with determination. "I'd like to know how you're not dead, so I can figure out who to sue."

Mia chuckled. Guess she thought he was joking...

"Tell me what happened after the rescue," Michael directed, eager to fill in the gaps of their disjointed story. As Mia recounted her experiences, he couldn't resist reaching out to touch her arm or brush a strand of hair behind her ear, reaffirming to himself that she was truly there. Real. And alive..

"Your turn," Mia said once she had finished, her gaze filled with curiosity and concern. "What have you been up to since..."

"Nothing of note. Playing football," he said with a shrug. " Just trying to...move on. But I never stopped thinking about you, Mia. I tried to find you, but a nurse told me you had died. Otherwise, there's no way wouldn't have kept my promise to find you"

Mia twisted her lips together and her eyes shuttered.

What was that about?

Michael adjusted closer to her. "I wish I had known...I would've done something, anything, to find you sooner. I swear."

He explained the situation with the hospital and what he was told to cause him to give up on her. She shared about her PTSD and the therapy sessions she'd been attending. His heart ached for her as he listened, silently vowing to support her in any way he could.

"Thank you for telling me," he murmured, reaching out to take her hand. "You got me, Mia. For whatever you need. I promise." He paused. "And even though I meant it last time, I *really* mean it this time."

She gave him a small smile. There was an ache in her expression that broke his heart. Where was his innocent and bubbly artist? Had the accident really taken that joy for life from her?

She squeezed his hand, their fingers intertwining like pieces of a puzzle finally coming together. "And...I'm here for you too."

Those words said with their hands twined together? It sent a jolt of electricity through him. The touch sparked a vivid memory of the way Mia had admired and fawned over his hands on the plane.

Mia's eyes darkened and she started to avoid eye contact. Michael tensed.

That couldn't be good.

Mia hesitated before admitting a recent struggle. "I...I've been having a hard time with water since...you know."

Michael's heart squeezed in guilt, feeling responsible for her newfound fear. He couldn't shake the feeling that he had done this to her, that his decisions on that fateful night had caused more harm than good.

Maybe he could give her this one tidbit. This one morsel of sharing. If it would help her, he'd open up the floodgates for just a second...

"Sometimes, I can't help but think about the choices I made that night," he confessed, his voice heavy with remorse. "What gave me the right to decide who was allowed to go where? Just based on people's appearances? There are a lot of invisible illnesses...I carry the burden of knowing that some people died because of my decisions."

Mia winced and looked down. "Michael, you weren't responsible for any of it. Especially the deaths-"

He cut her off, nicely, but firmly. "I don't want to talk about it, Angel."

Mia reached out, placing a small, cold hand on his arm. "Michael, you can't let that eat away at you. You did the best you could under impossible circumstances. We all did. Plus, no one from our side-"

"Please. I've done a good job of avoiding it. I just want to move one and not think about it too much if I can help it. Okay?"

She stared at him with so much compassion and understanding in her brown eyes that he started to hate himself even more. He didn't think it was even possible.

Of course, his angel wouldn't condemn him. She still had too much hope and optimism in her heart. If she really thought it through...she'd realize that he was responsible for many deaths that night.

He appreciated her support but she was wrong. The weight of his guilt still anchored his heart, refusing to release its grip.

"Okay," she agreed softly, her bright eyes on him. "I won't push. When you're ready. I'm here."

Man, when was the last time she slept? The hollows under her eyes were filled with dark circles and she looked like she had lost weight.

His heart ached for her.

"Thank you," he said softly, grateful for her understanding and compassion. "It means more than you know."

Around them, Michaels's teammates started filing out of the room. Glancing at his watch, Michael swore.

He had a meeting to get to.

He wished he could spend more time with Mia, but they'd have to reschedule this reunion.

"What are your plans for the evening?" he asked her, not wanting to lose the connection they'd rediscovered.

"No plans," Mia replied, brushing a strand of hair behind her ear. "I have this visitor's pass, so I'll be staying with Jen for the day for something to do. Not sure what time she plans to kick me out." Mia ended with a soft smile.

"Maybe we could grab dinner?"

Her big, dark eyes widened further, and she chewed slightly on her lower lip as she stared up at him, weighing his offer.

What was the debate?

Rather than pushing her into it, Michael waited her out. She sought him out here but maybe that was all she wanted. One and done, then move on.

His heart beat erratically when her lips turned up into a radiant smile, a spark lighting in her face. "I'd love that." She breathed as she beamed up at him.

Thank fuck.

"Good. I'll walk you back to Jen's office before I head to my meeting?" Michael offered, eager for any extra moments together.

"Perfect," she agreed, her voice soft and appreciative.

They strolled arm in arm, the silence filled with light conversation of topics that didn't dredge up painful memories. As they neared Jen's pre-hab room where she worked on the guys, Michael felt both hope and anticipation swirl in his gut.

What did her being here mean?

He hesitated at the door, looking into Mia's eyes. "I'll call you when I'm done for the day?"

"Sounds good," she said, her smile genuine and warm.

As Michael walked away, his mind raced.

What did this mean for both of them? Did she want to be friends? Something more?

Maybe she just wanted to connect with a fellow survivor to help her process the trauma?

A flash of anger bubbled up inside him as he recalled the hospital telling him she had died when she clearly hadn't. As much as he'd like to sue the fucking floor out from under them, in good conscience, he couldn't. Plus, given that he wasn't even supposed to have had that tidbit of information, he knew there was nothing to be done to fix the time together that the miscommunication had stolen from them.

He shook his head, trying to dispel the frustration and focus on the present. The fact remained that Mia was alive and they had found each other once again. In some strange way, it felt like the universe was giving them a second chance.

Michael stepped into the meeting room, ready to face whatever challenges lay ahead, buoyed by the knowledge that Mia was back in his life.

The sun pierced through the windows, casting the room in a brightness that reflected the sunshine that Mia's miraculous arrival had brought to his life. Michael leaned against the back wall as they waited for the final stragglers to show up, his thoughts churning wildly. He couldn't stop thinking about the way Mia's eyes had lit up when she saw him, the faintest hint of a smile tugging at the corners of her lips – it was all so surreal. He let out a sigh, running a hand over his shortly shorn hair as he tried to make sense of the whirlwind of emotions gripping his heart.

Danny sidled up next to him and reclined back against the wall, matching Michael's pose. "So, who was she?"

Michael blinked, returning to the present. "I'm still processing." He mumbled, his eyes staring blankly ahead.

Danny cocked his head in question and Michael sighed, turning his head to answer.

"Mia."

"Mia, who?"

Well, fucking shit.

Once again, he didn't get her last name.

Jesus Fucking Christ.

He bit his cheek instead of sprinting down the hall and demanded she tell him it just in case they got separated again.

That would probably be an overreaction...probably.

Their phones weren't likely to erase each other's numbers, not with the 'hi', 'hi' text chain they made as they walked down the hall.

A truly riveting way to start a conversation...

But it served the purpose of exchanging numbers. So unless the one in a million chance of both their phones breaking at the same time came to fruition...

The way the odds of a plane dropping out of the sky had done...

Shit.

He had to fight the urge to run to the front of the room and track her down. Maybe he could get her social security number as well.

No, he fought the urge to run to the front of the room and grab a marker so he could rewrite her number on his arm. He wasn't going to lose her. Not again.

"Michael? Mia, who?"

"Mia from the plane."

"Wait, what?" Danny's eyes widened in shock. "I thought she was-"

"Dead, yeah, I know." Michael shook his head. "But she's not. And now..."

"Wow, that's...amazing!" Danny grinned, nudging Michael playfully. "So, what does this mean for you?"

"I don't know." Michael's gaze fell to the floor. "I just feel like I've been given this incredible second chance, and I don't want to waste it. But I'm also not entirely sure what to do with it. Just be friends? Something more? I can't read what she wants." Michael swallowed. "She's not exactly..."

"Like your other women." Danny finished the thought.

Michael gave him a dry look. "I don't have 'other women.'"

Danny just shrugged and turned forward again.

"I *don't*. So I've dated a bit. It's not like I have four different baby mamas out there all demanding child support or something."

"Dude. Didn't say a word." Danny pursed his lips and fought to keep the smile off his face.

Danny needed a nut shot. He didn't want kids. So no harm, no foul. He didn't need the jewels to be healthy.

Michael settled for a less violent retort. "Dick."

Danny let one of his arms fall from across his chest and swing down to his side. On the way down, it conveniently made a trip to knock at Michael's own dick.

As Michael wheezed and bent over, trying to catch his breath and quell the nausea, Danny said with a chuckle, "Well, she looks sweet. Not your usual type. Be nice and don't fuck it up."

"Douche."

"Pussy."

He glanced around the room, taking in the familiar surroundings before settling his gaze back on his friend. "Ball tap, really?"

"It was preemptive." Danny shrugged. "It was either you or me. I chose you."

Michael grinned and was finally able to straighten back up against the wall, which was good timing because, at that moment, the coaches stepped up to the board to discuss the game from two days ago and talk about the upcoming home game against Dallas.

Michael couldn't help but feel a touch of hope coursing through him – a feeling he had been lacking since the accident. The memory of Mia's laughter rang in his ears and for the first time in what felt like forever, he allowed himself to entertain the possibility of a future filled with a little peace.

CHAPTER TEN

September 20, Tuesday
Michael

Later that night, when Michael stepped into Mia's quaint apartment, the aroma of sizzling garlic, onion, and soy enveloped him instantly. His stomach rumbled as he eyed the spread of pancit noodles, lumpia, and adobo chicken that was laid out on the counter.

"Wow, you really went all out. This looks incredible," he said, leaning against the doorframe as Mia finished up the last touches.

She shot him a shy smile over her shoulder. "It's not much, just some dishes my mom used to make. I hope you like it."

Michael chuckled. "Are you kidding? A home-cooked meal after a grueling practice is heaven. Though, I do wish you would have waited so I could have helped...and learned the recipe."

She wiped her hands on her jeans and then started to fiddle with the ends of her maroon sweater. "I, uh...wanted to do something nice. Not put you to work."

He gave her a small smile to say he was teasing and waited for her to point him where to go.

They settled down at the dining table to eat. Michael had eagerly piled his plate high and Mia watched in amusement when with the first bite, his eyes closed in bliss.

"Mmm...so good," he mumbled through a mouthful. "Seriously, this is restaurant-quality."

Mia's cheeks flushed pink at the praise. "Thanks. Cooking helps me relax. It reminds me of my mom."

Michael slowed from his ravenous eating, sensing the wistfulness in her voice. "I can't imagine growing up without my parents. I don't see them much anymore but the thought of not having them around when I was a kid...I can't imagine how hard that was..." His voice trailed off, not wanting to stir up what might be painful memories for her.

"Yeah." Mia shifted, staring down at her plate for a moment. Then, her eyes lifted to Michael's and she offered a weak smile. "Some days are still tough. But you make do, you know?"

Michael nodded, holding her gaze with empathy. "I know you have others..." Like Sean...He'd have to get more details on *that* situation at some point. "But I'm here too, whenever you need an ear. About your parents...or whatever."

Just because he wanted to avoid talking about his experience in the crash didn't mean he couldn't listen to her feelings and fears. It was messed up but...that's how his brain was handling it.

He reached over, giving her hand a supportive squeeze. His belly swooped when he touched her and he pulled his hand back.

Fuck, he felt like he was thirteen again.

Mia smiled gratefully. "Thanks. It's not easy dealing with the nightmares and panic attacks on my own." She hesitated, then added softly, "Water...I can't...I'm scared to even shower now. Sean has to sit in the doorway with his back turned in case I have a panic attack."

Michael's heart ached, hating to see her bright spirit dimmed by fear.

It was his fault.

How many others were also suffering because of his decision to allocate them to the water?

"I get it. Water...still gets to me too sometimes."

They moved the conversation to easier topics, ones less nightmare-inducing. Michael marveled at how easy she was to talk to, how she made him feel at peace. He realized that he wanted more of this – more time together, more cozy meals, more...her.

Who would have thought he'd want to trade in the night clubs, parties, and near-naked women for the soulful serenity of nights like this.

Michael smiled at the thought.

Mia shyly returned his smile.

As they finished dinner, Mia placed her silverware on her plate and moved to stand. "I should make us some tea," she said, starting to gather up the dishes.

Michael gently stopped her with a touch on her wrist. "Hey, don't worry about cleaning up. I'll help you later. No rush on my end..." He hesitated, then took a chance. "Would you want to grab dinner tomorrow, too? Maybe that Italian place on Cooley?"

Mia's eyes lit up. "I'd love that."

Just then, the front door opened and a man walked in.

Ahh.

This must be the infamous Sean.

Not the hulking ogre that Michael was hoping for.

He just fit through the front door, was bricked with lean muscle, with perfectly styled chestnut hair and stark hazel eyes.

6'3", 210 pounds of muscle.

Fuck. Not an ogre at all.

Michael felt the need to sidle up next to Mia and wrap an arm around her shoulder.

Sean was doing his own inspection on him. He had frozen in the doorway at the sight of Michael sitting at the table with Mia. Sean's eyes narrowed slightly at the snuggly place settings beside one another, the candles glowing, and the bottle of wine that Michael had brought.

Fuck. This was a complication Michael didn't see coming.

Michael stood up. "Hey man. Michael. Nice to meet you, I've heard a lot about you." He extended his hand.

Sean slowly approached and shook it firmly, jaw tight. Michael could feel the tension rolling off him in waves. Sean's eyes ticked back to Mia, who had remained at the table, watching them curiously. Sean gave Michael's hand a little extra squeeze before releasing it.

"Yeah, man. Same. Sean. Thanks for taking care of my girl on the plane."

It took every ounce of willpower to not stiffen when Sean called Mia 'his girl.'

Fucking shit. The roommate was going to be a problem.

Sean turned to Mia, "I hate to interrupt your evening, but I'm starving. Can I join?"

Yeah sure, he'd just *hate* to interrupt...

"Of course!" Mia beamed up at him and went to bring a fresh plate to the table.

Shit. No wonder the guy was in love with her. The trust and happiness in her eyes when she looked at him was palpable.

And also very much a sibling adoration.

Bad news for the poor guy.

And great news for Michael.

Michael was helping Mia with the dishes when his phone started ringing in his jacket pocket across the room. Normally he'd ignore it, but Sean was catching Mia up on his day, so he decided to step away to give them some privacy.

"Hello?"

"Dude. I need help. I'm trying to get this fucking playset assembled in my back yard and it's impossible."

Michael frowned and pulled the phone away from his ear to double check he saw the caller ID correctly.

"Danny?"

"Yes, you dick. It's me. I bought a playset for Megan's kids, for when they come over to visit and I unpacked everything this afternoon after practice and just assumed it would be easy as shit to assemble."

"And?"

"And it's pitch fucking black out, given that it's eight o'clock and the end of September, and the kids are coming over tomorrow with Megan and I want this shit assembled."

"A lot of work for kids who aren't yours..."

"Shut up and come help me?"

"Man, you said it yourself, it's dark out. Just hire someone to do it tomorrow, when we're at the stadium."

There was a pause and then Danny mumbled, "I don't know, that just doesn't feel right. I want to do it myself."

"With me." Michael added. He turned toward Mia and Sean, who were now both laughing over something she'd said to him.

He itched to join them.

"Yes, with you. Also, Kenny and John are coming over. And Ryan got included, though I'm not exactly sure how. Will you just come so we can bang it out and go the fuck to sleep?"

Michael sighed and looked down at his feet.

"Sure, man. Be there in a bit." Michael rubbed at his eye with his knuckle and dragged himself to the table where Mia and Sean were talking about the New England Revolution game that Sean was going to that weekend.

"Hey, I hate to bail, but I need to get going. My buddy is trying to impress a girl by playing stepdad of the year to her kiddos. He needs a hand setting up their new jungle gym before they have a play date tomorrow. He's all twisted around her finger, but she's great, so I want things to work out for them – otherwise I'd tell him to pound sand. I don't want to leave you with this pile of dishes, but he sounds like he's ready to have an aneurysm. Can I call you tomorrow, about finalizing dinner?"

The hero worship and adoration glowing on her face was certainly not the reason he shared so many details.

Nope. Not at all.

Suck on that, *Sean*.

Mia leaped up from her seat and wheedled close, nearly vibrating in excitement for this unknown-to-her friend. "Oh my gods, yes, absolutely, that's totally fine. And no worries about the dishes, you go play Cupid and just call me tomorrow when you have a sec to iron out dinner."

Mia walked him to the door, cheeks still flushed.

Aware of Sean's eyes burning a hole in the back of Mia's head, Michael took his time saying goodbye and even leaned down to press a little peck to the side of Mia's soft cheek.

There. If that didn't declare his intentions, he didn't know what would.

Roommate needed to get with the program.

As Michael left, he felt a glimmer of something new awakening inside. Hope, happiness...possibility.

He shook his head to get some clarity. When did his intentions toward Mia become so...romantic? When had he decided that he wasn't okay with being just friends?

Maybe around the time he had to fight off his second boner of the night, when Mia had laughed and leaned her head on his bicep.

Fuck, she was adorable.

And sexy as an angel in lingerie.

Shit.

And now he had to walk to his car with yet another boner while he imagined Mia made up heavenly, white lingerie.

Worth it.

CHAPTER ELEVEN
September 20, Tuesday
Mia

Mia closed the door behind Michael, leaning her forehead against it for a moment as she gathered her thoughts. The evening had been filled with unexpected emotional intimacy.

It was intoxicating. Exhilarating. Terrifying.

And addicting.

She wasn't quite sure what she was looking for when she asked Jen to bring her into the stadium so she could see him again...but a sexually charged dinner certainly wasn't it.

Not that she was complaining.

Turning back to the kitchen, unable to hide her smile, Mia saw Sean standing there with his arms crossed, scowling.

"What?" she asked defensively, trying to drop the smile from her lips and failing.

"Nothing," Sean muttered, not meeting her eyes. He turned and started clearing the table with more force than necessary.

Mia watched him for a minute. "What's up?"

Sean froze, then slammed down the plates in his hands. "I had no idea you were going to have Michael Dillon in our house tonight, Mia! You could have texted me to let me know."

She blinked. "I told you I was making dinner for a friend."

He gave her a 'please', look and went back to wiping down the table,

"Hey! Dude. What the heck? I was having dinner with a friend! What's the issue? It's not like we were doing lines on the coffee table."

He rolled his eyes and continued cleaning the table at an irritated pace.

Mia reached for his arm, "Sean—"

But he viciously threw his arm up and away from her grasp. He shuffled away from her, sucking in a deep breath.

"You've been talking about this guy for weeks. I thought you just wanted to shoot him a thank you letter or something, not invite him and his drama into our house!"

Mia blinked and cocked her head. "His drama? What are you talking about?"

"Mia, I know you. You're getting attached. This guy...he's not long-term. He's not a white knight. He's a love 'em and leave 'em kind of guy." He leveled her with a sad look. "The kind that would break your heart in two-point-oh seconds. You guys just don't play in the same league."

Mia jerked back. "Ouch."

Sean winced. "That's not what I meant and you know it. You're so far out of his league, it's not even funny. But he's playing...twister, while you're playing...chess. They're just two very different games and...I'm just worried you're not quite aware of the rules of his type of Twister."

Mia shut her eyes so he wouldn't be able to see them as they rolled into the back of her head.

He was just looking out for her. He was just looking out for her. He was just looking out for her.

It didn't mean she didn't want to bang his head with a frying pan, though.

"Miachel and I are friends, Sean. Believe it or not, we actually had a good time on the plane before we fell from the sky. And yeah, he was incredible during the crash, but that's not what this is. This is something else. And there are no games being played. We're just...friends." She shrugged.

What else could she say?

Sean scrunched his lips and looked away before gazing back at Mia, compassion in his eyes. "I've been here for you since the crash, through all the panic attacks and the nightmares. And now this guy shows up out of nowhere and suddenly he's your new best friend? Do you really think Michael Dillon is going to hold your hair back and rub your back as you throw up during one of your panic attacks?"

Fuck.

A burn started in her sinuses and worked her way down her throat. She swallowed hard and looked at him while shaking her head. "No, I don't think he's going to sit in the doorway while I shower, Sean." She choked out. "But why can't you let me have this? Something that makes me feel good. Alive. Someone who brings a smile to my face. Even if he's going to leave. Even if I'm not his type because I'm quiet and boring." When Sean looked like he was going to interrupt, Mia spoke over him. "I get it. I'm nobody. But can't I just have someone for a little bit who understands what I've been through? Who has that shared trauma? For as long as it lasts?"

"Mia....I'm sorry...I..." Sean trailed off, looking away.

"Forget it." Mia turned away. Luckily, Sean took the hint and backed off, leaving her to deal with the mess in the kitchen.

Then her phone buzzed. It was a text from Michael: a picture of a completely unassembled playset in a dark backyard, surrounded by a couple of men setting up spotlights with extension cords. Mia couldn't help the little flutter in her stomach as she read his message.

Thanks again for dinner, I had a really nice time. I'll call you tomorrow.

Mia smiled softly. She wished she was clever enough to write something witty and flirty back.

But nope, that was not the hand she was dealt.

Instead, she settled for: *Goodnight.* With a little smiley face at the end.

Mia set her phone down with a quiet sigh. At least one relationship in her life seemed to be progressing smoothly. She could only hope Sean would come around eventually. For now, she'd give him space and focus on this fragile new bond growing between herself and Michael.

For however long it lasted, that is.

Mia headed to her bedroom and got ready for bed. As she climbed under the blankets, her mind drifted back to Michael.

She thought about how he'd opened up to her over dinner, confessing his own aquaphobia that stemmed from the crash. The way he looked at her so intently as they talked, his warm brown eyes radiating kindness and understanding. His gentle touch when he bid her goodnight, lips grazing her cheek.

Mia felt her face flush at the memory. There was an undeniable attraction between them, but it was more than that. Michael saw her – not as the girl from the plane crash or Sean's roommate, but as *Mia*. He made her feel safe, respected, and clever.

She wondered if he was thinking about her right now. The idea made her stomach flutter. Still, she hesitated to get too carried away. Sean was probably right. He probably would get bored of her soon enough.

With a sigh, Mia rolled over and tried to quiet her racing mind. This was all so delicate and new: she didn't want to rush in, overcommit, and get hurt.

But as she finally drifted off, Michael's face lingered in her dreams, offering a vision of hope she desperately needed.

And that night, she dreamed of sketching him.

Chapter Twelve

September 23, Friday
Mia

The Italian restaurant that Michael had taken her too went beyond her expectation, as did the way they flirted all night. The dinner went so well that three days later, Mia was stepping through the front door of Michael's home. He'd invited her over for a Friday night not-date date.

Intrigued, but nauseous with anxiety, she naturally agreed.

Now, Mia meandered into the warm glow of the Springfield sunset bathing Michael's living room. The trees were aglow with both the sunlight and the unmistakable palette of autumn.

Look at those huge windows.

Wow.

How had she missed the foliage starting to turn?

"Welcome to my humble abode," Michael said, stepping next to her. "Mi casa es su casa."

Before Mia could respond, he held out a bag of her favorite saltwater taffy from a candy shop back in Seattle. Her eyes widened.

"How did you get these? I can't find them anywhere here!"

"I have my ways," he said with a wink.

Her heart fluttered.

Mia unwrapped a piece and popped a taffy in her mouth, the sweet cherry flavor transporting her back to lazy summer days on the pier. "So," she mumbled around the candy, "did you already have these or did you get them after I mentioned them on the flight."

He simply winked again. "My secret."

Mia laughed, feeling a weight lift from her chest.

Sean had been...difficult the past few days. Overly curious about where she was going, who she was seeing, if Michael had called. After the oh-so-wonderful warning on Tuesday, and his watchful, and judgmental, eyes on Wednesday, as she got ready to meet Sean for dinner, Mia had avoided him for the rest of the week. She didn't want to hear him say that another dinner date on Friday was a bad idea.

She didn't need another reminder that she was playing Cinderella with the notorious Springfield Spartan's prized Bachelor.

"So, you want the tour?"

"Please."

Michael walked her around the beautiful house, giving her time to 'oh' and 'ah' over all his art pieces. The man had a good eye.

"I'd love to see your woodshop shop, if that's okay?"

Michael hesitated, rubbing the back of his neck. "Yeah, sure," he finally said. "It's kind of a mess right now."

Mia followed him through the spacious modern kitchen to a door that was next to the assumed garage door. When he opened the door, that familiar scent of sawdust and stain oil hit her. It smelt like nothing but Michael.

She caught a glimpse of tools glinting, heavy machines lining the walls and half-finished projects scattered around the workshop before Michael suddenly pulled the door closed.

Oh.

She thought they were going to go in...

Michael had already started moving away.

"And now, the moment of truth." He paused at a sliding glass door and faced her. "I'm sorry, but if they don't like you, I'm going to have to ask you to leave."

"What?"

Michael slid the door open, and a beat went by before she heard the thunderous clop of four-legged feet approaching.

Mia barked out a laugh as two enormous dogs came bounding at the doorway, both trying to squeeze through at the same time.

Both dogs gave Michael an adoring sniff of greeting before whipping around to face her.

The Stranger.

"Hi, guys!" Mia immediately dropped to her knees.

Michael had spoken about 'his boys' a lot on the flight. She felt pretty confident that she wouldn't be kicked out.

The two brindle pitbulls greeted them eagerly.

"This is Ace." Micheal squatted down to give one an affectionate rub, "And this softie is Rookie."

Their bodies moved wildly as they left Michael and vied for her attention, sticking their noses in her face and neck when she squatted down too.

"Sorry, guys, you know the rules," Michael said, gently nudging them out of her space. "No licking faces."

Mia laughed as she stood, wiping at her now-wet cheeks. "It's okay, I don't mind."

Michael gave her a small wince. "Yeah, that's cool that you don't mind, but some of my friends have little kids, and I don't want the dogs getting used to licking faces. It's just...easier to keep it a uniform rule."

Mia fought off the blush of embarrassment.

He wasn't chastising her for Pete's sake, but she still felt like she wanted to crawl into a hole and never make eye contact with him ever again.

Michael led them to the living room and settled onto the couch before inviting her to do the same. The dogs flopped down at their feet, gazing up longingly as Michael pulled out an assortment of snacks he'd picked up for their not-date date night.

"Mia?" Michael called out, pulling Mia from a deep observation of her feet.

"Hmm?" She kept her head down.

"Mia."

The seriousness of his voice caused her to look up. "What's up?"

He gave her a heavy look, taking in her expression. "I don't want to play games with you. I want to be able to be me, be honest."

"Okay..."

"I just wanted to explain why I don't let my dogs do something. I wasn't...yelling...at you or something. I was just...explaining." Michael was watching her closely, monitoring her every blink.

Shit, she was ruining this.

She turned to face him, tucking one leg under her. "I'm so sorry, I get a little—"

"Uh, also, please don't put your shoes on my couch."

Before he even finished speaking, both feet were on the floor and her face was on fire.

He started chuckling and slid over to her, throwing an arm around her shoulder and tucking her in close. "Mia, Angel, baby. That was a joke. Put your shoes all over anything you want. I was just trying to lighten the mood." He swayed their bodies a bit, trying to get her body to loosen up.

"Oh, okay..."

Shit. Now she made things awkward.

Gah!

Watching her closely, Michael frowned and put a finger under her chin to make her look up. He peered down into her eyes.

"I'm sorry, it was an ill-timed joke. It's easy to forget that we still don't know each other that well." He pulled away after giving her one last squeeze and started dragging more snacks from the box on the coffee table.

Michael suddenly looked over his shoulder at her with a soft expression on his handsome face. "Yet. We don't know each other that well, *yet*."

Mia took a deep breath, trying to hide the horror coursing through her veins.

Gods, she was such a dork!

"So tell me," Michael said, plowing ahead out of the awkwardness and offering her the bag of pretzels. "How's the art piece coming along for the gallery show?"

Mia sighed, running a hand through her hair. "It's not...It's difficult to get inspired lately. I stare at the blank canvas and nothing comes."

Michael nodded thoughtfully. "I get that. Sometimes I hit walls with my projects too."

"You always seem to have it together though," Mia said.

"Nah, I just hide it well." He gave her a gentle smile. "Is it the medium? Maybe you shouldn't do a canvas piece if it's not vibing for you. What about your sketches? Those were breathtaking."

Ahh, that was sweet.

Mia opened the bag and snagged a pretzel, chewing thoughtfully as she said, "I feel like sketches aren't...powerful enough for this exhibition. I need something unique. Something flashy. Something...heavy. I don't know. It's hard to describe."

"Especially hard when you're not feeling inspired with anything in particular."

Mia chuckled and toasted him with her pretzel. "Bingo."

"Well, if you ever need a place to retreat to, feel free to come here. I'm at the stadium a lot and the dogs would love the company. Plus, I have great natural light and a fantastic view."

He wasn't looking at the windows when he said that last part. It was cliché, but holy heck if her toes didn't start to curl with satisfaction.

Mia's face reddened for an entirely different reason this time. "I'd love that, thanks." She crunched on her snack, feeling a sense of lightness at the sweetness of Michael's flirtation.

She wasn't sure what they were, but yikes, she was all in.

She hadn't felt this alive in...

Ever?

"Okay, so here's my plan for this lovely Friday evening. I have every stupid streaming service imaginable draining my bank account every month and I never have the time to watch any of them. So, my gift to you, my angel…" Dramatically, he held out a TV remote. "Is my controller. Take me on an adventure. Your pick. Then, after, I was thinking Scrabble, or another game that you'll probably destroy me at. I think some of my friends have a Bullshit game happening in a couple of weeks, so if you want to try your hand at that, let me know, and I can wrangle out an invite."

"You don't…" How did she put this delicately…"You don't want to go…out?"

He blinked at her, and his forehead got some adorable little wrinkles as he frowned at her. "What?"

Mia squirmed in her seat. Shit! She overstepped again.

"I guess I just assumed you'd want to go out at some point. Not do all this boring…Mia stuff."

His frown grew deeper as he stared at her.

"You're not a project," Michael said, suddenly, with a sincere firmness in his voice that startled her. "I'm not trying to 'fix' you. You're not a way to kill my boredom. I don't find you, or your interests, boring. Did I like to go out dancing and to clubs? Yes. Do I also find myself thinking of ways to spend time with you that allow me to actually get to know *you*? Yes. If you want to go out, we totally can. I just figured you'd be much happier with a low-key night in."

She couldn't stop herself. "But which one would you be happier with?"

Michael leveled her with a heavy look. One she couldn't read.

Finally, he said. "I'd be happier with the one that got you to laugh and smile more."

Oh.

And there goes more toe-curling.

"Oh." She repeated her mental thought aloud.

He gave her a slow smile and waved the remote. "So, are we going to watch something, or should I go get my car keys so we can head back into the city?"

Mia laughed and looked down at herself. Skinny jeans and a peasant top.

"I'm not exactly wearing my clubbing best. Not sure we'd get in anywhere." She said with a grin.

Michael didn't smile back. "You look perfect. There's not a bouncer in the city who wouldn't let you in."

His words hung there between them, heavy and important. Mia felt heat travel through her body as she stared into Michael's warm, genuine eyes.

"Oh."

A few more heated seconds passed before Michael directed the remote away. "So...stay or leave?"

"Stay," Mia whispered, taking in the beautiful expression of relief that overcame his face.

He grinned and handed her back the remote. "That's what I was hoping for." He then gave her one of his signature winks.

Mia's lower stomach tightened dubiously.

Bless his heart – he didn't even blink when she put on *How to Lose a Guy in Ten Days.*

He even chuckled when he was supposed to!

Mia found herself unable to shake the smile from her face throughout the entire movie. The third-act breakup didn't even phase her – she was too hyperaware of the man beside her.

When the credits started to roll, Michael put down his jar of peanut butter – which he had been eating from with a spoon – and flicked off the tv and its accompanying sound system. In a blink, the room was doused in darkness, before he pushed another button on the remote to make the overhead lights slowly brighten again.

Fancy.

Michael then turned to Mia. "Okay. What do you think? Are you tired? Or do you want to get wild?" he asked, with a playful glint in his eye.

"I'm still hanging, party boy. Scrabble time?"

"Scrabble time." He confirmed with a grin. He walked over to a dark wooden cabinet and started rifling through the various boxes of board games stacked within.

Mia grinned at his back. "I used to play all the time with my grandma when I was a kid."

"Ah, first mistake. You set up expectations. Now it will be double embarrassing when I kick your ass." He trumpeted, as he plopped down on the ground beside the coffee table and tossed the box on the table. "Okay, Queen Scrabble. Let's see what you've got."

Mia smiled and lowered herself to the floor opposite of Michael.

The dogs curled up close near her crossed legs.

Michael frowned as he glowered at them. "Turncoats." He mumbled, the smallest hitch in his lip belied how pleased he was at their approval.

Mia chuckled and gave the dogs some rubs – which she had been doing nonstop since the movie started. It seemed she had two new best friends.

Friends who *didn't* think that Michael was the scum of the Earth or were judging her for seeking him out....

It was an upgrade.

Mia sighed. She should probably try to patch things up with Sean. Sean later. Michael now.

As they drew their letter tiles, Mia said, "I hope you're ready to get your butt kicked."

"Pretty much daily" Michael laughed. "Our offensive coordinator isn't exactly the gentlest guy."

Mia shot him a grin, not having the slightest clue what he was talking about. He didn't say anything more so she went back to looking at her tiles.

They became engrossed in the word game, exchanging good-natured trash talk and trying to out-maneuver each other. Mia bit her lip in concentration as she laid down 'quixotic' on a triple word score.

"Not bad, but I can do better!" Michael countered with 'xylophone' off the X.

Mia giggled. "You cheater!"

"How? Show me where I cheated." He asked, as his hand crossed hers when they both indicated at the board at the same time.

Mia wiped a happy tear from the corner of her eye.

This guy.

He was freaking hilarious. And holy guacamole, Michael was competitive.

It was absolutely adorable.

His eyes sparkled like Christmas. The delicate muscles of his face painted a myriad of emotions as he stared at the board, then his pieces.

He was stunning.

That fierceness, the caring, the intelligence, the beauty.

It was all just so...surreal.

The night was filled with competitive banter intermixed with laughter and smiles. For a moment, it felt like the outside world faded away, leaving just the two of them, content in their bubble.

Fat raindrops began to splatter against the dark windows as a storm swept through.

At some point, Michael wandered up and over to the tall window to stare out at the branches waving in the wind. "Well, that came out of nowhere," Michael remarked, peering outside.

Mia scrutinized before getting up to approach him. Who knew what lows he'd stoop to in order to win the latest round. She'd already caught him 'dropping' a tile and sneaking a peek at her letters while 'looking for it' once already.

Satisfied this wasn't his latest ploy to cheat, she got up and went over to the window as well.

The lightning was impressive as it left silhouettes of the trees around his property.

As long as the water wasn't touching her, it didn't bother her. "It's really coming down out there. We're lucky it wasn't like this when the crash happened."

Thunder rumbled above them.

"No kidding..." His eyes took on a faraway look and a small frown puckered his smooth forehead.

Right...he didn't like talk about it.

She mentally zipped her lips.

With a jerk, he pulled away from the window and walked over to the small docking station that was currently playing the latest hits. His confident fingers reached out and twisted the volume dial, so the catchy song filled the room. Michael then turned and held out his hand to Mia. "May I have this dance?"

Mia's eyes widened and she glanced at Michael in disbelief.

He wanted to dance with *her*?

Here?

"I think I recall a little birdie on a plane telling me about a love of improv dancing..."

Oh, gods. Her heart pounded hard.

How on earth did he remember that?

He was seriously super human.

Either way, improv dancing with him was not something she was mentally prepared for.

She could hardly think straight enough around him as it was!

But the way Michael was looking at her, his eyes sparkling with a playful invitation, was just too irresistible to resist.

Slowly, she accepted his hand, feeling an instant connection as he slowly reeled her into his arms. The mismatched socks on her feet met the warm, polished wood floor of his living room and the two of them began to sway to the music's infectious beat.

At first, they moved with cautious steps, hands held loosely as if testing the waters. Laughter bubbled between them, light and carefree. But as the song picked up its tempo, so did they. Michael twirled Mia gracefully and she responded with a laugh that filled the room with pure, unexpected joy.

There were no choreographed steps, no formalities, just the pure pleasure of moving together to the rhythm of the music. They laughed as they twirled and spun, their bodies responding to the whims of the melody.

The living room transformed into a stage for their impromptu performance. Their dance was uncoordinated, spontaneous and utterly charming. The dogs, their captivated audience. They moved around the room, twirling and spinning, their laughter a sweet serenade to the music. Michael couldn't help but mimic some comical dance moves, earning even heartier laughs from Mia.

Could this guy be any more perfect?

As the song reached its climax, they shared a moment of exhilaration, twirling and spinning together one final time. Breathless and elated, they stopped, their eyes locked in shared euphoria. As the music played on softly in the background, Mia couldn't stop herself from looking up at his beautiful, smiling lips.

What would it be like to have those lips on her?

Not for a little chaste kiss on the cheek like the other night...but for a real, passionate kiss.

A kiss that meant something to her. To...him?

Michael cleared his throat and stepped away, turning back to the volume dial to lower it somewhat. Mia's heart fell into her stomach.

Right. Of course.

She was just Mia. Not a supermodel. Not a princess. Not a starlet. Just her.

And girls like her did not kiss guys like him.

Michael turned back and met her eyes, his expression conflicted. "I'm glad you're here."

Sure. As a friend. Her stomach felt heavy.

Shock rippled through her at how disappointed she was. She hadn't realized that she wanted something *more* with him, yet here she was, disappointed that he didn't want it too.

Maybe Sean was right to have tried to steer her away. He saw her growing infatuation before she even did.

Mia's heart fluttered weakly. "I'm glad I'm here too."

The rain continued falling outside and they finished up their game of Scrabble – this time, much more subdued and contemplative.

Later, they worked side by side in the kitchen preparing dinner. Michael seasoned thick steaks while Mia prepared asparagus and mashed potatoes. The smells of sizzling beef and simmering sides filled the air.

Over the meal they chatted and laughed, swapping childhood stories. Mia's expression grew wistful as she recalled her parents. "I wish I could remember more of them, but most of my memories have faded with time. I'm not even sure which memories are real or imagined at this point. I miss them every day."

Michael reached across the table and gave her hand a comforting squeeze. "I'm sure they'd be so proud of you."

Mia nodded, swallowing hard and blinking back tears. "I do know I used to love swimming with them." Michael nodded, remembering her stories from when they met. "But since the crash, I can't even look at a pool without panicking." She sighed. "The thought of the water on my skin...it's become too associated with the plane crash or something." Kayla Frost, the best therapist in Springfield, had confirmed the connection and although Dr. Frost was probably right, Mia trailed off, not wanting to bore him with the details of her messed up brain.

"It's okay, you don't have to rush anything," Michael said gently. "It's not like you need to be in the water to make a living. There's no rush."

Mia managed a small smile but it was more of a grimace. "Unfortunately, my best brainstorming and inspiration comes to me when I swim...since the crash...it's been...missing."

The rain pattered softly outside as they finished their meal, talking about random pieces of their life.

After cleaning up from dinner, Michael and Mia settled onto the plush couch in the living room. The lights were dimmed low, and the glow of the TV illuminated their faces as they browsed through another movie list.

Mia initially sat on the far end of the couch, being careful to stick to her side but when Michael came back after filling up their popcorn, he hesitated for all of point-two seconds before sitting down right next to her.

With a flick of his thumb, he chose *Angels in the Outfield*.

There. Maybe he'd get her to be a sports fan yet. Not all sports were violent.

Mia curled into his strong frame. He draped his arm casually, yet protectively, around her shoulders and she breathed in his warm, masculine scent.

Had she ever felt this completely at ease and nervous at the same time?

Swim meets had nothing on the nerves bouncing around her belly right now.

As they settled in to watch the movie, Michael's fingers traced light circles on her arm, sending tingles up her spine.

Mia found it hard to focus. Being so close to Michael made her heart race and her skin flush. She couldn't concentrate on anything but the way his leg pressed against hers, his fingers dancing across her arm.

Glancing up, she caught his gaze, his eyes dark and intense. The air between them seemed charged, and Mia couldn't help but notice how dry her mouth was. She regretted her decision to wet her lips when Michael's eyes flicked down to follow the motion.

In slow motion, he gently cupped her cheek and leaned in, capturing her lips in a slow, sensuous kiss.

Mia's breath hitched, and then she melted into the kiss, savoring the softness of his full lips. Her hands slid up his muscular chest to twine around his neck, fingers spreading to feel the fine prickle of his buzzed fade. Michael's strong arms wrapped tightly around her waist, hauling her against him.

The kiss deepened. Mia's pent-up longing finally unleashed.

Mia sighed softly against his mouth as Michael's hands roamed her back, taking her in. She nipped his lower lip slowly and was rewarded with a groan.

Finally, they broke apart, both breathing heavily. Mia's lips tingled deliciously. Michael's dark eyes smoldered with desire. No words were needed. The kiss said everything. They came together again, losing themselves in each other. The movie played on, forgotten.

After a heavy, but fairly tame make-out session, Michael pulled away and rested his forehead on hers.

"Angel. We gotta stop."

She just stared at him, her breath heavy. She lowered her gaze to his lips.

"I'm serious, we need to cool it."

Again, she said nothing and just closed her eyes, leaning harder into him.

"Fuck, you're perfect." He groaned, matching her pushback.

She peeked up at him and his face was anguished.

Shit.

She sat up.

What did that mean?

He gently pulled away and fidgeted, adjusting his pants and how he was sitting, now leaving some distance between them.

Michael rubbed hard at his face, and then leveled her with a look that had her giggling.

"That wasn't supposed to happen. It was supposed to be a fun movie, some games, dinner, maybe another movie if the night was going well. It wasn't supposed to be me getting to first base."

First base? That was a football phrase, right?

She knew what it meant in the make-out world, but what did it mean in the sports world?

If she was going to be in Michael's life...she made a mental note to look up football terms when she got home.

"Okay, here's the deal. You sit there. I sit here. No touching. No kissing. No checking each other out."

Mia laughed quietly and one of the dogs picked up their head to watch her.

"And no giggling. And next time, you wear a parka and huge, baggy sweatpants."

Mia looked down at herself. Black jeggings and a white V-neck tee. Hardly seductive clothes.

But, by the way Michael's eyes were already breaking his 'no checking each other out' rule, it was working for him.

Noted.

She suppressed a victorious grin.

As they spent the rest of the friend-zoned night watching what little remained of the movie, Mia couldn't keep the smile off her face.

He liked her.

However that happened.

All-star, stud running back, Michael Fucking Dillon liked *her*.

And for once, Mia forgot about how normal and unremarkable she was.

CHAPTER THIRTEEN

September 28, Wednesday
Mia

The sun sparkled through the floor-to-ceiling windows onto the pool's surface, glinting off the water like tiny diamonds. Mia stood at the edge of the pool, her toes curled over the cool concrete as she breathed in deeply, inhaling the familiar tang of chlorine and steeling herself for another attempt at conquering her fears. Michael stood beside her, his hand strong and unwavering in hers, providing both physical and emotional support.

"Whenever you're ready," he murmured, his voice soft and encouraging.

Taking a deep breath, Mia stepped into the unheated pool, the water lapping at her ankles as goosebumps erupted on her skin. She focused on the sensation, trying to acclimate herself to the feeling. Each second back in the water felt like a triumph. The familiar sensations of buoyancy and resistance, the gentle caress of the artificial currents, and the chemical smell burning her nose – it was as if a part of her soul had reawakened.

"See?" Michael said with a smile. "You've got this. That was so much easier than it was a few days ago."

Michael had come up with the idea over dinner last Friday night. They'd figure out a time, and he'd go with her, daily, to the local indoor pool. He'd be there with her while she tried to convince herself to touch the water. This was the fourth time they'd come together and as much as her body was healing, her mind was still catching up. Inside her chest, anxiety churned like stormy seas, its waves crashing against the shores of her newfound confidence. So much of her art was inspired by her time in the water.

Mia had always felt an inexplicable connection to water. Its fluidity, its power, and its unpredictability drew her in like a magnetic force. But it was more than just the physicality of it; water held a deeper meaning in her life. It was her sanctuary, her escape, and now, her greatest fear, all rolled into one.

It was in her therapy sessions that she realized the inseparable link between her fear of water and her artistic block. Her therapist had encouraged her to reconnect with the element that had once been her muse.

It was a daunting task, filled with terror and trepidation, but Mia was determined. Even with just her feet in the water, she could already feel the pull of her need to create. Especially with Michael being the one standing beside her, holding her hand. She wanted to sketch the ripples on the surface, show the interplay of light, and the mesmerizing dance of bubbles.

The gallery submission piece weighed heavily on her, the expectations and pressure driving her to sleepless nights as she struggled to bring a vision, any vision, to life.

When she got on that plane, she thought she knew exactly what types of pieces she was going to feature at the end of October at the gallery exhibition.

Now...

Now, the same ideas that had filled her with hope, determination, and optimism felt...immature.

Naïve.

Too innocent and juvenile.

Frantically, Mia stepped from the water and Michael was waiting with a towel.

"Thanks," she whispered, her voice trembling slightly as she accepted the towel. Michael followed her to the bleachers and they sat, both staring blankly as others swam their laps. She began rubbing the droplets off her feet. "If I can't find it in me to create something inspired...why did I even come to Springfield? It makes the plane ride, the crash, all feel so...pointless. I want the pieces to be perfect, but nothing feels right."

He looked at her, his eyes warm and gentle. "Mia, your art was incredible. You have so much talent, and you're only going to get better as you continue to grow. Don't let self-doubt hold you back. You got this."

"Easy for you to say," she replied, attempting a weak chuckle to lighten the mood. "I mean, you're a pro athlete."

"Hey," Michael said, his voice laced with humor, "I wasn't always a pro. I had to work my way up, face my own doubts and fears. And trust me, there were plenty of them."

Mia tried her best not to pout, but failed if his smile was anything to go by. "Really? Like what? Give one example."

Michael hesitated for a moment, then sighed. "Well, I guess one of the biggest fears I had was not being good enough. I thought that no matter how hard I worked, there would always be someone better."

"And? How did you fix that?"

Michael blinked and turned to her, his face filled with chagrin. "I mean, I guess I haven't really tackled that one yet. I'm still in my prime, ya know?"

Mia chuckled and faced forward again, chucking her shoulder against his.

"Gee, thanks. That's a lot of help."

He nudged her back. "Anytime."

Gods. she wanted more with him. But she also didn't want to risk what they had – it was so special.

They sat in silence for a minute more before Michael interrupted their reverie. "Also, I think you're being too hard on yourself. I know you came out here for the exhibition opportunity and it could change your life. But...hasn't your life already been changed? You talk about Lexie, Jen, and Megan all the time—they've totally adopted you into their circle. And..." He cleared his throat and peeked a look at her before swiftly looking away. "And you have me. So maybe the whole trip out here wasn't completely wasted."

Mia's heart gave a solid thump in her chest and her stomach warmed.

Yes, yes she did have him.

She nudged him with her shoulder and looked forward, not making eye contact. "Here you are. Right again. Dropping truth bombs like they're candy."

"Like, I said, happy to help." His blinding smile was facing the opposite wall, but he'd never looked more beautiful.

Once again, her fingers itched to sketch him.

CHAPTER FOURTEEN

September 30, Friday
Mia

With Michael's encouragement echoing in her ears, Mia faced each of the following days with renewed determination. Her progress in the pool became a symbol of her strength and drive, a reminder that she deserved a spot in an apprenticeship with Asher Wielde.

Michael was her constant companion, even if he couldn't be there in person. He was always just a text away.

Their connection felt natural, but there was an unspoken tension simmering beneath the surface, waiting to be acknowledged and explored. However, Michael hadn't made another move.

She wanted to scream.

Why wouldn't he kiss her again?

Was it regret? A moment of weakness? Had he not felt that spark? What was it?!

Thankfully though, in the meantime, she had begun to mend the fences with Sean.

But because he was still pouting a little, Mia conveniently failed to mention that talking with Michael was an everyday occurrence at this point.

On Friday afternoon, Mia stood in the living room, holding a paintbrush poised above a blank canvas. The empty space stared back at her, daring her to make a mark, but the inspiration she craved refused to come. She sighed and glanced over at Sean, who sat on the couch, fiddling with his phone.

She wished she could call Michael and hear his voice. Something about his presence inspired her to *create*.

She could only imagine how Sean would react if she called Michael to come pose for her now.

Sigh.

Hiding her friendship with Michael from Sean filled her with the heebie-jeebies.

Okay, no calling Michael. She just needed to put the brush...on the canvas. Who cared if it was bad? She just needed to *start*.

"What are your plans this weekend? Want to hit up a baseball game with me tomorrow?"

Shit.

"I can't."

Mia had already made plans with Michael. His team had a bye week.

Which, based on her research, meant they had a week off. Michael wanted to take her somewhere and she had yet to guess correctly what he had planned.

And, given the climate with Sean concerning Michael...she was hoping to keep their day date a secret.

Well, not quite a secret, but...an exercise of discretion.

An omission of facts.

"Another day out with the girls?" he asked, not looking up from his screen. His tone was casual, but there was an edge to it that made Mia's brow furrow.

She bit her lip, unsure how to respond.

"Uh, yeah. They're taking me on a day trip."

"They're taking you on lots of trips lately. You should have them come by so I can meet them. They sound great."

The girls *were* great. She texted with them all the time, too. But all the white lies were stacking up and her house of cards was sure to crumble. All it would take is one of them to make a confused comment about not having gone on a day trip for her jig to be up.

Shit! She didn't want to live like this.

Lying to her best friend? What was wrong with her?

She chewed on her lip and stared at the blank canvas before slashing a line of paint across it, not even relishing the slide of the wet brush over canvas.

"Yeah, I'd like that. They're awesome. Maybe one day next week we can have them over for dinner?"

Sean paused and slowly looked up at her. "Yeah?"

"Yeah. I think it would be great to introduce you guys. I can have the girls come, maybe have their guys over too. You can get some of your buddies over too. It can be a delayed, 'We're-new-to-the-area' party."

Sean's face was pleasantly surprised until the smile fell somewhat. "You haven't mentioned Michael. Is he old news now?" His tone was concerningly neutral and he was watching her carefully, like he was afraid she was going to start crying.

Crap.

Mia rubbed her foot into the floor while she stared at the smear of red on her canvas.

What did she say to that?

"Um, yeah. I'd invite Michael too. He's friends with everyone. I wouldn't want to be rude."

There was a beat of silence, then, "Right. Wouldn't want to be rude." Sean smacked his phone down on the cushion next to him and out of the corner of her eye, Mia saw him turn to face her. "Might want to give him a plus one though. The headlines are boasting the latest fling between him and that sports reporter, Peyton Knowles. They were seen just last night, cozying up at Versailles, that fancy rooftop restaurant everyone is always talking about."

Mia willed every cell in her body not to react to Sean's bait.

She knew about the dinner date: it was an exclusive interview. Peyton had picked the place and Michael let her company pick up the tab for his meal.

He got a filet and a lazy lobster.

But Mia wasn't supposed to know all that confidential, insider information that wouldn't have been in the article Sean had read. The one he was all too gleeful to share.

"Yeah, I'll let him know he gets a plus one, too."

She knew Sean was protective of her, but...come on, dude.

Sean's comments were starting to feel less like concern and more like jealousy.

She was having way fewer panic attacks and could shower without him being in the doorway now. Maybe he was feeling not only jealous...but a little less...needed.

Still, she couldn't quite bring herself to confront him about it, choosing instead to focus on her canvas.

"Maybe I should take a break," she suggested after a few more moments of staring at the singular stroke she'd made. "Want to grab some food?"

Maybe a change of scenery and topic would help revert things back to normal.

Sean had...changed since moving here. He swore that he was moving here because he *wanted* to. Not because of her. But she couldn't help but wonder if she wasn't the only one keeping secrets.

"Sounds good," Sean agreed, while standing and pocketing his phone.

They walked to a nearby diner, falling into their familiar routine of friendly banter. But as they sat down at the booth, Sean just couldn't seem to resist taking another jab at Michael.

"Did you know that he's been seen with a different woman every week since the crash?" he asked casually, stirring his coffee. "He's not the most reliable guy, Mia. I'm glad you guys pumped the brakes and let that connection fizzle."

A different woman every week? Not likely.

He would have told her he was seeing people...right? Plus, they were spending a ton of time together - as much as his football schedule allowed - there was no way he had time to carry on other relationships.

"Where did you hear that?" she countered, unable to deny the squirm in her belly. "Besides, it's not like I'm dating him or anything. We're just friends."

"Friends who went through some shit together. That's bound to connect you, even if the similarities end there," Sean pointed out, his voice tight. Apparently, she wasn't being as sly as she thought she was. "And if he can't commit to someone, what makes you think he can commit to you?"

"Sean, like I said before, I appreciate your concern," Mia said, trying to keep her voice steady. "But I'm a grown-ass woman, and I can make my own decisions about who I spend my time with. Besides, you're the one who encouraged me to make new friends."

"Yeah," Sean admitted, frowning down at his silverware. "But I didn't expect you to cling so close to someone like him."

"Cling? What am I? A barnacle?" Mia squeezed her fists together so she would reach over and smack him upside the head.

Why was he being so judgmental about Michael when he'd done nothing to deserve it?

Not to mention, throwing shade at her in the process?

"Just..." Sean muttered, shaking his head. " be careful. And don't get too attached. That's all."

"Mhm."

Wisely, Sean finally shut up.

He hadn't been her best friend for two decades without learning how to read her 'piss off' expression. He knew he was on thin ice.

Yet he felt the need to warn her anyway, because he was worried about her.

Mia reached over and thwacked his wrist with her spoon. "I love you, ya know?"

Sean grinned and shook his head. "But shut the fuck up, now?"

"Mm."

Sean shot her a bemused grin and went back to people-watching as they waited for their food to arrive.

As they ate their dinner, she couldn't help but let her thoughts drift back to Michael.

She couldn't deny that there was a connection between them, something deeper than friendship. But Sean had no idea how right he was weeks ago when he warned her away from Michael.

Michael really *was* in a different league than Mia.

What chance did she have against his prior flings? She wasn't even on the same planet as them.

And given that Michael hadn't made any other moves on her...maybe he realized that, too.

Maybe she was his pity project, despite his words to the contrary.

Just the poor little girl who decided to 'cling' to him in the aftermath of the plane crash. Maybe Michael's charitable, good-nature made it too hard for him to look her in the eyes and just say no

CHAPTER FIFTEEN

October 1, Saturday
Michael

The next day, Michael watched Mia from the driver's seat of his blacked out Rolls Royce Ghost, as she gazed out the passenger window. She looked gorgeous, as usual, with her dark hair blowing in the breeze. The team had a bye this weekend, so he was taking full advantage.

He was going to give her a taste of New England living.

Apparently, she'd snuck out without telling Sean that she was seeing him Michael and knowledge of the defiant act sent sparks of adrenaline racing through his blood..

Fuck Sean and his judgmental attitude. Michael could see just how it weighed on Mia and how much lighter she looked out from under her roommate's thumb.

He wanted none of that poison to infect her today.

Mia turned to him, brown eyes glinting mischievously. "Thanks for being willing to meet me around the corner."

He grinned and tried to hide how much it actually bothered him; he'd never been anyone's dirty little secret before.

He didn't care for it.

"Anytime. What are friends for?"

Friends. The word stuck in his throat. His feelings for Mia had been growing steadily, though he hesitated to make a move.

He was no good for a pure soul like hers.

Still, he relished these stolen moments together.

Mia sighed, leaning her head against the window. "I hate fighting with Sean. He's been my rock since we were kids. But lately, he's just so..."

"Overbearing?" Michael suggested.

"Yeah." She gave a half-smile. "I get that he's just trying to protect me. But I'm not made of glass."

"No, you're not." Michael squeezed her hand.

Mia pursed her lips together and gave him a tight smile before shaking off whatever irritations lingered on her mind. "Okay, so what's first on our list."

"Berkshire Mountains."

"You know I grew up outside Seattle, right? I'm no stranger to mountains."

Michael shook his head, fighting off a smile. "Nah, these aren't like your mountains. Your mountains were a different beast. These...these are the things that dreams are made of. Especially right now." He brought his fingers to his lips for a chef's kiss. "The foliage will bring you to your knees."

Mia laughed, "Spoken like a true local."

"Well, adopted local. But local all the same. I think if I had to choose between renewing my contract for the Spartans, retiring, or being traded to some place in Texas..." He turned and gave her a wince. "Would you still hang out with me when I was unemployed and not even thirty?"

Mia thought about it. "Would you still be able to get me my salt-water taffy?"

"Not even a question."

She smiled and looked back out the window. "Then...sure. I could still be friends with a lazy bum."

Friends.

Fucking hell.

Michael fought back the twist in his gut. He wanted so much to explore what was growing between them – what overtook him last weekend when he kissed her.

But, nope.

Not going to happen.

He wouldn't risk hurting her like that.

What if they didn't work out?

Let's face it – they probably wouldn't.

She despised sports! And he was a fuckin' professional football player. They didn't get more opposite than that.

She asked him if he scored 'a try' last Sunday. He wasn't a damn rugby player!

Mia clearly had no idea what he even did for work...and honestly didn't seem all that interested in learning.

That couldn't have been a good omen.

Then again, when they were together...it didn't feel like a problem at all.

· · · · ● · ● · ● · · ·

After an hour of taking winding roads up and out of the concrete jungle, Michael threw the car in park at a small mountaintop rest area. They climbed out to soak it all in and the rolling hills in front of them didn't disappoint. A soft gasp escaped Mia's lips as she stood in awe at the breathtaking landscape before her. Reds, oranges, and yellows painted the trees, aflame against the diamond blue sky while the crisp breeze carried the scent of autumn.

"Wow," she breathed, her hand brushing his lightly as they shared the majesty of the view.

He smiled, reveling in her delight. "Told you. If you like this, I'll take you up to the Kancamagus Highway in New Hampshire. It's breathtaking."

Her cheeks flushed pink, either at his invite or at the beauty of the world stretched out in front of them. And as he watched her take in the vista, his heart swelled.

"Want to walk around a bit before we hit up our next leg of the trip?"

Luckily, Mia was down to head out early this morning so he didn't feel the need to rush, even though they did have a schedule to keep.

But with the way her eyes were soaking in the colors, they could take some time...

"I'd love that," she beamed, before pulling out her phone to begin capturing the landscape. She even decided to snap a few of him.

He returned the favor, taking longer than required to frame up the shots.

Damn, she was pretty.

After exploring for thirty minutes or so, they hopped back in his car for the next stage of their Saturday excursion. The two hour ride to Boston felt like it flew by; Mia mentioned that it didn't feel like the drive had taken that long, so apparently she felt the same.

The thought warmed his heart but also made him anxious.

What *were* they?

Friends?

Something more?

She smiled at him like she wanted something more...

Then again, maybe this *was* just friendship for her.

Look at Sean. The poor fucker had been reading her smiles wrong for years. Michael didn't want to be *that* guy.

Plus, she hadn't given him any hint she wanted him to kiss her again...so, there was that.

Once they arrived in Boston, Michael took her to the Museum of Fine Arts. While in the large crowds, Michael was cognizant of the people around them. He didn't want to be hounded for photos. He wore a flat-brim cap and sunglasses on, even inside. It made him look like a douche, but it gave them the peace to wander around without getting accosted by fans.

After exiting the museum, they boarded the infamous Duck Boats for a guided spin around the city. In a thick Bostonian accent, the tour guide gave the sightseers all the juicy intel on the city during their ride on the Charles River, past historic landmarks and through the heart of the city. Mia laughed hysterically at the ConDUCKtor's puns and would lean hard into Michael at every dad joke uttered. The tour guide was eating it up.

So was Michael.

Fuck, she smelled good. Like earth and art, all rolled into one perfect, pint-sized package.

Michael wished he had time to take her to the aquarium or on a sunset cruise of the harbor, but this would have to be enough for the day. They still had one more stop to make.

· · • · • · • · • · ·

As the sun began to set, Michael led Mia back to the car. "Stick with me. We have one more stop before we head home, and then you can crash."

"Crash? Hell no. I'm going strong. Bring it on. I can't see how you can possibly beat what we've done so far. Unless...is it puppies? Are you going to take me to play with puppies?"

Michael grinned at the windshield as he pulled out on the hectic Boston streets.

Fucking Danny.

"I believe Danny set the bar too high on that one."

Mia grinned and tucked a wayward piece of black hair behind her petite ear. "Megan told me about it. It was epic."

"So, you're saying I'm falling short?"

Mia shrugged and tossed him a disappointed look. "I mean…it was puppies. He took her to play with puppies. You fed me a lobster roll. I'm not saying it's a competition, but…"

Michael's head snapped back as he let out a roar of laughter. He had to force himself to look back at the road so they didn't wind up in a ditch – but it took a lot more work than he'd care to admit.

He couldn't stop the smile from spreading over his face.

Fuck, even his cheeks hurt.

Content to not push for any more details on their next destination, Mia filled the silence as Michael drove by recounting her favorite parts of the day so far. She even went on to daydream openly about all the places she wanted him to take her to next.

Imperial little angel.

He loved it.

When they finally passed the 'Welcome to Salem' sign, her eyes lit up. She strained against the seatbelt, looking out the windows as they drove through to the center of town. She was practically drooling.

"Salem? Really?"

"Hey, once upon a time, I said you should go on a ghost tour. I repay my debts. I'm basically a Lannister. Anyway, Lexie *finally* got back to me. She said this one was the best."

As Michael led Mia down a dimly lit cobblestone street, the evening air carried a small chill. However, Michael guessed that by the way Mia was practically vibrating next to him, she was probably too amped to even register the cold.

The street became narrower, the old brick buildings leaning in conspiratorially. The atmosphere shifted, the weight of history hanging in the air like an old, forgotten secret. She looked around, brows furrowed in amazement, trying to see…ghosts?

Michael shivered.

Fuck, he hoped that shit wasn't real.

As they turned a corner, they were greeted by the sight of a small group gathered outside an imposing, centuries-old building.

A flickering lantern hung by the entrance, casting eerie, elongated shadows.

As they joined the group, the guide, dressed in period attire, welcomed them with a dramatic flourish. His voice was rich and velvety, designed to send shivers down spines.

"Welcome, ladies and gentlemen, to the haunted heart of this city!" he proclaimed. "Prepare yourselves for a journey through the shadows of the past, where tales of the supernatural and the unexplained come to life." His eyes landed on Mia and he added, "If you need an arm to escort you across our unsteady roads, please feel free to use mine."

And then the bastard shot Mia a wink.

Asshole.

Michael wanted to rip his powdered-wig head off when he heard Mia's little laugh next to him.

He was standing right there!

For all that guy knew, Michael was her fucking husband.

Michael ground his teeth but quickly found himself distracted by the way that Mia then latched onto his elbow.

Okay. That wasn't so bad.

Mia glanced up at Michael, her excitement infectious.

"Oh, my gods. Oh, my gods. Oh, my gods." She gave a little jump onto her toes as she leaned into him and squeezed his arm tighter still.

Okay. This wasn't bad at all.

The night was filled with eerie stories and chilling legends and despite all of the beauty the old, moonlit city had to behold, Michael couldn't take his eyes off Mia. Her eyes twinkled with the telling of each tale, and she clung to his arm a bit tighter when the guide divulged some particularly spooky anecdotes.

As they moved deeper into the heart of the city, the cobblestone streets grew narrower, and the old buildings pressed closer. Shadows danced on the walls and the chill of the breeze made them draw closer together.

"Are you scared?" Michael whispered, his lips brushing her ear.

Mia shivered. From fear or something else?

"A little," she admitted, her voice barely more than a breath, exhaled from her pretty little lips as a puff of fog.

Well, if she was scared, the polite thing to do would be to comfort her.

That's what *friends* do, right?

He slid his arm over her shoulder and tucked her in close. Despite the slender allies, the group continued winding after the tour guide as he led them through Salem's depths. The city seemed to come alive with stories of restless spirits, unexplained phenomena, and spooky encounters.

As the tour came to a close, they found themselves standing outside an ancient cemetery, with the moonlight casting an ominous glow on the crumbling headstones. The guide shared a final tale of lost love and tragic endings, and Michael couldn't help but glance at Mia. Her eyes held a mix of wonder and apprehension, her vulnerability only making her more enchanting.

The group dispersed, leaving them alone by the centuries-old graves. Michael turned to Mia, his gaze unwavering. "Did you enjoy it?"

Mia smiled, a soft, genuine expression that reached her eyes. "I did. Thank you so much. This was...so awesome."

She seemed...lighter. Like she had when he'd first met her on the plane.

Michael itched to kiss her, to taste the sparkle of her joy on his own lips, but he held back. A cemetery wasn't exactly romantic, despite how amicable she seemed to be feeling.

As the tour group dispersed, they wandered hand in hand through the lamp-lit streets of Salem. In a quiet courtyard, an old stone fountain stood ringed by tall oaks. Mia hurried over to it, her excitement shimmering in her wide, dark eyes.

"I've heard this fountain is haunted," she said in a hushed voice. "People say if you toss a coin in and make a wish, it's guaranteed to come true."

Michael chuckled at her earnestness. "Well, let's test it out then. I don't carry change though. Think it will take a ten?"

Mia slapped at his arm and chuckled. "I have some coins. Keep your paper, you high-roller."

She fished some coins from her small purse and handed half to him. They closed their eyes, and tossed them into the burbling water. Mia's eyes were still closed, deep in concentration over her wish. Michael gazed at her upturned face, thinking his wish had already come true.

He had found his angel.

Mia's eyes fluttered open, meeting his tender look. She glanced away, tucking a strand of hair behind her ear.

Just then, a bloodcurdling scream pierced the quiet night air. Mia jumped, grabbing Michael's arm.

"What was that?" she whispered.

Michael scanned the courtyard, then laughed, pointing to a speaker mounted in a tree. "Just a Halloween sound effect, I think."

Mia exhaled in relief, "It's October first! We have a whole month to go."

"And yet, here we are. At a ghost tour." Michael teased.

Damn, she was adorable.

"Fine. But there could have been a sign. What if I had a heart condition," Mia grumbled, her cheeks visibly bright pink even in the dim light.

"Then you probably wouldn't be on a ghost tour in Salem."

Mia narrowed her eyes at him and the adorable scrunch of her nose had him laughing, raising his hands in placating fashion. "My lips are sealed."

She gave him a haughty look and perched on the fountain's stone edge, trailing her fingers along the stones.

"Scaredy cat." He couldn't resist adding before settling beside her, their shoulders touching.

After a beat of frozen time, Mia took a deep breath and slowly lowered her hand into the fountain's water. Her fingers continued to dive down and down until the water was up to her wrist. Michael stilled, knowing just how difficult this was for her. Yet, she held her hand under, gazing at the ripples spreading from her fingers.

Then, without warning, she flicked her hand up, splashing him across the neck and chest with the cold water and giggled at his stunned expression.

"Scaredy cat, my ass." Mia jested, "Who was clutching who during the ghost tour, hm?"

So, he jumped once or twice...everyone did...

"Oh, it's on now," Michael laughed, cupping water in both hands and tossing it at her.

Mia squealed, returning fire. They carried on like kids, laughing and splashing one another until they were soaked to the skin.

When was the last time he'd felt so carefree?

When Mia finally surrendered, shivering, he wrapped her in his jacket. She snuggled into its warmth, meeting his eyes again, coyly.

Shit. He was falling for this girl. Hard.

Michael studied Mia as she huddled in his jacket. Her wet hair curled around her flushed cheeks, eyelashes spiky from the water. She looked so vulnerable, yet so full of joy.

He thought back to when they'd first reunited after the accident, how timid and nervous she'd been. She'd come so far since then. Michael knew firsthand how trauma could change a person, make them afraid of living.

Yet here Mia was, laughing and playing in water, something she'd avoided for so long. Michael was amazed by her strength. He wanted to wrap her up and keep her safe even while he understood that she didn't need anyone to do that for her.

How had this introverted, cautious girl crept so deeply into his heart? She was the opposite of his usual type. But Michael found himself captivated by her sweet spirit, her resilience.

Mia tilted her head, cheeks pinking further. "What?" she asked self-consciously.

Michael brushed a damp curl behind her ear. "You're amazing, you know that?"

She smiled, ducking her head.

Nope, none of that. Not on his watch.

Michael tilted her chin back up and kissed her, soft and lingering.

When they finally drew apart, he kept his forehead pressed to hers, not wanting this perfect moment to end.

Well, she kissed him back. So, that was promising.

Taking things slow was...foreign. This dance they had going was fucking...glacial.

But for now, he was content with sweet kisses and wandering hands. It felt...wrong to push for anything more.

Michael knew his reputation as a ladies' man.

Yet here they were, strolling through a moonlit courtyard with a kind, gorgeous woman who saw him as more than just People's People's Sexiest Man Alive. Who liked his mind, as much as she liked his looks. Who didn't view him as a one-way ticket to fame.

Who made him feel worthy of a pure kind of love.

Michael smiled as he glanced down at Mia, her head nestled against his shoulder. He loved seeing the contentment on her face, knowing he had brought her exuberance after so much hardship.

He wanted more...and yet...

What if it ruined what they had?

As they left the courtyard, they had to walk past a statue of a witch burning at the stake.

Michael tensed.

Fuck, that was macabre. Though, fitting given the history.

As Mia leaned closer to read an information plaque, Michael sensed someone approaching through the misty night. He stiffened, not having realized anyone else was in the courtyard with them.

"Tragedy follows you, doesn't it?" An old woman said as she drew closer to them, staring up at the burning witch. She cocked her head as she inspected the statue before turning to Michael, and whispering to him: "I sense a lingering shadow in your past. Unfinished business, perhaps. Be wary of the weight you carry, for it may cast long shadows on your future. Remember, the past has a way of seeking retribution in the most unexpected of ways."

The woman then leaned forward and handed Mia some glow sticks, speaking in an entirely different voice, "Have a great rest of your night." And then she left.

Like she wasn't just a messenger from Satan himself.

Michael didn't buy into this shit...so why was the hair on his arms sticking up straight and why did he feel like he was going to vomit everywhere?

His mind was a whirlwind of doubt and disbelief. He clenched his jaw, trying to shake off the unsettling words of the old woman.

Mia, blissfully unaware of his internal turmoil, playfully dangled a glow stick in front of him, which painted her skin lime green. "I need the light. As a nonbeliever, you only get one, Mister I'm-not-scared," she teased, her voice teasing and carefree.

He forced a smile and accepted the glow stick, but as they walked away, the courtyard seemed different, darker, as if the shadows themselves whispered secrets. Michael couldn't help but glance back at the burning witch statue, as a sense of foreboding settling over him. He had always been a skeptic, but tonight, as they ventured deeper into the haunted world of Salem, doubt gnawed at the edges of his mind.

Michael compulsively wiped his hand on his jeans, feeling phantom water that was no longer there.

What in the actual fuck was that?

CHAPTER SIXTEEN

October 3, Monday
Michael

Michael stood at the edge of the field with Danny, watching their offensive coordinator's face turn a deep shade of crimson as he tore into their quarterback. Butch's arms flailed wildly as he gesticulated, spit flying from his mouth as he berated Ryan for some stupid, immaterial mistake. Michael winced in sympathy, remembering all too well the sting of Butch's sharp tongue from his early days with the Spartans.

Out of the corner of his eye, Michael spotted John Costner stomping over, his usually friendly face darkened with anger. As John reached Ryan, he stepped between the quarterback and the bellowing coordinator. Ryan's shoulders sagged in relief while Butch's tirade ramped up a notch at the interruption.

Michael shook his head, muttering under his breath, "Here we go again."

Beside him, Danny sighed. "He's really turned up the *dickhead* this season."

Michael took an offered water bottle from one of the staff and squirted it into his mouth through his face mask before handing it back. Danny did the same.

"So, uh, Jen mentioned you've been skipping out on your sessions with her lately," Danny said, keeping his eyes on the argument. "She's afraid she might've done something to upset you."

Guilt squeezed Michael's chest. He took off his helmet, scrubbed a hand over his face, and groaned. "Ah man, no, it's nothing like that."

How could he explain his aversion to the water without Danny prying further and getting even more worried than he already was?

Where Mia had seen progress...Michael had seen regression.

Even thinking about pools and tubs knotted his stomach lately.

And Jen's preventative rehabilitation work had a lot of water recovery weaved into her therapies. Michael just wasn't ready for that. Or ready to tell anyone the truth.

But Danny and Jen didn't deserve his silence. "I've just been...uncomfortable in the water recently."

Danny's forehead creased in concern. "Have you thought about talking to someone? Megan's therapist is great, despite all the shit I give Meg about her..."

"I'm fine, really," Michael cut in with a forced smile. "Mia sees her, too." He knew Danny meant well, but no stranger with a notepad could erase the sight of a lifeless body floating face-down in the water from a man's mind. Michael gave Danny's shoulder a gentle punch. "Tell Jen I'm sorry. I'll come by this week to smooth things over."

Danny opened his mouth like he wanted to push the issue, but seemed to think better of it. "Yeah, okay. Just let me know if you change your mind. I know it helps to have someone to talk to."

Michael nodded.

If only he could spill his guts, unburden his soul about the crash, the water, all of it. But the shame and regret sat like a lead weight in his core. He had made choices that cost lives – how could he ever forgive himself for that?

Michael sighed, turning his focus back to the escalating shouting match on the field. There would be no absolution for him, no matter how many therapists he saw. The best thing to do was keep his head down and power through this funk.

He owed that much to Danny, Jen and...Mia.

Michael's thoughts drifted to Mia, bringing an involuntary smile to his face. He hadn't shared much about her with Danny or anyone else. Their budding connection felt too fragile, too precious to expose just yet.

Michael remembered her standing in the aisle of the plane, petite frame trembling as she stared wide-eyed at the gaping hole where the emergency exit door had been. She had looked so small and vulnerable in that moment, but she had also been remarkably brave. He remembered the feeling of her hand clinging to his arm, her nails digging in with each violent lurch of the plane. She had trusted him to keep her safe. And against all odds, he had.

Somehow, through that trauma, a bond had formed between them. One that made his heart beat faster every time her name popped up on his phone. He wanted to nurture that connection, help her continue to heal from the scars left by the accident. But how could he do that when he himself was so damaged?

"I don't know, man," he said finally. "I'm not sure I'm ready to drag up all that stuff again."

Danny clasped his shoulder, his eyes filled with empathy. "I get it. But holding it all inside isn't healthy either. Megan's therapist has helped her a lot since her cousin died. Or so I'm told. The chick really knows her stuff apparently."

"It's just...hard, facing up to choices I've made. Decisions that cost lives." Michael explained slowly.

But maybe Danny had a point. The plane crash had dredged up old demons, and he could feel them creeping in, keeping him awake at night. Maybe he did need to talk to someone.

But not just with anyone – he needed to open up to *Mia*.

She was the only one who could truly understand the shadows he carried, because she had her own. He just had to work up the courage to let her in. To tell her the truth about his past. The stains he had on his soul. The darkness that the old lady at the ghost tour mentioned.

Then again, maybe it was a hoax. A generic enough quote that anyone could look into and interpret it how they wanted...

But if he ever wanted to have a real relationship with Mia, he had to confront them.

"All right," he conceded. "I'll think about it. After practice today, I'll clear the air with Jen. Don't want her thinking I have a problem with her."

"Good call. I'm heading to her rooms after we get released from this latest ring of spectator hell, I'll walk with you." Danny trailed off. "I also gotta track down Liam, if he can sit still long enough for me to ask him something."

"The who's your daddy thing?"

Danny nodded, his eyes scanning the collected players on the sideline. "Yeah, he's been uncharacteristically absent lately. He's one of the last on my list. After him...if he says no...I'm wondering what Megan will want to do."

Liam, one of their stud tight ends had been notoriously busy as of late. He was still a machine on the field and during practices, but the man disappeared as soon as it was quitting time.

"The rest on the list are the douches?"

"Putting it mildly." Danny's lips twisted and then he turned back to Michael. "And listen, if you ever want to talk more, I'm here. I know you've got a lot on your shoulders."

Michael smiled. Danny was a true friend, solid and steadfast.

"Thanks, man. I appreciate that." And as their tradition, he whipped his arm down and gave his best friend a rough ball tap that had him bending over and chuckling through his gasps. "I love you, too."

He then jogged over to where Mitchell, their head coach, was summoning him.

Time to go back to work.

•   •   •   •   ●   •   ●   •   •   •

Michael let out a long exhale as he entered the locker room after practice, his shoulders slumped with exhaustion. The conversation with Danny weighed heavily on his mind. His friend was right – it was time to stop running from his past.

Dropping onto a bench, Michael leaned forward and cradled his head in his hands. Behind closed eyes, visions from the plane crash flashed like a slideshow. The crying baby. The prayers and panic all around him. The feeling of helplessness as water flooded the cabin. And the guilt – the soul-crushing guilt of choosing his own life over others.

Michael gritted his teeth, fighting back the emotions rising like bile in his throat. He thought he could outrun it all – the trauma, the fear, the regret. He had just wanted to start fresh with Mia, to have a shot at happiness.

But Danny saw the truth. The pain was catching up to him. It was poisoning his chance for a future with Mia before it even began.

Michael knew Danny was right – he couldn't keep ignoring the darkness that lurked below the surface.

Ever since the accident, he'd been haunted by memories long buried. The panic and desperation on the plane had transported him back to a life-altering day at his childhood lake, when his best friend's limp body had been pulled from the water. Michael had stood there, frozen on the beach, as the EMTs silent as they conducted their useless compressions on a long since lifeless body.

He'd felt so powerless. Just like on the plane, when lives had been in his hands.

Michael exhaled shakily, lifting his head. His reflection in the premier locker room mirror stared back – eyes haunted, shoulders slumped in defeat. He looked like a ghost of himself.

Maybe he didn't deserve Mia after all. Maybe she was better off with someone uncomplicated. Someone who wasn't drowning in their own past mistakes.

Someone like Sean.

Michael shut his eyes again, tightly. He had to beat this. He couldn't let the darkness swallow him whole. He refused to be defined by a single moment of impossible choice.

He would fix this. He would confront his demons. He would do whatever it took to be the man Mia needed...the man he wanted to be.

Michael rose on unsteady legs and shuffled to the showers, jaw set with resolve. The road ahead would be painful. But if Mia could face her fears, then Michael could as well.

For his own peace of mind. For a chance at a future with Mia. It was time to heal.

CHAPTER SEVENTEEN

October 6, Thursday
Mia

Mia clicked off her phone and shoved it in her purse as she hurried to the front door.

"Hey, where are you going?" Sean called from his place on the couch.

"Out with Lexie," Mia said over her shoulder, already turning the knob.

"Now?" His eyebrows drew together. "It's almost nine o'clock."

"Yep!" She forced brightness into her voice. "Girl's night. Don't wait up."

Before he could respond, she slipped out the door, pulse racing. The swish of her short skirt and the click of heels echoed in the stairwell. She burst into the muggy night air and slid into her waiting taxi, exhilarated at the prospect of seeing Michael again.

She hadn't seen him since the amazing weekend they'd shared and she felt like she was missing a limb. Michael's best friend, Danny, who was practically dating her new friend Megan – and Megan's daughter had been in the hospital for a few days now. Michael had been busy making sure Danny and Megan were okay, while also attending practices and PR campaigns.

As the taxi sped away toward Michael's house, she tugged at her snug top, suddenly self-conscious. The clingy fabric and low neckline showed far more cleavage than she was used to, but Lexie had insisted it was flattering when they went shopping, even if it was skimpier than Mia's normal style.

She took a deep breath, trying to ignore the nervous flutter in her stomach. Seeing Michael always made her heart race, but after sharing their second kiss last weekend, she didn't know for sure where they stood.

She remembered the heat of his hands on her back, his soft, plush lips rubbing hers, and his warm woodsy aroma enveloping her. The memory sent a shiver down her spine.

Tonight would be different. They'd be completely away from prying eyes, with a chance to explore the simmering connection between them. She smiled, picturing his handsome face.

This was worth a little white lie to Sean.

Once, she got to his house and hustled up to his front door, she didn't even have to knock. The door swung open and there he stood, looking unfairly gorgeous even in a simple long-sleeved button down and dress slacks. Mia's mouth went dry.

How did he look so good in such a simple get up?

"Hey, you," he said, flashing that heart-stopping grin of his. He pulled her into a quick hug. His musky scent lingered on her skin from their brief contact, making her dizzy.

She stepped back, taking in his tired eyes and the slump in his broad shoulders. "Michael, are you sure you're up for going out? You look exhausted."

"Gee, thanks for the glowing compliment."

Mia shot him a dry look and bent to greet the pups who were wiggling their butts excitedly behind Michael. "Ace, Rookie, I missed you boys this week." She then continued in inane baby talk that meant absolutely nothing to human ears, but everything to the darlings who were ecstatic to see her.

"You know you're gorgeous, you dork." She brushed fur off her hands as she stood. "You just look wiped out."

He waved a hand dismissively. "I'm fine, don't worry about me. This week has just been a little rough on the Spartan fam. Danny had his...own drama. And now it looks like Kyle was holding out on us with some crap from his past, too. My head's just a little twisted from trying to keep it all straight. It was a rough one. But, it's been a couple of days since I last saw you and I was jonesing. I want to take my girl out on the town."

Warmth flooded her chest at his words. *His girl.*

That felt nice.

"If you're sure..." she said, uncertainly.

"Absolutely." He took her hand, sending tingles up her arm.

Soon they were winding through the city streets in his sleek car. He kept one hand tucked in hers, thumb idly stroking her skin. The touch was innocent but still made her pulse skip.

They pulled up to an elegant tower, the top aglow with golden light. "Versailles," he announced. "Best view in the city." He continued to hold her hand all the way up the elevator and Mia couldn't stop her mind from racing, wondering what that meant.

Mia gasped as they stepped out onto the rooftop terrace. The whole skyline glittered before them, a horizon full of countless lights.

Part of the roof had been encased in a glass dome to protect them from the elements.

"It's beautiful," she breathed.

He smiled, eyes fixed on her. "Yeah. Beautiful."

She nudged him halfheartedly for the cliché. Even so, it still made her toes curl.

Once the server brought them to a cozy table for two, Michael pulled out her chair with a flourish. "For you, my lady."

She chuckled, allowing him to scoot the chair in under her. The table was tucked into a secluded corner, giving them privacy.

"How are you doing?" he asked, eyes gentle. "For real. I haven't had a chance to really connect with you this week, and texting just isn't the same."

Mia traced the linen tablecloth, considering. The glittering skyline blurred as she thought of her lie to Sean, guilt gnawing at her.

"I'm okay," she said finally. "Lexie's been going to the pool with me so I don't stall my progress. But..." She bit her lip.

"What is it?" Michael prodded lightly.

"Lying to Sean. It sucks. Told him I was going out with Lexie tonight." She looked down, ashamed. "I just...I didn't want to fight with him again." She placed her elbows on the table and plopped her face in her hands. "Oh, and if I'm just airing all my laundry, then we also need to mention how far behind I am in getting my art pieces ready for the gallery at the end of this month."

Michael reached across the table, taking her hand in his warm grasp. "First, that's great Lex has been going with you while I've been busy. Two, it's okay to not share every detail of your life with Sean. You don't have to explain anything to him. He gets what he gets. He's not owed anything more."

That was harsh and probably untrue.

Or maybe it was true for dudes? Was it really that simple? That black and white?

Ah, the simplicity of that kind of life. She wished it were that easy.

She nodded, twirling her thumb against his dark skin and marveling at the way their intertwined fingers contrasted. "I know. I just feel bad about lying."

"Well, don't." His thumb traced returning circles on her skin. "You deserve to make your own choices."

Warmth bloomed in her chest. No one had ever made her feel so secure, so free to be herself.

"And as for your art pieces. You'll get there. Or you won't. Channel your inner Yoda. You have to decide: buckle down and get something together, or keep procrastinating until the perfect vision hits you."

Dayumm.

She gave him a surprised look over the leather-bound menu she had opened. "Ouch, good sir."

Michael shrugged. "I think you're talented as shit. And I've seen you daydreaming while you stare off at mountains, lakes, trees…me. The desire is there. I'm not entirely sure what's stopping you. Maybe direction? But it's not desire. You sure as fuck look like you're ready." He held up his hands and gave her a funny look. "Tell me I'm wrong?"

Mia rolled her lips between her teeth and broke eye contact, looking around the luxurious and still bumping restaurant. The late hour hadn't stopped anyone from enjoying it.

Her eyes moved to the windows where she could see the city lights aglow all around them.

Gods, it really was gorgeous.

"You're not wrong," she said in a small voice.

Confirming it aloud felt…weird. Uncomfortable. Embarrassing.

Something to process later.

She straightened with a somewhat forced smile. "Enough about me. How are you doing?"

He leaned back. "Oh, nothing much to report. Other than this new hobby I picked up."

Her ears perked up. "What's that?"

"Improvised dance parties with the dogs." His eyes sparkled with his laughter. "They love trying to figure out what the hell I'm doing. It's been great exercise for all of us."

Mia burst out laughing. "Oh Jeeze. I'd pay to see that. All three of you spinning around like nuts."

He grinned. "You're cordially invited to swing by any time and start one. It'd make it less embarrassing to have someone else there. Someone human." He paused and cocked his head, thinking. "Or more embarrassing. Not sure about that one. I'll get back to you."

Her laughter rose into the glass dome ceiling while the last of her anxiety faded away into the night.

Her chuckles subsided as she gazed at Michael, his smile still lingering as he watched her. A jolt of desire coursed through her as their eyes met.

She bit her lip, suddenly remembering an offhand comment she'd made on the plane about sketching him one day. At the time, it had just been a halfhearted joke, but now, the idea held an undeniable appeal.

"You know..." she began, feeling a blush rise on her cheeks. "I could sketch you again. To get back into things. My original drawings of you were obviously lost in the crash..."

Michael arched an eyebrow, watching her closely. "Oh yeah? What did you have in mind?"

Mia tucked a strand of hair behind her ear, heart pounding. "Well...I may have mentioned wanting to sketch you without clothes." She let out a nervous laugh. "For art, of course."

A charged silence strung between them. Michael's gaze turned smoldering, his burning interest all too evident in the dark depths of his chocolate eyes. "I think I could be convinced to model. I've been known to strip down for a good cause."

Mia's breath caught, hyperaware of her body's reaction to his enticing offer. Her skin tingled everywhere his eyes roamed, leaving a trail of fire in their wake. She could almost feel his hands on her, igniting her deepest fantasies.

Clearing her throat, she managed a teasing reply. "I think...I think that would be a good place to start."

Michael held her gaze a moment longer before glancing away, the sensual tension still simmering between them. Mia fidgeted in her seat, arousal and anticipation flooding her senses. She wanted nothing more than to touch him, to feel his sculpted body under her hands.

Hell, maybe she could sculpt him for real and use that as an excuse to touch him endlessly.

You know. For art.

She exhaled slowly, trying to rein in her runaway thoughts. But one look at Michael's handsome face made her pulse race all over again. This man would be the death of her, she was sure of it.

The waiter came, refilled their drinks, took their orders, and was gone in the blink of an eye.

Mia took a sip of her wine, grateful for the distraction. She needed to steer the conversation to safer territory before she threw caution to the wind and ravaged him right there in the restaurant.

"So, I have some good news to share," she began, an excited lilt in her voice. "I managed to make it waist-deep in the pool the other day when Lexie and I went swimming!"

Michael's expression softened. "Hey, that's great! I'm proud of you, Angel."

Mia grinned, thrilled by his praise, and turned on by the endearment. "Lexie was prancing around in this itsy-bitsy neon bikini, flirting up a storm with the lifeguards. It was quite a sight. I think one of the lifeguards was definitely gay, but the other guy and girl were definitely willing to be entertained."

They both laughed, Mia regaling him with the details of Lexie's antics poolside, including her attempts at provocative yoga.

"Lexie's a nut," Michael chuckled, eyes crinkling at the corners. "And a bit of a lost soul. The guys on the team...most of us worry about her. About the trouble that she's inevitably going to find herself in that a blank check won't fix." Michael frowned. "And I think some of the guys worry that she'll bring down her girls with her when it happens."

Mia felt her own frown form. She definitely got the sense that Lexie was...looking...for something. Something that even Lexie didn't know what it was. To hear that the guys on the team worried about their future owner...Mia made a note to keep her finger on Lexie's pulse going forward.

Michael reached across the table, giving her hand a gentle, reassuring squeeze. "I'm glad you have her in your corner. I'm here for you too. Whenever or however, you need me."

"Naked and posing would be a good start."

He barked out a startled laugh that had the other patrons looking over with frowns etched onto their prissy faces.

Mia mentally patted herself on her back for her quick comeback.

A comfortable conversation blossomed between them, sharing about their weeks and more tidbits about their pasts.

After dinner, Michael drove her home, the night feeling all too short. At her door, he hesitated, then asked softly, "So, uh, I'll text you tomorrow?"

She held his gaze. "Yeah, that would be nice."

He looked down at her lips and she tensed, more than ready to take whatever onslaught he wanted to unleash.

Hells, she had even shaved...everywhere...in the hopes that something would happen. She was smooth as a freaking veal cutlet. The only person getting beard burn would be hopefully her...when his head was buried between her legs.

She'd just have to remember to keep quiet with Sean down the hall...

Mia smiled up at Michael, waiting for him to make a move. He'd been staring at her breasts all night, he *had* to want her. Right?

As he stared down at her, his face conflicted, Mia's stomach started to tighten.

Oh.

Maybe he didn't.

Maybe he was looking at her chest for a different reason. Compared to some women – like Peyton Knowles – Mia's breasts were basically mosquito bites. She'd never have impressive cleavage or a thick ass booty. She was shaped like her mother: petite and lean.

Michael leaned forward and Mia held her breath, hoping for fireworks.

Instead, he veered off to the side and placed a light, lingering kiss on her cheek.

"Night, Angel."

And with that, he was gone.

Mia slipped inside and touched where Michael's kiss had warmed her cheek, conflicted.

She struggled with the conflicting emotions inside her.

How could she be elated and disappointed?

Turned on and exhausted?

Mia leaned back against her closed door, pulse racing. Being with Michael tonight had awakened a hunger in her she'd thought she'd never feel. Arousal throbbed through her body.

She pictured his muscular frame, those strong arms that had cradled her so tenderly time and time again. What would they feel like wrapped around her while she lay naked? Holding her close as his lips claimed hers, his own body moving in and out of her?

A soft moan escaped her lips at the thought. She squeezed her thighs together, desire pooling low in her belly.

"So, that was Lexie, huh?"

Fuck.

CHAPTER EIGHTEEN

October 6, Thursday
Mia

"Sean, what are you doing up? It's almost midnight."

Why did her voice sound so guilty?

"I heard a noise," he said, as he stood at the mouth of the hallway in the middle of their dark living room, "so I came to check it out."

Mia's bullshit detector started ringing.

"Right." She snarked, flipping on a light.

Sean sighed. "Fine," he backtracked, rubbing his temples. "I just don't think he's right for you, Mia. He's a famous athlete, and you're...well, you."

"Excuse me?" Mia huffed, her cheeks flushing with anger. "What is that supposed to mean?"

"Come on, Mia," Sean snapped, his own frustration boiling over. "You're this quiet, introverted artist who hates sports. You really think you have anything in common with someone like him?"

"Maybe I don't," Mia retorted, her hands balled into fists at her sides. "But he's been there for me, Sean! He's helped me face my fears and supported me when I needed it most. Can't you see that? Can't you just be happy that I found someone that makes me happy?"

"I see it, all right," Sean shot back, his voice laced with bitterness. "I also see how blind you are to the fact that he's just using you to boost his own ego. I mean, who wouldn't want a pretty, little artist following them around like a lost puppy?"

Woah. That escalated quickly.

"Is that what you really think?" Mia whispered, cursing herself for the burn in her eyes. "That I'm just some weak, helpless girl who can't see when she's being used?"

"No," Sean admitted grudgingly, his voice softening slightly. "But I know you, Mia. And I don't want to see you get hurt."

"Then maybe you should trust my judgment instead of constantly undermining it," Mia countered, wiping away the tears that had begun to fall.

Sean let out a ragged breath, his shoulders slumping. As he turned to leave the room, Mia caught a glimpse of the vulnerability beneath his anger, and she knew that something had irrevocably changed between them.

Mia's heart felt as if it were being torn in two directions, her chest tightening with each breath. Gratitude for Michael's presence in her life warred with the guilt she felt for moving on without Sean. As she stood there, biting her lip to keep from crying, she couldn't help but wonder if there was more to Sean's feelings than she'd ever realized.

"Sean," Mia finally found her voice, albeit shaky. "I get you don't like him, but he's done nothing to deserve it. Maybe the media just sees what they want to see."

Sean let out a choked laugh that had Mia's spine stiffening. "Oh, is that the line he gave you? That it's the media's interpretation of him? That countless hotel staff from across the country haven't found an ungodly amount of used condoms in his trash bins over the years? That the endless line of women ends with you? Is that what he's been filling your head with?" His derision made her want to punch him in his beautifully arched nose.

"No, that's not what he's been telling me—"

"What is he saying then?"

Now didn't seem like the right time to say that they hadn't really talked about it...

Sean read her silence anyway.

His face contorted with frustration; his hands balled into fists at his sides. "God, Mia! You want to know why I'm so fixated on this?" he snapped, glaring daggers at her. "It's because ever since Mr. Hotshot Running Back showed up, you've been so wrapped up in him that you've forgotten about me! I moved across the fucking country for you. I held you through your panic attacks, took care of you when you were sick. I was there during the worst of it. Not Michael. But then he gets to waltz back into the picture and get all the good shit. It fucking sucks to be strung along, Mia...but for your sake, I hope you're right." Sean leveled his gaze at her, a look that simmered with a rawness that was startling. "I hope he's not doing that to you."

And with that effective parting shot, Sean stormed out of the room, his footsteps echoing down the hallway. The slam of his bedroom door punctuated his exit, leaving Mia to stand alone in the heavy silence.

Shit.

CHAPTER NINETEEN

October 8, Saturday
Michael

Michael pulled his car into the driveway of a modest two-story house, the GPS announcing their arrival in a cool female voice. His hands gripped the steering wheel as he stared at the quaint home, anxiety stirring in his gut.

"You ready for this?" he asked Mia, glancing over to the passenger seat.

She nodded, though her body language radiated tension. "As ready as I'll ever be," she said, softly.

Michael reached over and gave her hand a supportive squeeze. "We got this. A team."

"Right. A team," Mia repeated with an apprehensive smile. She took a deep breath. "Let's do this."

They climbed out of the car and walked up the front steps. Michael gave Mia's shoulder a gentle rub before ringing the doorbell.

After a few moments, the door opened, revealing a smiling brunette woman holding a toddler on her hip. Michael heard Mia's sharp inhale at the sight of them.

"Mindy." Michael greeted her warmly, a grin breaking out across his face. "You look wonderful. It's so good to see you again."

Mindy's eyes widened. "Oh my goodness, you both look so good, too! Please, come in! The kids will be so happy to see you." She stepped back, allowing them inside.

Michael and Mia moved into the foyer, glancing around the homey interior. Mindy shifted Isla in her arms. "I'm so glad you found me. After everything that happened, I wasn't sure..." Her voice trailed off.

Mia cleared her throat. "Michael's been trying to track down the other survivors..." Her voice quivered slightly.

Mindy smiled warmly. "It's thanks to you two. I can never repay what you did for us that day."

Michael shook his head. "It wasn't enough."

Michael watched as Mia's eyes filled with tears. She reached out a trembling hand to gently stroke the toddler's hair. "Look at her. How can you say that?" Isla gave a shy smile.

Apparently, bonding during a traumatic event didn't rank in a toddler's memory banks, though she seemed willing enough to smile at them.

Mindy bounced the toddler gently. "Thanks to you two, Isla just turned two last week."

Mia let out a soft squeal and clapped her hands. "Happy birthday, sweetheart!"

Michael felt a swirl of emotion in his chest.

Just then, a wail sounded from the other room, and their heads turned toward the sound.

Mindy laughed. "That would be Charles waking up from his nap. Let's go say *hello*."

Michael followed Mindy and Mia from the room. Family photos and colorful artwork adorned the walls. The lived-in space radiated warmth and love.

In the living room, Mia perched on the sofa, accepting a squirming Isla into her lap. She bounced the toddler, eyes shining. Michael felt his heart swell, struck by how natural this seemed for Mia. Her inherent kindness and empathy were so evident in that moment. He could easily picture her raising a family of her own someday.

The visit stretched on for several comfortable hours as they caught up on life since everything. Mindy seemed to be doing...fine.

Being a mother of two kids under two...she said she didn't have time to give it much thought. The true danger they were in only struck her after they were safely home, so it didn't affect her like it had others.

"I've reached out to the airline for names of others from the flight. The airline only gives their contact information if the person has already called to authorize it. I guess we were all looking for that...connection...after the accident. There's a small circle of us that stay in touch."

Despite the lingering weight of memories it stirred, Michael found himself enjoying the visit.

Mindy was funny as hell, and Mia was entertaining them all, filling in any awkward lags in the conversation.

When the alarm on Mindy's phone went off, Mindy started shuffling the kids around to get them ready for swim lessons.

"Alrighty Miss Mia. I promised Mindy on the phone earlier this week that we'd head out when it was time for her to leave, so we need to say our goodbyes and start the trek back home.

"Actually," Mindy paused her packing of the diaper bags. "Do you guys want to come? I bet Isla would love to show you her 'big kid' pool." Mindy looked fondly at her daughter who was curled up in Mia's lap on the floor.

Michael tensed reflexively. "That's kind of you to offer..."

"We'd love to!" Mia gushed before tickling Isla's sides, causing giggles to erupt.

Shit.

Mia looked up at him and froze. "Or, actually...we might need to get going..."

Michael shook off the nerves that coiled tight. "Nah, we have time. Just can't stay too late because of the game tomorrow, though."

The excitement in Mia's face as she jabbered to Isla had his stomach clenching again, though for an entirely different reason this time.

Fuck, she was radiant.

And seriously tough as nails.

He bet, if she had her swimsuit, she would even have gone in with the tot, despite her own lingering anxiety.

Michael looked up to see Mindy watching him, a glint of comprehension flickering on her face. She knew the crash still haunted him in ways he couldn't articulate. Yet she kept silent, for which he was immensely grateful.

Michael marveled at how fully Mindy had healed and moved on with her life.

He envied her resilience, even as guilt squeezed his chest. After all, Mindy and her children had been the lucky ones he'd placed on the wing that fateful night.

They'd survived, while others had not.

Michael quickly shut down that line of thought. Now was not the time to spiral down the all too familiar rabbit hole of self-blame and wondering what else he could have done. He focused on the present – on Mia's clear joy in this reunion. That's what mattered most.

Like he had done for weeks, he shut it down and blocked it all from his mind.

Once they arrived at the indoor pool, Michael settled into the bleacher seats overlooking the pool, while cradling baby Charles in his lap. Across the walkway, Mia sat at the pool's edge, laughing and playing with Mindy's daughter in the shallow end.

When the instructor snagged Isla for her lesson, Mindy and Mia sat at the edge, their calves and feet resting in the cool water, their legs kicking in tandem as they spoke in low voices. Even just witnessing that amount of progress from Mia filled Michael with admiration and pride.

And, at the same time, it only highlighted his inability to face his own shit.

Ripples of unease moved through him as he imagined how events could have unfolded differently on that traumatic day. What if that panicked man had pushed Mindy and the kids into the water during their struggle over the wing space?

Michael shuddered, cuddling the baby closer.

What would Michael have done if the guy had pushed the issue? Fight with the man in the middle of a sprawling lake that had no land in sight?

How would that have played out?

Regardless, it just would have resulted in even more blood on his hands.

Why couldn't he be strong like Mia? Confront his fears head-on? The fear had started when he was a kid. It began with lakes but now even a dousing of ice water left him paralyzed.

He hated this weakness, his inability to move forward.

He was a fucking wuss.

Mia's quiet laugh drew Michael's gaze again. Watching her find even a glimmer of healing gave him hope.

Maybe he wouldn't be like this forever...

The baby squirmed then, drawing Michael's attention. He slowly rocked the little one, murmuring soothingly. As he did, some of the tension ebbed from his shoulders. While part of him was still trapped in the past, he began to realize that this moment was about life, about living fully after loss. He had to focus on that.

For now, it was enough to take one small step forward. The rest would come in time.

After the swim class, they all gave each other hugs goodbye. Michael sighed as they walked to his car in the parking lot. Bringing Mia here had been the right decision, even if his own healing still felt out of reach.

Before they got back to the car, Mia slipped her hand into his, gratitude shining in her eyes.

"Thank you," she said softly. "For this. For connecting us."

Michael lifted her hand to his lips. "Nothing a couple of phone calls couldn't manage. I hardly did anything."

She needed to stop looking at him like he hung the moon and stars or he'd push her up against the car and the kids visiting the local Y would get a lesson on the birds and the bees.

Mia waved his dismissal away. "You know it wasn't that easy. And to top it off, it was incredibly thoughtful. It was easier with you here. Having you near..." She trailed off, brow furrowing as she watched him. "I wish you could have that too."

Ah, so she had noticed his aversion.

Fuck.

Michael tensed, the familiar weight settling on his shoulders. "Maybe someday," he said after a moment. "But today was about you. And it was beautiful to see."

Mia studied his face. She knew he was still haunted, still struggling. but she smiled at him like she also saw the care and compassion that had led him to bring her here, to this place of healing.

Rising onto her toes, she kissed his cheek. "We'll get there," she promised. "Together."

Michael's throat tightened with emotion.

He didn't think so, but it was nice to pretend.

He gave her hand a grateful squeeze.

Michael held the car door open for Mia, watching as she slid gracefully into the passenger seat. As he walked around to the driver's side, his thoughts drifted back to the pool.

He could still picture Mia sitting at the edge, her legs dangling in the water. The joy and relaxation in her face as she played with the children that day had made his heart soar. It was the most carefree he'd ever seen her.

And yet, even in that moment, the darkness had crept into his heart. The familiar guilt, the what-ifs.

What if he had made different choices that day on the plane? What if she really had died because of him?

Or...

What if the nurse hadn't mixed up the flight manifest and reported back to him about another elderly passenger with the name Mia who had died from hypothermia? If the nurse hadn't made that mistake in thinking it was *his* Mia...would he have even left that hospital without finding her? Without demanding a chance to see her?

What if they had had the chance to deal with the aftermath together, immediately, rather than so many weeks later? Would he, and she, be doing better?

Michael gripped the steering wheel, jaw tightening. No matter how hard he tried to outrun it, his past and his doubts clung to him like a shadow.

"You okay?" Mia's soft voice drew him back to the present.

He glanced over, taking in her concerned eyes.

"Yeah," he said, forcing a smile. "Just...thinking."

She reached over, covering his hand with hers. "You did a good thing today," she said gently. "The best thing. I know it was hard for you, too."

"I'm glad it helped you," he said. And he meant it. Whatever lingering ghosts haunted him; it had been worth it to watch Mia reclaim a piece of herself.

She gifted him a smile that warmed him like sunshine. "So," she said brightly, "home we go?"

Michael turned his hand over, lacing their fingers together. The future awaited, and they would face it together.

"Home it is," he said.

"Good. Because I think I have an idea for a theme for my submission collection..."

CHAPTER TWENTY

October 9, Sunday
Mia

The next day, Mia's heart raced as she unlocked the door to Michael's house. She needed this escape today, away from her own home and the awkward tension that seemed to have settled there. She didn't want to deal with Sean.

As she entered the living room, Ace and Rookie greeted her. Their bodies writhed against her legs, as if they knew she needed the comfort. She bent down to give them both a quick scratch behind the ears. "Hey, boys, mind if I set up shop here for a little while? Daddy said he didn't mind."

Michael had a home game at one, so he'd be at the stadium for most of the day. He'd said that Mia could take over the house while he was out. It was like he sensed her burning need to *create*.

Finally!

Ace and Rookie seemed content with her presence, so she took that as a yes and moved on. She had brought a mountain of art supplies with her. There was something about being in Michael's house that made her feel safe and inspired.

Maybe it was that it just smelled so much like him.

Once she got her art supplies spread out across the dining room table, she stepped back to survey the situation.

Canvases, sketchbooks, paints, colored pencils, and even some digital equipment were all within reach. She picked up a sketchbook and began to flip through it, scanning her past work for inspiration.

Where to start...

"Okay, boys," she said, her voice a light coo, "I've got this gallery exhibition coming up, and I'm feeling a little stuck. But I think I might've figured it out yesterday, so let's see where that goes." She scratched her head, deep in thought. "You see, this stupid plane thing...it gave me...some issues. And it got me thinking."

Mia picked up a pencil and started to sketch a rough idea in her notebook. "I want to show what we've all been through, Ace. The fear, the confusion, the grief. It's not easy, but we're survivors." She looked down at the dogs. "Thanks to your Daddy." She chewed on her lip as she stared down at her chicken scratch. "The other side of the plane wasn't nearly as lucky. They didn't have a Michael to save them." Mia finished on a mumble, trying to chase down a fleeting idea.

Rookie, seemingly understanding that he didn't need to participate in the conversation, curled up at her feet. Mia continued to brainstorm out loud as she sorted through her supplies. "I think I'll use watercolors for the fear, and acrylics for the confusion. Grief...that's a tough one. Maybe some pastels to capture the depth of emotion."

As she explored her art supplies, she picked up an epoxy kit, turning it over in her hands. "I've been toying with the idea of adding epoxy to one piece," she said, her voice contemplative. "To give it that glossy, almost lifelike texture. And maybe a wooden piece, too, to represent strength and grounding. Ironic, given Michael's woodworking hobby." She paused and looked back at the dogs. "Ironic? Coincidental? I can never tell which one to use. The song messes me up."

She set the epoxy kit aside and continued to brainstorm. "Sculpting...that's another possibility. I could shape something...Oh! Or metalworking. Metal has this raw, unyielding quality...Like the wing in the water..."

She picked up a blank canvas and set it on an easel. She stared at the daunting whiteness and took a deep breath, recalling her tarot reading this morning.

The High Priestess card had appeared, a symbol of intuition, inner knowledge, and the subconscious mind. She felt a shiver of recognition at the connection between her reading and her artistic inspiration. With a determined look, she started mixing some paint, looking to find the perfect combination of blue and gray.

Her body was antsy - it just wanted to get it all done at once.

So many paths to choose! So little time.

"Water. That's what we all have in common. I lost my ability to swim after the crash, but I want to face that fear and I want to show the world what it's like to fight through that."

Her brush moved swiftly across the canvas and her thoughts drifted to Michael. "Michael's been my rock through this. I'm falling for him, you know? He's dealing with his own demons, and he's tabled that to help me." She bit her lip and cocked her head as she stared at the canvas. "Not that I needed him to, I'll have you know. I would have gotten there." She looked down at Ace who was still watching her, his little eyebrows cocked as if he were truly listening.

Was there judgment in his eyes?

Gah! Little snob.

Mia turned back to the canvas with a grin.

As she painted, the colors on the canvas began to blend and meld, capturing the terrifying chaos of their shared experiences. "This submission combination," she mumbled, "is going to be breathtaking. The trauma, the survival, and the love that's helping us through."

Ace and Rookie watched her, as though they understood the weight of her words. With a small smile, she bent down to pet them again. "Thanks for listening, boys. You're the best audience a struggling artist could ask for."

Mia turned back to her canvas, her heart lighter and her mind clearer. She was ready. This was it. She was going to create something beautiful from the pain. Her collection would be a testament to resilience and healing, a reflection of the...love that was blooming from the seed that trauma had planted between her heart and Michael's.

CHAPTER TWENTY-ONE
October 16, Sunday
Mia

A week later, Mia dipped her paintbrush into a mug of murky water, watching the bristles expand and contract as they soaked up the liquid. She glanced over at Ace and Rookie who were curled up together in a patch of sunlight streaming in through the bay windows of Michael's living room. Their chests rose and fell in sync as they napped, peaceful and content.

Mia sighed, pushing her cotton paper away. While she was waiting for glue to harden and some paint to dry...on two completely different pieces...she resorted to doing a couple mindless sketches that were for fun rather than deadlines.

She was running out of time to complete her exhibition set.

Don't panic. Don't panic.

She had tried to capture the dogs' sweet faces in pencil for the last hour, but her mind kept wandering. Wandering to thoughts of her submission collection...and Michael.

She felt a pang of guilt in her chest. Here she was, staying at his beautiful house, surrounded by everything that was important to him – his dogs, his trophies, his workspace – and she couldn't even be bothered to turn on the TV and watch his away game.

What kind of friend was she? Sean would have watched, she thought. Her best friend had never missed a swim meet, even when they were kids.

Swim meets were boring as hell.

And yet, he always went.

Mia stood abruptly, nearly knocking over her mug of paint water. She began to pace, her socks sliding over the smooth hardwood floors.

Gods, just thinking about Michael set her body on fire these days.

She wanted him. Badly. And she hated not knowing what she was to him.

Did he 'like her', like her?

What was she? Twelve?

Mia worried her bottom lip between her teeth. Michael was her friend. Her savior, even.

But this was more than gratitude. More than friendship. She yearned for his touch, his kiss. Again.

He'd only kissed her twice, but...wowza. The guy could turn a nun against the convent.

Mia sank down onto the couch, face in her hands. She had to get a grip. Michael was kind, caring, brave. And what was she? A mess. A boring, plain-Jane, starving artist.

Well, not technically starving, but still.

She was in no position to be in a real relationship with someone like him. They worked when they were together...but that was a bubble fantasy.

He had opened up about his past flings this last week. She didn't know for sure, but she thought that seeing Mindy had helped him...maybe.

It seemed like it. Otherwise, the timing was just very coincidental.

Michael had also opened up a bit more regarding his hatred of cold water and his contentious relationship with the media and his image.

He put it all out there.

And boy, did it come out.

It was like trying to drink from a fire hose.

The man just...*unloaded.*

It was glorious and overwhelming all at once.

The trust there, though, was astounding.

Rookie lifted his head sleepily, blinking at Mia. She smiled softly and patted the cushion beside her.

"Come here, boy."

The pitbull lumbered over, nuzzling his cold nose into her palm. She stroked his back, taking comfort in his presence.

She missed having dogs around. Spending so much time with Michael's was like a blast from her past. If only matters of the heart could be as simple as the unconditional love of a dog. She envied their peaceful existence.

After hours of frantic painting, Mia needed a break. If only just so she could stretch out her fingers, which were cramping around her brush.

Damn, it had certainly been a minute since she'd last held a brush for that long.

Mia cleaned up her brushes and left the dogs snoozing in the living room. She wandered into the kitchen, admiring the gleaming granite counters and stainless steel appliances. Everything was tidy and organized, reflecting Michael's orderly nature.

Opening the fridge, she found it well-stocked with fresh produce, proteins, and meal prep containers – the diet of an elite athlete.

Oh, an apple. Perfect.

She bit into it with a satisfying crunch and paused.

He had laughed earlier when he invited her to snoop...was he serious?

Because suddenly...snooping seemed...fun.

Chewing thoughtfully, a smile on her lips, Mia used her phone to take pictures of her standing in front of open drawers and cabinets. She sent the photos to Michael and then followed up with a text asking him where the 'real goods' were.

Mia paused and wandered over to Michael's extensive spice collection. She opened some up and took a whiff. Delicious.

The man loved to cook. She could get on board with that. Sean and her usually just ran out and grabbed to-go.

Her heart fluttered as she pictured Michael making her breakfast. She could almost imagine his strong arms wrapping around her from behind as he leaned in to kiss her neck...

Mia shook her head, banishing the fantasy.

"You guys smell a gas leak? I'm hallucinating."

The dogs didn't reply. In fact, she didn't even hear a jingle of their dog tags that signified they even lifted their heads.

Little devils.

Next, Mia found Michael's home office. A plush leather chair sat behind a dark wood desk stacked with papers and playbooks. Shelves displayed football memorabilia and trophies marking his success.

This room exuded competence and achievement. But it lacked warmth. Mia yearned to make it more personal, more inviting. She could picture exactly what artwork would look best. The simple exercise gave her a thrill - it had been so long since she felt that spark, and now here she was, drowning in ideas.

She ran her fingers over the spines of books about coaching, finance and Black history. Michael had eclectic interests and a wicked thirst for reading.

Michael in his reading glasses was a recurring fantasy for Mia.

Holy hells bells, the guy was a god when he was wearing those puppies while reading a book.

Woof.

He knew he was sexy as fuck as well. Which made it even more frustrating that he hadn't made any more moves!

Hand holding was great and all, but...damn. How much build up was one woman expected to take!

Sighing, Mia left the office and wandered down the hall, she paused outside a closed door. Michael's bedroom.

She took a picture of her standing in front of the door and sent it to Michael.

This is me wondering if it's a total invasion of privacy to go into the inner sanctum or if you'd be cool with it. The boys said it was fine, but you know them. They're pathological liars.

She knew he wasn't going to text back, given that he was in the middle of a game, but it still felt nice, sending him a message he'd see later. Something to make him smile.

Her pulse quickened as she stared at the door.

She shouldn't go in there, should she?

That felt like prying.

But before she could talk herself out of it, Mia turned the knob and stepped inside.

Okay, so guess she was going in.

Mia's breath caught as she stepped past the threshold, hit with nothing but the encapsulating scent of sawdust and musk. Nothing but masculinity and *Michael*.

On the opposite wall were floor-to-ceiling windows, draped by long velvet curtains. A lounger was tucked in the corner, a stack of books on the small black table next to it. In the center of the room was a king-sized bed, neatly made, with a black and gray geometric comforter with dark wooden nightstands on either side.

She pictured waking up tangled in those sheets, Michael's sculpted arms around her...

Down, girl!

To stop her wandering thoughts, she studied the photographs on the walls. Most featured Michael with his teammates, celebrating victories. In every shot, his megawatt grin made her heart flutter.

But one photo drew Mia closer. It showed a younger Michael, maybe high school age, with his arms slung around another boy, their heads thrown back in carefree laughter as they stood on a dock by a lake.

Mia brushed her fingers over Michael's image. Even then, his eyes had held that magnetic warmth.

Who was this? A family member of some kind? A friend?

She hoped they kept in touch despite Michael's schedule and fame. Childhood friendships that thrived into adulthood were hard to come by.

Poor Sean. She just didn't see him that way.

As Mia's eyes lingered on his big bed, she felt heat curl in her belly.

With a start, Mia realized she'd spent too long invading Michael's private space. She turned to go but couldn't resist running a hand along his dresser as she passed.

Would he mind her being in here? Or would it thrill him to know she'd imagined them together in his bed?

Shaking her head ruefully, Mia left the bedroom.

It was stupid to miss him. She had just seen him yesterday morning before he courageously boarded another plane.

Yet, here she was: wishing he was home.

The house felt too big without Michael's larger-than-life presence helping to fill it out.

Eager to send him a photo of herself in a less personal space, Mia made her way to the closed door of Michael's workshop. He had told her she was welcome to go in there anytime, but so far she hadn't taken him up on the offer.

Maybe now was the perfect time to explore his studio. Maybe she'd find some new art supplies to experiment with?

If nothing else, it would be a good distraction from overthinking things with Michael.

Mia walked over and gingerly turned the doorknob, pushing the door open. The smell of stain, turpentine, and sawdust washed over her as she stepped inside.

Canvases leaned against the walls, some blank, some splattered with vivid abstract designs. Tables displayed jars of brushes, tubes of oils, boxes of pastels and charcoals. An easel held a half-finished painting of a woman's face emerging from swirling blues and greens.

A woman...who looked a lot like her.

Mia moved further into the studio, taking it all in. This space felt like Michael – bold, passionate, outgoing. She could imagine him spending hours here, channeling everything he felt into his art.

Her eyes landed on a shelf lined with sketchbooks. Unable to resist, she slid one out and opened it up. It only had a few pages filled in, showing figure drawings, intimate studies of the human form. Mia's breath caught at the beauty and fluidity of the sketches.

He'd been holding out on her! He had mentioned painting and woodworking! Never that he sketched too!

"Michael, my dear. You are an onion." She muttered as she flipped through the pages.

One drawing in particular made her heart skip a beat – a nude woman reclining on her side, back arched, head tilted up in ecstasy. Though the face was featureless, the rendering of the body was exquisite, sensual and unapologetic.

But on her wrists were two very distinct angel wing tattoos.

Mia looked down at her own forearms...at the same tattoos there.

Mia's cheeks flushed warm, her pulse racing, skin tingling. She couldn't tear her eyes away.

Okay.

Safe to say, Michael was attracted to her.

Probably.

At the very least...he pictured her naked.

She could work with that.

Or...maybe it was just an artist's appreciation? She had sketched tons of nude people throughout the years. Maybe this meant nothing.

But...

He did tell her to check out his studio today...did he want her to find it?

Gah! What was happening to her? This rollercoaster of giddy attraction and gnawing doubt was exhausting. She needed perspective from someone she trusted.

Sean was out, for obvious reasons.

As she walked back to the living room, and with the hot image burned in her mind, she pulled out her phone to call Lexie.

Mia sighed, collapsing onto the couch. It was time to make sense of these growing feelings for Michael before she lost herself completely. Michael's dogs scrambled to snuggle up next to her. She smiled as she scratched behind their ears, taking comfort in their warm, furry presence.

The phone rang three times before Lexie's cheerful voice greeted her. "Mia! Are you finally calling to have me explain football to you?"

Oops. Yeah, she probably needed to do that, too, at some point.

She'd been friends with Sean for two decades and it never even occurred to her to ask him about soccer. How self-centered was that? And now, here she was, trying to shelve her aversion to violence for the sake of *a guy*.

Well, not just any guy.

Michael.

No wonder Sean hated her.

Man, she needed help - stat.

Hence, why she called Lexie in the first place.

Mia took a deep breath. "Actually, it's about me. And Michael. I'm just confused about..everything. And I wanted some girl talk. If you're down?"

Lexie shrieked. "Girl. I'm always down for a dish sesh. Lay it on me."

"You know most of it. Just being around him is so amazing, but it's getting more complicated and I don't know what to do."

"Complicated how? Tell me everything, don't leave anything out."

With Lexie's gentle prodding, the whole story came spilling out - including Michael's sexy sketch of her.

"It's like I can't get him out of my head!" Mia finally burst out. "But I'm afraid if we take this further, everything will fall apart. He's used to dating models and actresses. I'm just...me."

"Oh, Mia," Lexie said surprisingly gently. "You're selling yourself short. You're talented, kind, beautiful inside and out. Any man would be lucky to have you."

Mia smiled slightly, even as doubts continued to linger. "I don't know, Lex. What if it ruins what we have? I care about him so much already."

"It's risky for sure," Lexie agreed. "Opening your heart always is. But don't you owe it to yourself to find out if this could be something real?"

Mia traced her finger along the couch cushion, considering Lexie's words. As terrifying as it was, she knew her friend had a point. The longer she ignored these growing feelings, the more tangled up she would get.

Glancing around his living room, she smiled as she took in the surroundings that were becoming so familiar. She could picture lazy weekends here, curled up together watching movies and stealing kisses.

When they were together, she felt like the best version of herself. He didn't make fun of her scars or see only the baggage of her past. He saw her spirit and her passion. He made her feel whole.

What had started as fascination had grown into something so much deeper. She cared about him in a way she never expected. The thought of losing him, of not having him in her life, made her heart ache.

"I...uh...ah! I don't know."

"Girl, say no more. We'll be there in twenty."

"What?"

Mia could hear movement in the background of Lexie's call.

"I can hear the doubt in your voice from miles away. I'm coming to you and I'm bringing the girls. You need more than just me to change your mind."

"What are you talking about?"

"You're good enough. And we're going to make you see that. See you soon. Ciao, babycakes."

And with that ominous sign off, Mia was left holding a silent phone to her ear.

What kind of floodgate had she just opened?.

CHAPTER TWENTY-TWO

October 16, Sunday
Mia

About 30 minutes later, Mia's eyes scanned the room as she took a seat on Michael's plush leather couch. She never pictured herself as a hostess, yet here she was, surrounded by chattering women, floating in a sea of endless catered foods and drinks, and throw pillows that probably cost more than her monthly rent.

Lexie got shit done.

Or...her chauffeur did. The guy was a magician.

"Okay ladies, let's get this emergency meeting started." Lexie clapped her hands dramatically as she perched on the edge of the adjacent armchair. Mia had to stifle a laugh at the idea of this being an 'emergency.'

On the plus side, it finally gave her a chance to meet the rest of the legendary book club babes. She'd heard enough stories and now she was finally able to put some faces to their names...and deeds.

Chloe and Rose, two of the regulars from the book club, squeezed together on the loveseat across from Mia. Megan claimed the remaining armchair, while Julie parked herself cross-legged on the floor, not bothered in the least by the lack of seating. From what she heard, Julie spent most of her life in a saddle so sitting on the floor was probably wickedly uncomfortable, but the woman didn't complain at all, sipping happily at the mixed drinks that Lexie's personal driver had brought them.

Where did he even get them?

"So..." Lexie began, leaning forward with an eager glint in her eye. "Mia, darling. I believe you have some juicy tidbits to share with the group?"

Mia felt her cheeks grow warm as all eyes in the room turned to her. She should've known Lexie would throw her under the bus like this.

"Oh, uh, I don't know about juicy," Mia mumbled, suddenly finding a loose thread on her shirt remarkably interesting.

"Girl, I've had the week from hell. I could use something else to think about besides criminal deeds and super shitty family members." Megan chimed in. "Spill the fucking tea."

Well, at least Megan was handling her most recent drama with her standard poise. The woman was an unflappable rockstar. Mia couldn't even imagine.

Mia sighed, knowing there was no getting out of this. "I mean, we've been spending a ton of time together. He's sweet and thoughtful, always doing little things to make me smile. Obviously wickedly smart and sexy. But..." She trailed off, unsure whether to mention Sean.

"But what?" Julie prodded gently.

"I don't know. We have this amazing connection, but he hasn't exactly made a move. Well, not exactly. He's kissed me. Twice. But that hasn't happened for weeks now. I'm worried I'm misreading things or that he just sees me as a friend."

"Michael Dillon, 'just friends' with a woman?" Rose laughed into her drink. "Yeah, right."

Mia felt a twinge in her chest. Rose's comment reminded her of the nagging insecurities Sean perpetuated that she tried to ignore. Michael had model-worthy women fawning over him daily; what made her think she stood a chance?

"It's not like that," Mia said quietly, more to herself than the group. "He's different with me. There's something real between us, something special. I can feel it. I'm just scared to take the next step in case I ruin everything we have going, now."

The women exchanged thoughtful glances as they considered Mia's options.

Mia was surprised to feel a rush of gratitude for this makeshift sisterhood. For the first time, she didn't feel quite so alone in her doubts and worries.

"You know," Chloe began gently, "I was terrified when Kenny and I started transitioning from friends to more. I kept thinking 'what if this ends horribly and I lose him altogether?'"

Megan nodded along. "Same. Danny and I were in that weird in-between for weeks before we finally caved."

This launched the group into more stories of romantic milestones, missteps, and lessons learned. Mia found herself laughing along and opening up more than she expected. With each new tale, her own worries seemed to grow a little smaller.

Maybe she had been overthinking this, letting fear hold her back from potential joy. Her friends' encouragement gave Mia a spark of courage she hadn't felt before. She and Michael had something special brewing between them, she just knew it. It was time to silence her doubts and follow her heart.

As the evening wound down, Mia hugged each of her new friends goodbye with squeezes of genuine gratitude. As she cleaned up the remnants of their impromptu gathering, Mia found herself lost in thought.

These women had walked similar paths. Her friends had all felt the same doubts and fears at some point. They made themselves vulnerable and it paid off.

And here they were living their happily-ever-afters while she was still chasing hers.

She now knew that she couldn't ignore these feelings. She had to tell Michael how she felt, no matter how scary it would be.

Even if he didn't feel the same way, their connection deserved to be acknowledged.

Besides, she couldn't stop thinking about how glorious it could be if he felt the same way...

No more hesitating – she had to take control of her love life. It was time to transform this spark with Michael into a burning flame; time to turn their flirty friendship into something real, and time to find out if sparks could ignite into lasting love. She was ready for the next chapter, whatever it held.

This was her moment. She was ready to be brave.

Chapter Twenty-Three
October 17, Monday
Mia

Mia perched on the edge of the sofa, clad in silky pajamas with lace trim that clung to her curves.

If he didn't make a move after seeing her in this, she was joining a convent.

She fidgeted with the remote control, glancing between the TV and the front door as she waited for Michael to come home.

Uncharacteristically, the team had stayed the night in Las Vegas after their game and Mia couldn't stop the gut clench at the thought of what the guys – and Michael – were up to. They just weren't *there* yet. And even with Michael's honesty this week about how he was a whore in the past, they weren't technically dating...so did that give him a free pass to get wild in Vegas?

She didn't have the nerve to ask.

She didn't care. She didn't care. She didn't care.

If she said it enough times, it would make it true, right?

That was then. This was now. And she was going to make him forget those past conquests if it was the last thing she did on this Earth.

When she heard his key turn in the lock, Mia leapt up, pulse racing. Michael stepped inside, his travel bag slung over his shoulder. His eyes widened at the sight of her. The duffle bag dropped to the floor.

"You didn't have to wait up for me," he said with a smile. "But I'm glad you did. Hi there, Angel."

Mia rushed forward and wrapped her arms around him. His solid warmth enveloped her.

The dogs bounded over, too, their tails wagging. Michael chuckled and scratched their ears. "Smells good in here. You made dinner?"

Mia nodded, cheeks flushed. As he took in the meal laid out on the table and seemed to make an approving assessment of her pajamas, the flutter in her stomach intensified.

Michael met her gaze. "Thank you. I needed this. This last week has been awful. Danny's been a wreck and I just...mentally haven't been myself. Thank you."

Mia's pulse leaped at the sincerity in his eyes. "Of course. Anytime."

While Michael unpacked his bag in the bedroom, Mia reheated the food and set it out on the kitchen island. He emerged a few minutes later, freshly showered, and took a seat on one of the stools.

"So how was the game?" Mia asked, sliding a plate of chicken parmesan toward him.

Michael's eyes lit up. He launched into a detailed recounting of the plays and scores as he ate, complete with expressive hand gestures as he reenacted every play from his stool. Mia nodded along, trying her best to keep up, despite her limited knowledge of sports.

"I don't get how you remember all that," she said, shaking her head in amusement.

He grinned. "Years of practice. You gotta have a mind for the details and the bigger strategy. It's like a chess match out there."

Mia raised an eyebrow. "I'll take your word for it."

She loved these moments where their opposite natures collided – her artsy quietness meshing with his athletic intensity.

When he finished eating, Mia gathered her courage. "If I haven't said it yet...it's pretty amazing how you're flying again after...everything."

Michael's expression turned solemn. He rotated his water glass in his hands. "There was a while there I just couldn't do it. Had to take a car if we were traveling."

Mia's heart ached at the vulnerability in his voice. She reached out and gave his hand a gentle squeeze, hoping it conveyed what words could not.

Michael gave her a small, appreciative smile.

"I could've driven myself those times, I guess," he said with a shrug. "But I like having someone else there, you know? Another set of eyes on the long stretches. Someone to keep you awake."

He took a sip of water, gazing into the distance as if picturing those difficult days.

"Plus it gave me a chance to really rest during the trips," he continued. "Couldn't do that if I was behind the wheel."

They fell into easy conversation as they finished up dinner, the atmosphere warm and intimate. Mia noticed Michael's eyes occasionally wandering, taking in her body in the silky pajamas. A flush crept up her neck at the attention.

Finally!

She thought back to her friends' encouragement last night - the time was now.

Michael helped her clean up, their hands occasionally brushing, igniting sparks.

As they bid goodnight, Mia didn't want the evening to end.

"You know, I could just sleep on the couch tonight," Mia said lightly as Michael walked her to the bedroom. "Let you have your space after traveling."

Michael shook his head with a small smile. "Don't be silly. You take the bed, I'll take the couch. Plus, you've already made yourself at home, if the photos were anything to go by."

She laughed and leaned her shoulder into him. "Hey, I was just doing what you said. You said to explore. Call me Magellan."

"Okay, then, Magellan. Now go curl up in my comfy, King sized bed while I attempt to squeeze onto the couch." He pouted ridiculously and she slapped him on the shoulder.

"See! You know you should be in your bed. You're huge, the couch is not. Plus, you just got back from being away! You should sleep in your own bed."

"What kind of host would I be if I let my guest take the couch?" Michael countered. "Really, I don't mind."

They continued playfully debating the sleeping arrangements, both endeavoring to let the other have the bed. Finally, Mia said, "How about we...just...share? We're both adults here."

Well, that worked out nicely.

Even so, her heart still skipped a beat as he studied her closely. "You sure?"

"Yeah, of course," she managed, suddenly feeling shy. The thought of lying next to Michael's muscular frame all night made her pulse quicken.

In the bedroom, Mia perched nervously on the edge of the mattress. Was she on his usual side? Would he think it presumptuous of her to already be in his bed?

Michael came in a few minutes later, wearing low-slung sweatpants and a soft long-sleeved Henley. He paused in the doorway, eyes widening and nostrils flaring at the sight of Mia sitting on his bed.

Was that a flicker of desire?

"I hope I'm not in your spot," Mia said, heart pounding.

Michael blinked then gave a small laugh. "Actually, I'm a psycho. I don't really have a set side of the bed." He rubbed the back of his neck. "I just kind of...sleep in the middle, I guess."

Mia giggled and started to back away slowly, making a show of it. "Maybe I should go..." She moved to escape and he tackled her down onto the bed.

"Nope, no takie-backsies. You liked me before you knew I was crazy. Now you're stuck."

She smiled up at him.

Channeling her inner Chandler, she thought: *could he be any more perfect?*

Michael watched her fondly for a moment before sliding under the covers. He rolled onto his side to face her, his eyes wide-awake and warm. Mia shifted under the covers as well, careful not to touch him as she did so.

Her whole body hummed being this close to him. She contemplated making a move, but then Michael winced slightly and rotated his shoulder with a grimace.

Crap. He was probably exhausted.

And beat up as all hell from the onslaught of tackles he'd endured.

Okay, no move tonight.

Patience.

There would be time to explore this growing connection between them. For now, she just wanted to savor the feeling of falling asleep next to this kind, fascinating man.

Michael groaned and settled onto his back, staring up at the ceiling.

Mia studied his profile, taking in the strong line of his jaw and the way his muscular chest rose and fell with each breath.

"How's your shoulder feeling?" she asked.

Michael glanced over, lips quirking up. "Just a bit sore. Occupational hazard. I'll be fine."

"Let me know if you need an ice pack or anything."

"Thanks, doc," he teased.

Mia smiled, enjoying their easy banter. A comfortable silence fell between them. She was hyperaware of Michael's proximity, his body heat radiating across the scant space between them. The domestic intimacy of sharing a bed felt both thrilling and natural at the same time.

Michael's eyes drifted shut, his breathing evening out. Mia continued gazing at him, marveling that someone like him could make her feel so safe.

With that comforting thought, she finally let her own eyes fall closed as Michael's rhythmic breathing lulled her into a peaceful sleep.

CHAPTER TWENTY-FOUR

October 18, Tuesday
Michael

Michael stood at the stove, absentmindedly stirring pancake batter while images of Mia curled up beside him in *his* bed flashed through his mind. His heart raced and he shifted his weight, trying to hide yet another erection that had been plaguing him all morning.

He chuckled under his breath. Damn, she was a late sleeper.

As he poured the batter into neat circles on the griddle, Michael's thoughts drifted to Mia.

He didn't deserve her. Not with the trail of death he dragged behind him like chains. Mia was too good, too pure. He had no right to want her, yet here he was, taking advantage of her time. Her affections. The familiar weight of guilt pressed down on his chest.

The sizzle of the pancakes jerked Michael back to the present. He slid the golden brown circles onto a plate just as he heard Mia's footsteps. His pulse quickened at the sight of her, hair mussed from sleep and wearing an oversized sweatshirt over her sexy as fuck PJs.

Damn, she was adorable.

"Morning," she mumbled through a yawn.

"Morning, sleepyhead." Michael grinned. "Hungry?"

She jerked to a stop and stared at him, processing him cooking breakfast.

Why were her cheeks suddenly so red?

She shuffled to the table and ducked her head.

Interesting...

Over breakfast, they chatted casually about their plans for the day. He had the day off. The game on Sunday did not go as planned and

Coach kept them in Vegas for the night to berate them about their performance against the Raiders.

And then again on the flight home.

And again, on the bus.

Today was their one day off this week, so he was taking advantage of the lazy morning.

As Mia updated him on her art progress from the weekend, Michael was captivated by Mia's smile, her laughter.

He didn't want to lose this, whatever it was growing between them. He just didn't know how to move forward.

Would she care for him if she knew the truth about his past?

Mia's voice cut through the storm in his mind. "Hey, can I ask you something crazy?"

Michael nodded, bracing himself.

"Are you finally ready for me to sketch you? You know, without clothes?" She bit her lip, eyes hopeful and cheeks blazing red.

Michael froze, his body reacting in a very primal way. He was shocked. And intrigued.

Who was this minx and where did Mia go?

And even though she was very clearly embarrassed for asking...there was an empowered spark in her eyes. The way she held her chin up, looking somewhat down at him...she wanted this and she was nervous as hell to ask.

Yet, here she was...asking.

Fuck. She was so fucking *brave*.

There was nothing that could stop her.

Slowly, he nodded. "I think that could be arranged."

He led her to his bedroom where it was a bit warmer, while anxiety and anticipation twisted his gut. When they reached the middle of the room, he hesitated, suddenly self-conscious.

Mia gave him a reassuring smile. "It's okay. Take your time. Where would you be most comfortable?"

"Bed?"

"Works for me." She swallowed and looked away. "I'll step out for a minute…"

Shit. Did she want him posed a certain way?

She was gone before he could ask.

Michael took a deep breath and removed his shirt and sweats.

Okay…how to sit…

"Michael?" Her soft voice came through the door and he froze.

Fuck!

He looked around for something…he didn't know what.

What was he going to do? Cover up? She was going to sketch him naked for fuck's sake. It didn't really make sense to get modest now…

"Um, if you would feel more comfortable," she said through the cracked door, "there's a pose we sketched a lot in that might be less invasive…"

Oh?

"So, you can leave your underwear on and recline back on the bed. One arm can go behind your head and the other can rest on your upper thigh. Your right leg can be bent a bit, and your left leg can be steepled. So, uh, yeah…with underwear…or a sheet can be used…or also not. Yeah…okay…" Her voice trailed off.

Michael couldn't stop his smile.

Fuck, she was perfect.

Well, let's start with the underwear option.

He crawled onto his white sheets and pushed the black, top blankets away, to the floor. He settled into the pose she suggested and paused…

Fuck, why not.

In a hurried movement, with an eye on the door, he shucked his briefs and tossed them in the hamper across the room. He then tugged the sheet up under his thighs just enough to cover the goods.

There.

He was basically naked, but…not.

If Mia wanted more…she'd get more.

And he wouldn't be worried about trying to protect her from him at that point.

At that point, his angel would have clearly made a choice.

"Are you ready for me?" She called, shyly, a twinge of eagerness audible in her voice.

He'd been ready for her his whole life; it was she who wasn't ready for someone like him.

"Come on in."

Chapter Twenty-Five

October 18, Tuesday
Mia

Mia's hands trembled as she clutched her sketchpad to her chest, her palms growing slick with nervous sweat. She blinked rapidly, struggling to process Michael's agreement to model for her – naked. After months of casual flirting and coy suggestions, she'd never imagined he would actually say yes.

Now here he was, reclining on the bed with a soft grin, ready to bare himself to her artist's eye. Mia swallowed hard, arousal and anxiety twisting hotly in her belly.

Mia nodded mutely, pulse racing. She smoothed her sweaty hands down her jeans, willing her nerves to settle. It's just art, she told herself. Just shapes and lines on a page.

Nothing more.

She took a deep breath, exhaling shakily.

Get it together.

It's not like she'd never seen a naked man before.

Yeah, but none of them were Michael Dillion.

Apparently running backs were built like brick shithouses. Holy fuck.

That morning, her confidence soared after she'd pulled her daily tarot, drawing The Queen of Wands and The Tower. She just didn't anticipate experiencing their hinted-at events so swiftly. Hot damn.

Gripping her pencils tightly, she walked on unsteady legs into the bedroom. Michael lay prone on the bed, muscular body bare, a sheet draped casually over his groin but that was it. He left everything else exposed.

Holy fucking fuck.

Mia's mouth dried. Her eyes drank in the sight hungrily, cursing the sheet for obscuring even an inch of his flawless form.

Well, from what she could see...there were actually a lot of inches that it covered.

Down girl.

Mia dragged a chair over and flipped open her sketchpad, taking a deep breath before looking back up at him.

It's just art. Just art.

She sketched him for hours on the plane...this was no different.

Oh, how she had wished to see his skin and muscles under the suit at the time. And now here she was, living that dream. And she couldn't even make herself look at him without ruminating on how hot her cheeks were.

Okay, she needed to stop being a chicken.

Just art.

And...she'd start at his feet. There. Easy peasy.

A compromise with the thirsty bitch inside of her.

She began to draw, losing herself in the soothing motions of her pencil, occasionally sneaking glances up Michael's perfect body. Maybe art and fantasy didn't have to be mutually exclusive after all.

Mia worked steadily, pencil gliding over the page as she captured every contour and curve of Michael's sculpted physique. Her earlier nerves faded away as her artistic passion took over. This was better than any fantasy – the real thing laid bare before her.

She shifted her chair closer, studying the strength in his calves, the scar on his knee. A tiny moan escaped her lips before she could stop it.

Michael's voice rumbled softly. "Everything okay down there?"

Mia flushed, grateful his eyes were still closed. "Yup, great! Just, uh, messed up the shading a bit there."

"Mhm," he murmured, a smile in his voice.

They lapsed back into silence. Mia's gaze traveled higher, lingering on the sheet barely clinging to him. One little tug and it would slide right off, revealing...

Gah!

She squeezed her eyes shut, willing her thoughts away from naked places.

Just finish the damn sketches.

Something about his body fascinated her. It wasn't just because it was gorgeous – he was so much more than that. But...his body told a story. Each muscle served a purpose, added another layer to him.

Michael. Her onion.

With a deep breath, she continued, carefully detailing his muscular thighs and hips on her newest page.

Mia's stomach churned, her head swimming. She tried to focus on not staring, but he was definitely getting aroused and *it* kept drawing her attention, saluting under the sheet.

Ten-hut!

Okay. She needed a change of pace. The groin region was far too problematic.

She started a new page and stared at the contours of his chest, the subtle wea of hair disappearing under the sheet...

She shifted in her seat, heat pooling in her core.

Taking a shaky breath, she continued sketching the lines of his neck and shoulders. As she reached his biceps though, something caught her eye.

"You have tattoos?"

How had she never noticed before?

"Just a couple. An old buddy of mine owns a shop."

Maybe the kid from the picture.

Mia leaned closer, examining the intricate designs inked on his skin. Her breath caught when she recognized the wings on the inside of his biceps...where they would be close to his heart.

They were identical to the ones on her own wrists, the wings she had gotten to honor her parents.

And underneath, in flowing script: *My Angel.*

She looked up at him wordlessly, heart pounding. His eyes had rolled up and he was watching her with a soft smile.

"I got it after the crash. After I...thought I lost you." He swallowed. "I thought I killed you by directing you into the water..." his voice was broken. "You were my angel then...and you still are."

Mia's eyes filled with tears. Unable to speak, she leaned forward and put her hand over his heart, pressing adoringly where is heart thundered under her touch. The moment hung suspended between them, weighted with meaning.

After a long moment, she found her voice again. "They're beautiful," she whispered. As she blinked, a tear slipped down her cheek. "Thank you."

He nodded, eyes never leaving hers. The air simmered between them, full of unspoken words.

Clearing her throat, Mia reluctantly pulled her hand away, brushing the trickle of tears from her cheek before picking up her sketchpad again. There would be time later to explore what had just passed between them. For now, she had a drawing to finish.

Mia took a deep breath, refocusing her attention on the sketch in progress. As she continued to study Michael's muscular frame, she made a few light strokes to capture the contours of his shoulders and beck. His skin seemed to glow in the now afternoon light streaming through the window.

She worked steadily, losing herself in the process. The scratch of pencil on paper was the only sound as she added the fine details.

Mia smiled to herself. She was surprised by how comfortable she felt, how intimate this moment was between them. Her heart swelled with emotions she wasn't quite ready to name.

After some time, she sat back to survey her work, flipping through the pages. "I think I'm good for now," she said.

Michael lowered his legs, stretching his arms overhead. The sheet slipped down, causing Mia's heart to jolt. She tore her eyes away, her throat too dry to swallow nervously.

He grinned at her reaction. "So, how did I do as your model?"

"You were perfect," she said, meeting his gaze. "This is my best work yet."

His expression turned serious then. Reaching out, he caressed her cheek with his fingertips. "You're pretty perfect, yourself," he murmured.

Mia's pulse raced at his touch. This was uncharted territory for them, but it felt right.

Be brave.

Leaning in, she brought her lips to his in the lightest, lingering kiss.

CHAPTER TWENTY-SIX

October 18, Tuesday
Michael

Michael sat up in the bed, ignoring the breeze from the falling sheet. He reached out and took Mia's hand, intertwining their fingers. The fact that he was naked and had been aroused for hours didn't faze him in the least; all that mattered was the tender connection they were sharing together, now.

As if propelled by a force greater than themselves, Mia launched herself at him and their lips met in a soft kiss that immediately turned heated. Michael welcomed her passion wholeheartedly, wrapping his strong arms around her as they explored each other's tongues.

"Fuck, Mia," he breathed between the ravenous kisses, his hands roaming the length of her back. "I've wanted this for so long."

"Me too," she confessed, her cheeks flushing with heat.

The warmth of their embrace was intoxicating and the electricity between them was undeniable. As Michael's hands moved along Mia's body, curiosity mingled with desire, each touch leaving a a burning imprint. He tentatively ran his fingertips over the delicate fabric of her thin PJs, under her sweatshirt, feeling her shiver beneath his touch.

"Is this okay?" he asked, looking into her eyes for confirmation.

"More than okay," she whispered, a hint of urgency in her voice that emboldened him to continue.

With careful hands, Michael unzipped her sweatshirt, revealing the alluring curves of her body. Then, seeing her hungry gaze, he also pulled the tiny pajama top up and over her head.

Mia's breath hitched as his fingers brushed against her skin, each new touch igniting a spark within her. She watched him with hooded eyes, her chest rising and falling with anticipation as his fingers seared dark paths of his adoration all over her pale skin. The contrast between them was striking.

And fucking hot.

"Michael," she murmured, her own hands crawling down his chiseled chest. "I need you."

"Patience, Angel," he teased gently, his own eagerness evident in his lap. "I want to savor every moment. Finally."

He continued undressing her at a maddeningly slow pace, driving Mia wild with a mixture of frustration and excitement. Mia groaned as her shorts fell away, leaving her vulnerable and exposed in front of him.

"Finally," Michael breathed again, taking a moment to admire the sight before him. She was still standing on the side of the bed next to him where he sat. He leaned back to get the full effect. "You're even more incredible than I imagined." He shot her a look. "And I imagined a lot."

Mia blushed at his words and gave him a shy, pleased smile. She stepped forward and pressed herself against him, the heat between them nearly unbearable.

They were going to burn his house to the fucking ground.

"Please," she begged, her voice thick with need. "You're not the only one with an imagination."

"All right, baby," Michael relented, his own restraint faltering as he captured her lips in another scorching kiss. "Let me show you what I've come up with."

Michael turned and lay Mia down on the bed, his body covering hers. Their kisses grew more heated, hands roaming and caressing. He trailed his lips down her neck as she arched into him, soft moans escaping her.

Michael slowly kissed her, worshiping every inch of exposed skin with his mouth. Her hands tugged at his head, wordlessly urging him downwards. He teased her nipples with his tongue before continuing lower.

When he finally tasted the slickness of her, Mia cried out. He stroked her with his fingers and tongue until she trembled on the edge of release.

"Michael, I want you inside me," she panted.

Needing no further encouragement, he grabbed a condom from the nightstand drawer and positioned himself above her. They locked eyes as he slid inside her and his body shivered, overwhelmed by the intimacy of their joining.

It had never been like this before.

It had never been this...*consuming*.

Michael moved slowly at first, giving her time to adjust. He was no slouch in the size department.

But after hearing her small grunts and feeling her heels digging into his glutes, pushing him in deeper, a primal need took over and he quickened his pace. Mia matched his rhythm, nails raking down his back as her moans bellowed into his ear. The mounting tension crested and broke like stormy waves as they climaxed together, both grunting inelegantly at the force of it.

Fuck!

It had been a month of constant blue balls and he'd just had an erection for pretty much the last twelve hours.

That was the hardest, most explosive orgasm of his entire fucking life.

The wait had been torturous, but holy shit.

Had he just unlocked a new kink for edging?

In the aftermath of their combined release, Michael held Mia close, both spent but profoundly connected.

No more doubts or guilt, just clarity.

She was his now, body and soul.

· · · ● · ● · ● · ● · ·

Hours later, Michael couldn't help but marvel at the way Mia's body seemed to glow beneath him, her every curve and contour illuminated by the soft afternoon light that filtered through the curtains. As he traced his fingers along her skin, he felt a shiver run down his spine.

Was this love?

"Michael," Mia whispered, still somewhat breathless from their latest round. "I never thought we'd be here like this."

"Neither did I," he admitted, gently brushing a strand of hair away from her face. "But now that we are, I can't imagine being anywhere else."

As their lips met for another passionate kiss, Michael flexed his hips against hers, reveling in the skin-to-skin contact.

He didn't even have to be fucking *in* her and it was still heaven.

At this rate, he was going to need to see a doctor about how many times a man could orgasm in twenty four hours and not die. He was probably setting a World Record.

Michael started kissing his way down her soft neck again. They could play while he recharged...

That wasn't the first time he'd thought that either. And just like last time, he'd probably recharge with superhuman speed.

With each new revelation of her body, he took the time to appreciate and explore, savoring the sensation of her warm skin yielding to his fingertips.

"God, you're beautiful," he murmured, his voice thick with the intensity of his emotion as Mia blushed under his gaze and arched her back at his touch.

"Thank you. You're not awful either," she replied softly, her eyes locked onto his, conveying a trust and vulnerability that had his recovery speed increasing.

As they continued their passionate exploration, Michael found himself holding back, keenly aware of his massive size compared to Mia's small body. But as the heat between them grew, so too did Mia's impatience.

"Michael, I'm not glass," her voice strained with need. "I want more."

"Are you sure?"

"I'm sure," she assured him, her gaze unwavering. "Gimme gimme."

Grinning, he heeded her greedy request.

Michael allowed himself to succumb to the magnetic pull between them, losing himself in the rhythm of their bodies as they moved together in perfect harmony. However, this time, he refused her demand for "harder, faster."

This time he set a slow, deliberate pace that had her moaning and writhing beneath him, unable to form words.

Mia climaxed first, letting out a shattered cry while clinging tight to his shoulders. He slid his hand away from where they were joined and threaded it deep in her hair, looking down at her in fascination as she shuddered in her aftershocks.

Fuck, she was magnificent.

When she opened her eyes and looked up at him, it was a look of pure peace. Michael followed her lead as he soared into his own oblivion, his hips jerking roughly against hers.

And the sun began to set, burning in golden beams through the window and they lay entwined in each other's arms, bodies slick with sweat and trembling from their impassioned exertions.

This was it. This was happiness. Peace. Maybe even love.

It was more than just physical attraction – it was a soul-deep connection that transcended time and circumstance, binding them together in a way he had never thought possible.

"Are you okay?" he asked softly, brushing a tender kiss across Mia's forehead.

"Better than okay," she murmured, snuggling closer to him. "That was...incredible."

"Agreed," he chuckled, his heart swelling with happiness.

As they nestled in each other's arms, Michael felt something shift within him. It was as if a door had been unlocked, revealing a future filled with hope and healing. Though the journey ahead would be far from easy, at least he wouldn't have to face it alone. And with Mia by his side, maybe her strength could rub off on him, and he could finally forgive himself for what he had done.

CHAPTER TWENTY-SEVEN

October 29, Saturday
Michael

Michael walked into his woodshop, stopping short when he saw Mia perched on a stool, brow furrowed in concentration as she worked on a large canvas. Sawdust sprinkled her hair and smudges of charcoal darkened her cheeks. The oversized flannel shirt she wore was covered in splotches of paint. She was so focused on her work that she didn't even glance up.

Pride swelled in Michael's chest. Over the past two weeks, Mia had transformed into a woman possessed. She barely left the shop, pouring all her creative energy into painting, sculpting and sketching. Having an active sex life had clearly awakened her artistic spirit.

Michael leaned against the doorway, content to watch her work. The morning sun streamed through the windows, framing Mia in its warm glow. Seeing her so vibrant and passionate for her art filled him with joy. This was the Mia he had glimpsed on the plane, not the one who had been muted by her trauma. Not only was she creating art again, she was also hitting the indoor lap pool almost every day. She still couldn't fully submerge, but she could swim with her head above water, and she no longer needed the bathroom door to be open when she showered.

Mia paused and studied the canvas, forehead wrinkled with the intensity of her thought. Michael crossed the room and wrapped his arms around her from behind. She leaned back against him with a happy sigh.

"It's really coming along," he said. "It's gorgeous."

She tilted her head up for a kiss. "I couldn't have done it without you."

Michael nuzzled her neck, breathing in the faint scent of some earthy essential oil mingled with paint and clay. Right here, holding this amazing woman in his arms – this was exactly where he was meant to be.

Mia slipped out of his arms and headed for the bathroom. "I need to wash up before we go over the plans for the show."

Michael smiled, watching her disappear into the other room. She had showered yesterday before he even got home. Alone. With no accompanying panic attacks.

It was just another sign of her strength.

He glanced around the studio, taking in the organized chaos. More canvases leaned against the walls, bearing the fruits of her creative labors. A pottery wheel occupied one corner, blobs of clay drying nearby. The surface of the worktable was littered with paint tubes, brushes, charcoal sticks, sketch pads. She'd practically been living here lately, immersed in her art. He couldn't even see his feeble attempts hidden in amongst the beauty of her pieces.

His sketchbook was flipped open on the table to Mia's favorite page.

She was a sly fox, that one.

He wandered into the kitchen and got some food out while Mia washed her latest art project from her skin. The shower turned off and Mia emerged a few minutes later, toweling her inky black hair. "So get this," she said. "The venue for the art show got switched this afternoon. Asher decided an outdoor locale would be better given the nice weather. And you know Asher."

He didn't. Not really. But he knew of him and the guy was known to be imperial and dramatic.

Maybe they should introduce him to Lexie...

She tossed the towel on the table and pulled a hair tie from her wrist. "It's going to be on a floating dock out on the Quabbin

Reservoir. Should make for some gorgeous scenery. I just hope my pieces complement the backdrop."

The mere mention of a dock on a lake sent a shiver down his spine.

Ace whined from the floor by Michael's feet and started pushing his body against Michael's legs.

"I have no idea how they're going to get it set up safely in time..."

Walking out over the water, the rickety sensation beneath his feet, the gentle rocking...

His stomach protested violently, as if it were already trapped on that precarious platform, and his pulse quickened.

Ace wound his way through his legs and leaned harder against him.

"We're all taking small rowboats out there—" Mia's voice trailed off as her focus shifted to tying up her hair. She bent over, her wet hair obscuring her face as she drew her wet locks together. Michael watched as she whipped her head back up, and cold droplets sprayed across his face.

For a moment, he felt only the freezing water droplets, a stark contrast to the warmth of the room.

Waves and thunder crashed in his ears.

His hands curled into fists at his side.

Rookie gave a small bark that caused him to blink and flinch away. There was too much stimulation. Too much...everything.

The dread sat heavy in his chest, making it hard to breathe as her words faded into a muffled buzz. The idea of small rowboats bringing them to the docks was his worst nightmare.

Michael's mind raced with images of himself, struggling to stay afloat outside a capsized rowboat, the violent lapping of the water against the sides, causing him to inhale chunks of it at a time. All the while, not being able to hear. To see. To find his friend...

"—there might be a small storm rolling in but Asher is apparently convinced it will hit *after* the show. It's like he doesn't know New England weather at the end of October at all." She looked at him, pleased with herself for assuming the role of a 'local', but Michael couldn't respond. Couldn't move.

His body was suffocating.

Drowning.

He could feel the small drops speckling his face.

He could hear himself calling out for his friend, his voice barely audible over the pounding rain…

"—so, I figured we'd leave at—"

"I'm not going."

Mia paused and fully turned to take him in, her face turning pale and worried.

"I'm sorry?"

"I'm not going. I'm not fucking going."

Mia blinked and her head jerked back. "Michael. What the heck happened? What's going on?"

He couldn't breathe.

He couldn't fucking breathe.

Now Rookie was whining too. Why wouldn't they be quiet!

His hands were shaking and he stared at them, his mind seeing the pruny hands of a fifteen-year-old boy.

And then the pruny hands of a twenty-eight-year-old man.

When he was near water, people died.

He caused people to die.

He killed them.

He'd killed Wayde all those years ago.

Just like he'd killed all those people from the plane.

What in the fuck was he doing with Mia?

"Michael? Honey? Look at me. Are you okay?" She stepped close to him, her hand out as if she was unsure whether to touch him or not.

What *the fuck* was he doing with Mia?

"I need to go." He looked toward the door, desperate to leave. "Take your stuff and get out."

Mia blinked and looked toward the door as well. "What?"

"Take your fucking stuff and get the fuck out of my house. Go to your art show on the fucking lake and then go back to your own apartment with Sean, where it's—."

Mia's eyes went wide, and she grabbed a necklace laying against her chest, twisting it between her fingers as she studied him. "Michael, I— "

"Just get the fuck out!" He roared.

Ace and Rookie abandoned and his legs and started barking.

His skin was on fire.

He was on fire.

No, he was freezing.

He was drowning.

Why wouldn't the dogs stop making noise!

As tears started welling up in Mia's eyes, he was able to unstick his feet from the floor.

Like he was moving through molasses, he made his way out the door, to his car in the driveway, and down to the player parking at the stadium.

On autopilot, not even remembering the drive to the stadium, he scanned in and made his way to the locker rooms. As he walked, he ripped his clothes from his body, dropping them on the floor, and entered the showers.

Turning the showers on the coldest possible, he stepped in, collapsed to the ground, and screamed.

CHAPTER TWENTY-EIGHT

October 29, Saturday
Michael

After leaving the deserted stadium, Michael drove aimlessly, lost in the torment of his memories.

He saw Wayde's young, smiling face – his friend from that ill-fated camp, more than a decade ago. They had laughed and joked as they pushed the boat into the water, ignoring their camp counselor's warnings from earlier in the day about the upcoming storm.

"Don't be a wuss," Michael had said, tossing his life jacket back onto the shore.

Wayde had paused, looking down at his own vest, before following Michael's lead and dropping his on the rocky shore, too.

The storm had come out of nowhere, violent and unforgiving. Michael remembered the terror as the boat capsized, the desperate struggle to keep their heads above water. Wayde had panicked, swallowing mouthfuls as he thrashed and tried to find some part of the boat to hold onto. Michael had tried to reach him, but the waves kept pushing them apart. Michael clung to his oar, cursing himself for losing the other in the waves.

He'd never forget the sight of Wayde's terrified eyes disappearing below the churning surface.

They found his body hours after the storm passed, washed up on the shore several miles downstream.

Guilt consumed Michael.

If only he hadn't teased him about the life jackets.

If only he had listened to the counselors about the incoming storm.

If only he'd had the strength to fight the waves, grab Wayde, and keep them both afloat.

Michael rubbed his chest against the raw ache of regret.

Then there was the plane crash.

He'd prioritized the most vulnerable passengers for the wing, but had he chosen right? Had he condemned the others to a watery grave? How was he not hated by Mia for judging people solely on their appearances? Who knew what kind of hidden troubles each of those passengers had.

And there he was: playing judge, jury, and executioner.

Michael pulled into his driveway and squeezed his eyes shut, trying to block it all out.

The witch in Salem had been right.

The ghosts of his mistakes would haunt him forever. Maybe he was cursed; anyone near him seemed destined to drown.

He couldn't risk it happening again. Not with Mia. She'd just begun healing from her own trauma – he refused to be the cause of more pain for her.

Coward.

Michael slammed his palm against the steering wheel in frustration. "I know," he whispered. "But she deserves better."

He killed the engine but made no move to exit the car.

Coward. Selfish. Weak.

The cruel taunts battered his mind as he gripped the steering wheel. He should be there for Mia, supporting her big moment. She'd worked so hard, overcome so much, to reclaim her passion for art. After everything they'd shared, he owed it to her to be by her side.

But the thought of standing on that dock, surrounded by open water, made panic rise in his throat. His heart raced as he recalled the plane's violent impact on the lake, the screams of the terrified passengers as they were plunged into the icy depths.

Michael pressed his palms against his eyes until bursts of light exploded behind his lids. He focused on slowing his breathing, pushing back against the dark memories threatening to pull him under.

Gradually, the anxiety ebbed. But shame still coursed through him. He should be stronger than this – for Mia's sake, if not his own. She deserved more than a man still chained to the ghosts of his past.

Maybe Sean was right. Maybe he wasn't good enough for her.

Michael sighed heavily and stepped out of the car. The sun shone brightly overhead, mocking his inner turmoil. It really was a beautiful day for an art show.

If the storm held off.

Michael entered the house cautiously, conflicting thoughts swirling through his mind. "Mia?"

Every time he closed his eyes, he saw Mia's face, her expressive eyes filled with hurt and confusion. He couldn't shake the guilt that weighed heavily on his chest.

She was no where to be found. And neither were her things.

Fuck.

The dogs stayed at their spots in front of the big windows, sunning themselves. Even the pups didn't bother with greeting him.

He'd yelled at their mom. Hell, he wouldn't have greeted himself, either.

"Dammit," he muttered under his breath, tossing his keys on the counter. "Why didn't I just tell her the truth?"

As he turned to go to the living room, he noticed a small, brown cardboard box with shipping labels all over it, sitting on the entryway table. Mia must have put it there before she left.

Naturally. Even stung by him, she still did the right thing. Another blinding example of why she was too good for him.

With a sigh, be brought the package back into the kitchen and perched on a stool, staring at it.

He didn't order anything recently...and if Mia had, she would have taken it with her.

He brought a shaking hand up to his face, pinching the bridge of his nose irritably. Holy fuck, he'd messed things up.

Okay, this package was a later problem.

Right now, he had to focus on anything other than the fact that he was supposed to be getting ready to go to Mia's show.

That was supposed to be inside an art gallery in the fucking city.

Fucking Asher Wielde and his stupid fucking whims.

An art show on the middle of a fucking lake? During October? With a storm on the radar...

"Asshole," he grumbled as he shuffled into the living room to flick on the TV. He had film to review for tomorrow's game and was hoping that the familiar routine would help distract him from his self-imposed heartache.

Two hours later, Michael slumped back against the couch and cursed the headache plaguing him. The internal debate had taken its toll, leaving him feeling hollow and guilty. He glanced out the window, taking note of the late afternoon sun shining down everything it touched.

"Beautiful day for Mia's art show," he said to the dogs, who were both still ignoring him. He shot them a betrayed look. "Look, I lost my temper, okay? I'm allowed. People make mistakes. I'll explain myself and everything will be okay." He hoped, aloud.

A pang of sadness washed over him. This was so important to her. This art show was the entire reason she'd been on that plane in the first place. The whole catalyst for how they'd met.

Maybe it wouldn't be okay.

The dogs didn't even look at him. "The next time Danny says he has a couple of rescue dogs that need a home, I'm telling him to look elsewhere."

No reaction.

Traitors.

He wondered what kind of pieces Mia had created, knowing she had kept them secret from him to surprise him. Now, he would never get the chance to see them, and it tore at his heart.

"Maybe I could have explained myself a bit more," he mused, staring blankly at the screen. "But I wasn't exactly processing things...healthily? Of all people, Mia will get that...right?"

Michael stood up from the couch, his body aching from the hours spent sitting in one position. With a deep breath, he walked back into the kitchen, approaching the mysterious parcel.

"All right," he thought. "Time to see what this is all about."

He picked up the package, then he gave it a slight shake.

Huh.

Slowly, Michael tore open the wrapping, revealing the contents.

First, there was a small piece of artwork sitting on top. It was just scribbles, really, a child's drawing. There was a note attached. The drawing was Isla's and the note, in Mindy's handwriting, explained that the artwork was an interpretation of them all swimming together. His heart caught in his throat..

Also included was a thick, paperclipped stack of photos and newspaper clippings. The pictures captured moments from the rescue that he had never seen before, articles that he had avoided at all costs. They featured families huddled together on the wing of the plane, old people clinging to any dry surface they could manage as they were hoisted into safety by the rescuers, the hypothermic being loaded into ambulances on the closest beach...

The images brought back a flood of memories and feelings that had him swallowing through a burning in his throat.

"Wow," he whispered, his eyes welling up as he took in each photograph and every article.

Among the haunting scenes of the crash were also pictures of Mindy with her kids after the rescue, smiling brightly as they held toy airplanes and stood with others he didn't recognize. The contrast between the two sets of images tugged at his heartstrings, sending his emotions spinning in every direction.

A small card stuffed into the side of the box caught his eye, and he picked it up, his hands trembling. Written in Mindy's delicate handwriting, it read: "If it wasn't for you, we might not be here. You saved our lives. You saved *all of our* lives. I got the sense from your visit that you might have forgotten that. So here's your reminder."

"Damn," Michael choked out, tears streaming down his face as the weight of her words settled on him.

Michael's fingers trembled as he turned the card over, revealing an attached newspaper clipping. The headline detailed the imperfect water landing, and his heart clenched at the sight of the highlighted death toll: twenty-three. None of them from impact. His eyes traveled to the next highlighted section – the total number of passengers on that fateful day: one hundred ninety-seven.

The weight of it all settled heavily on his chest, guilt: his ever present companion.

His gaze shifted to a line highlighted on the bottom of the article. It explained that out of the twenty-three who had died, all of them were found on the left side of the plane...

On the opposite wing to where Michael had been directing the passengers...

Chaos had reigned supreme there and he wondered for the millionth time if he could have made a difference for those people as well.

"Thank you for being our angel," Mindy had written alongside a small heart drawn in ink. "You couldn't do it all, but you did everything for all of us. It's not about the lives you couldn't save, but about honoring the ones you did."

Tears filled his eyes, blurring his vision as he gripped the paper tightly in his hands.

He collapsed against the kitchen island in a heap of hopeless sobs. Michael let the emotional turmoil wash over him, feeling the burden of both guilt and gratitude vying for dominance within him.

As his tears began to subside, Michael stared at the newspaper clipping, at the heart Mindy had drawn.

He took a deep breath, his resolve strengthening.

For Mindy, for the survivors, and for Mia – he needed to fix himself. Properly. He didn't need to force this atonement on himself. He...wasn't at fault...

He glanced at his watch. If he hurried, maybe he could still make it. His heart stuttered at the thought. But then he pictured Mia's radiant smile – one he hoped he'd earn, when she saw him arrive. That alone would make facing his fears worth it. He had to try. For her.

Michael rifled through his closet, pulling out a crisp white button-down shirt and dark jeans. He dressed quickly, checking his appearance in the mirror. As ready as he'd ever be.

His hands trembled slightly as he locked the front door. He paused on the step, taking a deep breath.

He could do this, he reminded himself.

For Mia.

For himself.

CHAPTER TWENTY-NINE

October 29, Saturday
Michael

The drive to the reservoir was a blur. His mind raced as he drew closer, heart pounding against his ribs. Finally, he pulled into the packed parking lot overlooking the glittering water.

Michael scanned the crowds milling along the floating docks displaying artwork of various sizes and mediums. No sign of Mia. Wiping his sweaty palms on his jeans, he started down the grassy slope toward the water's edge where the transport boats were waiting.

This was ridiculous. Part of him hoped that Asher didn't choose Mia, so she didn't have to be subject to this whimsical and capricious, spoiled bullshit that he was sure to pull during her understudy time.

Immediately, he felt guilty for the thought.

Shit.

The dock bobbed as he stepped onto it. Michael froze, images of the plane's wing flashing through his mind. Breathe.

It was going to be fine.

He stepped onto the boat and the rower pushed off, carrying them toward the floating docks.

Jesus, how much did the guy pay to get this all set up in the span of ten hours?

Michael's eyes kept darting up to check out the sky...no storm clouds in sight.

Yet.

It was okay. They'd be gone in time.

Once he was off the rowboat, Michael took a minute to settle his stomach as he grew accustomed to the soft swaying motions of the dock and the volatile lake they were at the mercy of.

He then weaved between patrons admiring the art, searching for Mia's familiar face. His courage wavered with each step further onto the undulating dock.

Just when he thought he couldn't go any farther, he spotted her.

Mia stood before a striking abstract sculpture; her hair swept up in a messy bun as she gestured enthusiastically to a small crowd. Michael edged closer, heart swelling at the passion in her voice.

"...the fluidity of the bronze represents water's capricious nature," Mia was saying. "Both beautiful and dangerous at times. I wanted to capture that dichotomy."

Her dark eyes suddenly met his through the crowd. Surprise flickered across her delicate features. Excusing herself, Mia hurried over to Michael.

"You came," she said, her eyes worriedly taking him in.

Michael rubbed the back of his neck, avoiding her intent gaze. "Hey, Angel." He swallowed hard. "I'm sorry about earlier."

Mia tilted her head, her face concerned...and a little angry. "Yeah, what the heck was that?"

Michael took a deep breath, the words heavy on his tongue. "It's not that I didn't want to be here..." He trailed off, shame creeping in.

Mia tilted her head, brows furrowed. She waited for him to continue.

"I have this thing with lakes," he finally said. "Bad stuff always happens when I'm near them. I know it doesn't make sense, but I'm cursed or something." He shook his head, laughing darkly. "Or maybe it's just happenstance. I don't know. But my friend...he died in a lake when we were kids. And It was my fault. Then...the plane crashed, too. Lakes just...aren't good for me."

She watched him closely, her brow furrowed. "Okay...so this was because of it being moved to a lake?"

He fidgeted and looked away, not wanting to tell her the second part. "When you flipped your hair up, it splattered me with some droplets. It's stupid, but the water, it's been a...thing...for me, too. And I just wasn't ready for it." He ended on a rush, trying to stop the horror that was spreading over her features.

"Michael..." Her regret was causing his stomach to clench. That wasn't the point of this.

"I'm just...sorry. For taking it out on you. That wasn't cool. And I'd like you to forgive me. I'll do whatever it takes to get it under control. I'm so sorry, Angel."

She was shaking her head.

Why was she shaking her head?

Michael tensed.

"Michael...I, of all people, get it. I'm not going to hold that against you. Though...I wish you had opened up to me about this all earlier than now..." She shook her head. "But, that's up to you to process as you see fit. I just...you're my soul, Michael. I want to be there for you like you were for me. Let me in. Let me help you?"

Michael met her earnest gaze. "I'd like to think it was fate that brought me to you on that plane. But if I thank fate for that, then what does it say about my friend? Or the other people on the flight." His voice grew hoarse with emotion.

Mia stepped closer and embraced him.

"I don't have answers for you. But thank you for telling me," she murmured against his chest.

Michael exhaled in relief, holding her tightly.

Okay.

He could do this.

"Come on, let me show you my stuff to get your mind off everything?"

Michael nodded. "That would be fucking fantastic. I'm already sweating through my undershirt with my nerves out here right now."

Together, they turned back to the exhibit, her arm slipped supportively through his, a soft smile on her face.

Michael took a deep breath as they approached the sculpture, the sun shining off the tangle flowing copper forms.

"It's beautiful," he said sincerely.

Mia smiled up at him, cheeks flushing pink. "I'm so glad you like it. I was a little nervous about the concept."

"Don't be. It's amazing."

As Michael gazed down at her, Mia's eyes darkened alluringly. She traced a finger along his jaw.

"Thank you for being here."

As she turned to speak with a few more of the attendees, Michael watched her admiringly. The breeze off the water ruffled her dark hair and brought out the golden undertones of her skin. She glowed with creative fulfillment.

Pride swelled in Michael's chest. Mia had come so far, facing her fears and rediscovering her passion. Witnessing her growth and being a part of her journey was a gift.

He knew then, without a doubt, that he was ready to face his own demons. For her, he would find the courage.

Michael took a deep breath as he stared out at the shimmering water of the reservoir. Mia's hand slipped into his, squeezing gently.

Mia studied him with knowing eyes. She understood what it had cost him to be here.

"Come take a closer look - now that I have another free thirty seconds." She gave him a wry grin as she tugged him closer to where the art piece stood.

Mia took a deep breath, her voice quivering with emotion. "This is my way of turning a traumatic experience into something beautiful, something healing," she began.

She gestured toward the first piece, a canvas brimming with vivid colors and dynamic brushwork. "This one," she said, "depicts the initial spark of connection, the handsome stranger on the plane. It's called 'Intrigued.'"

Michael smiled, his heart squeezing in his chest.

Fuck, he didn't deserve her.

He bowed his head respectfully, acknowledging the nod to his presence in her life.

Mia moved to the next piece, a powerful portrayal of the plane crash in all its chaos and terror. "This is the fear, the moment everything spiraled out of control." It was all done in dark charcoals with heavy slashes and thick texture.

Next was a sculpture crafted from twisted metal and debris. "This one represents the wreckage, the aftermath. It's about finding strength in the midst of chaos." She gave him a small smile. "To finding other healing souls."

Her collection was an eclectic mix of various mediums, each piece arranged around her small corner, hanging from racks and tied in place. In wood, she burned a series of images, each one depicting a different moment from the emergency landing that had ripped her life apart. On metal, she painted and etched scenes of chaos and destruction, while pottery moldings of planes served as a haunting reminder of the tragedy.

Finally, they reached the heart of the exhibit, the grand resin piece that glistened brilliantly in the late afternoon sun.

Mia's voice quivered with a mix of pride and vulnerability as she spoke. "And here is 'Unbreakable.' This is the moment when courage and hope triumphed over fear. It's about healing and discovering love in the most unexpected of places."

The resin piece was a mixture of assorted styles. In a resin box, she had created a miniature crash. A plane in dark water, surrounded by passengers, subtle waves on the 'water's' surface. His chest tightened as he stared.

Holy fuck.

How did she turn something so terrible into something so...beautiful?

Michael shifted his gaze from the art to Mia, touched by her sincerity and the deep emotions woven into each piece. He reached for her hand, giving it a reassuring squeeze. "They're incredible, Mia," he said, his voice filled with genuine admiration. "These pieces tell a powerful story, your story. I'm honored to be a part of it."

Mia flushed with pleasure. "Thanks for letting me weasel my way in."

He kissed her forehead. "Not much weaseling needed. I was all too willing to bring you down with me."

She leaned up on her toes to brush a kiss across his jawline, lips grazing the stubble there. "You forget. You're the hero in my story, not the devil."

Michael shivered gratefully, closing his eyes.

Witnessing Mia conquer her fears to rediscover her artistry was a privilege.

And being a part of her journey was a gift he would always cherish.

CHAPTER THIRTY

October 29, Saturday
Mia

Patrons of the art exhibit strolled along the floating dock, sipping wine and admiring the unique installations that lined their path. The ambiance was electric. Some applicant artists posed in their designated spots, wearing their art pieces like armor – chains, metal, and wood hanging from their bodies as they held their painted poses with pride.

Michael wandered off to see the other pieces and left Mia to talk about her pieces with any interested guests.

As patrons approached her display, Mia felt a wave of anxiety wash over her.

This exhibition was a chance to win a spot in the coveted art residency with Asher. A year-long mentorship and inclusion in his network of galleries awaited the winner. It was a big fucking deal. She couldn't screw this up.

"Excuse me," a woman asked, drawing Mia's attention to the wooden piece she was examining. "Could you tell me more about this one?"

"Um, yes," Mia stammered, her nerves causing her to babble. "This piece, it represents the moment when...when the plane first hit the water. I...I wanted to capture the raw emotion and the...the heartbreak."

"Interesting," the woman murmured, her eyes scanning over the rest of Mia's collection. "Your work is very moving."

"Thank you," Mia replied softly, feeling a small sense of relief.

Glancing across the dock, she spotted Sean standing in front of another artist's section, an attractive woman by his side. Her stomach clenched as she remembered the rift between them and wondered if they could ever truly be friends again. She didn't see him the same way he saw her, but she couldn't deny that she missed him. She offered an awkward wave, which he returned with a tight smile before turning away.

At least he came...that must mean something...right?

As the exhibition continued, Mia did her best to engage with the guests who stopped by her corner. Each compliment brought a flush to her cheeks, but her nerves refused to subside.

Mia's fingertips brushed over the epoxy resin surface of her statement piece, feeling the subtle waves she had created to mimic the waters around their sinking plane. Her heartbeat quickened as she looked at the intricate details of each miniature person, all one hundred ninety seven passengers captured in various states of emotion – some panicking, others patiently waiting for help.

"Wow," a man breathed out from behind her. "This is incredible."

"Thank you," Mia replied, forcing a smile onto her face as she turned to face him. She knew her art was meant to evoke strong reactions, but it still felt surreal to hear someone appreciate her work so openly.

"Did you really paint all these faces?" he asked, his eyes wide with amazement.

Mia nodded. "I did. It took hours and hours, but I wanted to make sure I got it just right."

"Your dedication shows," he said sincerely before moving on to examine the rest of her collection.

As more guests approached her corner of the dock, Mia couldn't help but feel exposed. Each piece she had crafted told a story – a story that was deeply personal to her – but now they were on display for everyone to see. Would they understand the pain she had poured into each stroke of paint, each etched line in wood? Or would they only see the tragedy and chaos that had consumed her life?

"Your work is incredible," a woman whispered, leaning in close to study the facial expressions of the tiny passengers. "You've captured something very raw and real here."

"Thank you," Mia managed again, her voice barely audible amidst the chatter around them.

"Is this based on a true story?" the woman asked.

Mia hesitated for a moment, debating whether or not to reveal the truth. But then she remembered why she had chosen this theme in the first place: to honor the strength and resilience she had witnessed on that fateful day. "Yes," she finally admitted. "It's a portrayal of my own experience during a plane crash."

The woman's eyes widened and Mia braced herself for the inevitable questions that she was sure would follow. But instead, the woman simply nodded her understanding and moved on.

As the sun started to set and dark clouds started to roll in, Mia continued to engage with each person who stopped by her collection. Some were curious about her story, while others offered their condolences or shared their own experiences with trauma and loss. With every conversation, Mia felt a little lighter, as if sharing her art was somehow helping to heal the wounds she carried within her.

Mia's fingers trembled as she adjusted her metal wire sculpture one last time, ensuring that it hung securely from the wooden frame. The recycled airplane materials glinted under the warm lighting of the floating dock, casting a subtle glow over her artwork. Lexie had pulled some strings for her to get some of the actual wreckage. Lexie refused to disclose how much it cost her to get the materials. Mia decided to bury her head in the sand on that one. She took a deep breath, trying to calm her nerves as a new batch of admirers stepped up to view the piece.

When he found a rare moment to breathe, she looked around for Michael. Was he still here?

Given his...issues, she couldn't blame him for wanting to get the hell out of Dodge. Maybe she could track him down and explicitly say that she didn't expect him to stay. Would that help his anxiety if he knew she was okay with him leaving? She didn't want him to be there under duress.

She scanned the bustling crowd, looking past the other artists who wore their creations like armor. There were chains of metal woven into intricate patterns, wooden sculptures draped across bodies like living vines, and even a few daring souls who had painted themselves from head to toe, holding poses that showcased their work to its fullest potential.

"Excuse me," came a voice from behind her, jolting her out of her thoughts. Mia turned to find none other than Asher Wielde standing before her collection. Her heart raced, and her breathing hitched as she took in the stern expression on his face. The famous artist was known for his capriciousness and extravagance, but in this moment, he looked entirely unapproachable.

"Hello, Mr. Wielde," Mia managed to say, her voice barely a whisper. He didn't acknowledge her greeting, instead focusing intently on her artwork. Minutes passed, each second stretching out like an eternity as Asher continued to study her collection without uttering a word. Mia's nerves skyrocketed, her hands wringing together behind her back.

Please say something.

Anything.

Did he hate it? Love it?

As if sensing her silent plea, Asher finally broke the silence. But rather than offering any indication of his opinion, he only asked, "What inspired this piece?"

"Um...well, the plane crash," Mia replied hesitantly. "It was a traumatic experience, and I wanted to capture the raw emotions and chaos of it all. The trauma it wrought on all of us." She glanced at her statement piece, the epoxy resin creation depicting the harrowing moments of the water landing.

"Interesting," was all Asher said, his eyes flicking between the artwork and Mia. It was impossible to read his expression, and Mia felt her stomach twist into knots. Was he impressed? Disgusted? She couldn't tell, and it was driving her mad.

His opinion could make or break her career. He glanced at the swaying grid panels of accompanying art, his eyes skimming over the various pieces with an unreadable expression.

Mia's heart hammered in her chest, her palms growing damp with nervous sweat.

For a moment that felt like an eternity, Asher remained silent. Then, he turned back to her resin statement piece, and Mia braced herself for his verdict. Finally, he spoke, his voice slow and weighted with emotion. "It's said that art is a reflection of the human soul," he began, his dark eyes locked on hers. "But your piece, it's more than that. It's a testament to the human spirit's incredible power to endure and emerge stronger from the darkest of moments."

He gestured toward the figurine of Michael in the scene. She was trying to capture the essence of heroism and salvation in his positioning. "This figure here, it speaks volumes. It's a reminder that even in the face of tragedy, there are individuals who rise above, who become beacons of hope for others." Asher then turned back to the artwork, his eyes returning to the chaos and calm sides of the scene.

"Your art," he continued, "it's not just about the crash though, is it? It's about the beauty of resilience, the way humanity can find solace amidst turmoil. It's a tribute to the indomitable human spirit." He paused and looked up at the wall one more time, his eyes resting on one of the many paintings of Michael that she had displayed. "Well done," he remarked, and then walked to the next piece.

Oh.

Oh gods.

She was going to puke.

Mia bent over and held her stomach, unable to process what just happened.

Oh gods. Asher Wield had just complimented her work. *Her* work!

Mia's heart soared as she hyperventilated.

She had impressed Asher Wielde. *The* Asher Wielde.

The setting sun was split by the horizon, illuminating Mia's artwork in a soft, golden light. She couldn't help but steal another glance at where Asher Wielde had been standing just moments before, her heart still fluttering with excitement.

"Way to go, Angel."

Mia whipped around and threw herself in Michael's arms, trying not to scream out in the elation of her in excitement.

CHAPTER THIRTY-ONE

October 29, Saturday
Michael

"Thank you for coming," she said. "For sharing this with me. I'm honored you're here."

Michael took a deep breath, steadying himself. Mia's empathy and warmth were a balm, easing the rawness of his confession. He managed a small smile, ready to tell her that he'd be there whenever she needed him because that's what people do when they love each other.

But then chaos erupted as the dock rocked below them, splintering a part under the prolonged weight of the art pieces and patrons that had only grown as the event stretched on

Screams echoed over the water as part of the dock suddenly collapsed into the water. Michael instinctively grabbed a rope that was part of the 'fence' of the dock, preventing them both from being thrown into the lake. Panic spread as others were less fortunate, tumbling into the churning water. Mia's artwork teetered precariously on the edge of where the dock had snapped.

More sections gave way, sending even more people and art pieces flailing helplessly down into the lake's depths. Mia's wobbly gridwall panels and its attached paintings toppled over with a mighty splash, their vivid colors bleeding into the dark water.

The warmly dressed patrons struggled to stay afloat, weighted down by heavy clothes. Artists that had been wearing their metalwork were pulled down, although they were able to dislodge themselves and swim back to the surface.

Michael tensed, ready to leave Mia clinging to the rope while he rescued the others. But to his surprise, she leapt in before he could move.

He stared in a panic as she submerged herself and swam quickly over to an artist, thrashing with her artpiece trying to save it from sinking to the bottom. After a moment's hesitation, Michael jumped in to join Mia in her rescue efforts.

Together they worked to disentangle the thrashing victims and boost them onto the slanted docks.

Though soaked and shivering, Mia met his gaze with determination.

"You okay?"

He gave her a weak grin. "That's my line?"

She gave a dark chuckle and spun in the water, looking for another person that needed a boost out of the water, or a hand while they untangled themselves from the various debris.

How the fuck was this actually happening?

Again?!

Maybe he really was cursed.

Once everyone was relatively secure and the rescue boats were on their way, Michael and Mia swam over to a partially submerged dock, hanging on the ropes there. Michael noticed Mia hesitate, her eyes drifting to where her artwork had sunk below the surface.

She wouldn't...

In shock, he watched her glance back at him, then to the spot her paintings had disappeared. She took a deep breath, steeling herself.

Apparently, she would...

Before he could react, Mia arched gracefully into the dark water. Michael's heart seized with fear as the ripples faded where she had been.

CHAPTER THIRTY-TWO

October 29, Saturday
Michael

Mia had been under the water for too long. Michael's heart pounded as he peered into the murky lake, searching for any sign of her.

Just as he was about to dive under, she popped up.

In her arms she clutched the waterlogged canvases, blurred colors running down the frames.

Relief flooded Michael even as confusion furrowed his brow.

Why was she doing this? Was she going to do this for every piece of her collection?

For everyone's collections?

She was going to get herself killed.

Or be run over by a fucking rescue boat.

Mia swam with one arm, determinedly, toward him, her paintings tucked in close. As she reached the dock, Michael stretched out his hand.

"Here."

Mia smiled softly, handing over the ruined paintings.

"I had to try," she said simply. "Those paintings...they're how I found myself again. After the accident, I was lost in grief for so long. When I started painting our meeting, it was like the fog finally lifted." She glanced down, cheeks flushing. "I know it sounds silly, but painting our story gave me hope. It reminded me that life can still be beautiful, even after tragedy."

There were still cries and panicked murmurs cascading around them but Michael took the moment to pull her close, rubbing at her shivering shoulders as he had once done so many moons ago.

"It's not silly at all," he murmured into her hair. "I'm honored you find beauty and hope in me. But please, don't risk your life over it."

Mia nodded, then looked up at him with a rueful smile. "Nope, no dice. An artist will do crazy things for her muse."

And with that, his headstrong little introvert, turned towards the water and dove right back down.

Fucking hell. Okay, yup. He was going in.

He dove under as well, pushing his way through the murky water, his vision limited by the setting sun at the surface and the debris that floated in the lake.

Where was she? His own lungs burned for air.

Just when panic started to set in, he spotted a flash of color. Mia.

She struggled to free a large, abstract sculpture from where it had become ensnared by weeds on the lakebed. Michael swam hard, his muscular arms cutting through the water.

Together, they freed the sculpture. Michael's chest ached as he lifted it, kicking for the surface.

She better be right fucking behind him.

They broke through, water streaming down their faces. Michael sucked in a painful breath as he swam for the dock. After setting the sculpture down, he turned to find Mia treading water, her head tipped back with an expression of peace.

She was so beautiful it made his heart skip.

Why was she smiling?

And then, his crazy woman dove back under.

Of course.

Michael took a deep breath and dove back down into the dark depths. His eyes burned as he propelled himself deeper, searching for some of her art pieces. There – he spotted the edge of the metal sheet poking out from under a layer of silt.

Wrapping both arms around it, he kicked powerfully, racing for the shimmering light above. The need for air was overwhelming now, his chest tight. Just a little further.

With a gasp, he broke the surface, gulping oxygen into his starving lungs.

Fuck, shouldn't he have better lung capacity than this?

He was a professional athlete, for crying out loud.

Treading water, he angled the art piece and inspected it. Amazingly, it was still in one piece.

Michael swam for the dock, heaving the metal artwork onto the weathered planks. It landed with a hollow clang.

Mia swam over, dumped an armful of items and away she went.

Rest time over.

He dove back down after her.

At the bottom, he found Mia already at work disconnecting her art pieces from the submerged stand. Her hands moved swiftly, detaching sheet metal and wood with ease. Michael joined her efforts, gathering up the rescued artwork in his arms.

His lungs burned for air but he pushed on, determined to recover as many of her creations as possible. Mia worked tirelessly at his side, her movements graceful and efficient despite the challenging conditions.

As the last piece came free, she turned to him with an exhilarated smile. Michael's heart stuttered at the unbridled joy on her face, her hair fluttering wildly in the water. Wordlessly, they kicked for the surface.

Breaking through the water, Michael gulped grateful lungfuls of air.

Let's get you two out of there!" one of the rescuers called out, gesturing for them to climb aboard.

But Mia floated calmly in place, treading water as she gazed up at the sky, the hint of a smile on her face.

Michael's breath caught at the look of utter peace and contentment that transformed her features. With her hair fanning out around her and her lips parted slightly, she had never looked more beautiful, nor more angelic.

The desperation and panic from moments just minutes before had vanished, leaving behind a profound sense of belonging.

Here in the water, she was in her element.

Michael found he couldn't look away, transfixed by this serene, almost ethereal version of the woman who had captivated his heart. He ached to share in the joy and wonderment that radiated from her.

"Hey!" The rescuer's voice broke through his reverie. "We gotta get moving here. It's not safe for you to still be in the water."

Michael nodded absently, his gaze never leaving Mia's face. Yes, they would leave this water soon enough. But first, he silently promised her, they would find a place to swim together, always. A lake, an ocean...it didn't matter. All that mattered was seeing her like this again, unguarded and free.

With a contented sigh, she righted herself and dove beneath the surface once more. Michael followed close behind, his powerful strokes cutting through the murky water.

Mother fucker.

She was searching for more artwork, wasn't she?

Of course, she was.

Again and again, they came up, they went down, ignoring the shouts from one of the rescue boats whenever they surfaced. Before long, they had a collection of art stashed haphazardly on the remaining floating dock. The rest of the guests had already been removed to shore.

One lone rowboat bobbed there, a grouchy looking rescue member pouting at them.

There would probably be consequences for their refusal to be rescued later...

Mia treaded water beside him, her hair streaming around her like a dark halo. "Thank you," she said softly.

Michael's breath escaped in a rush, his voice husky with emotion. "Anything for you."

Together, they swam for the boat to deposit their recovered treasures. But Michael's mind was already leaping ahead, envisioning a place by the water for his Mia. A sanctuary where she could float and dream and create.

A home for them both.

Mia hauled herself up the ladder and into the boat, water cascading off her lithe body. Michael followed, unable to tear his eyes away as she emerged from the lake. Even soaked and bedraggled, she was captivating.

They sank down side by side on the metal floor, the boat's engine rumbling as it sped toward the shore. Adrenaline still pumped through Michael's veins, his heart hammering against his ribs.

Mia tipped her head back and laughed, the sound clear and melodic over the drone of the motor. She kicked her feet playfully, giggling like a child.

Michael studied her profile, enraptured by her unconcealed joy. The clouds had lifted from her soulful brown eyes, leaving them bright with mirth. She seemed lighter somehow, unburdened.

He ached to pull her into his arms. To cradle that slender body against his and promise that he would always protect her radiance. But Michael held back, giving her this moment of innocent delight.

Mia tipped her face up, as the now-gray sky started releasing small droplets on them. "Wasn't that incredible?" she said. "It was like the lake was calling to me. I could've stayed down there forever."

The rescuer grunted irritability.

Michael studied her profile. Droplets of water clung to her thick lashes. "You surprised me. I had no idea you were able to go underwater now."

She turned to him, a guilty smile on her face. "Yeah, I surprised me too. I haven't been able to go under. Today was...the first." She let out a wild laugh and yelled to the sky, "Oh my gods! I'm back!" Sobering, she reached across, giving his hand a squeeze. Her thumb absently stroked his knuckles. "Thank you for coming in with me."

Letting his gaze sweep over her, he committed each detail to memory. The elegant angles of her face, her skin glowing golden under the now dark and stormy sky. The way she moved with such fluidity and grace, even on land. His beautiful mermaid returned to her natural element.

Michael smiled to himself, picturing their future unfold. A secluded beach house, open and airy. Vaulted ceilings to display her sculptures, gauzy curtains fluttering in ocean breezes. Mia would bloom there like the most exquisite orchid.

And he would bask in her light, no longer haunted by past demons. Together, they would build something wondrous. A sanctuary, a home. For his angel, his mermaid. For them both.

For now, it was enough just to sit here together. Watching her bask in her element.

Chapter Thirty-Three

Epilogue: September 16, Saturday
Mia

The following September, Michael made sure to get a jump start on all the best autumnal activities. The past year proved he was intent on giving her every New England experience he could. In the time since her art exhibition, life had settled into a harmonious rhythm.

The morning sun streamed through the window as Mia stood in front of her easel, brush in hand, carefully adding the final touches to her latest masterpiece. Her eyes danced over the vivid colors, awash with pride at the growth she'd made – not just as an artist, but as an individual.

"Hey," Michael's voice called from behind her, causing her to jump slightly. He stepped closer, towering over her petite frame, his hands resting gently on her shoulders. "Whoops, sorry. I didn't mean to startle you. I think Asher's going to love that. He seems to prefer your paintings the most."

Mia blushed, tucking a strand of hair behind her ear, humming in agreement. "He does, doesn't he." She glanced around the studio, filled with her recent works – each piece reflecting a part of her soul, her experiences, and the love she and Michael shared. Michael still tinkered in the workshop but his newest hobby was sketching her nude.

"Just returning the favor" he would say when he would take all day sketching her.

"Are you ready for our day at The Big E?" Michael asked, excitement bubbling in his voice.

"Almost," Mia replied, placing her brush down and turning to face him. "I just want to finish this last part before we leave. I want the paint to be wet for it."

Mia's art was being showcased in galleries across the country and she was quickly making a name for herself within the art world. It was a dream come true, but more importantly, it was a testament to the strength she'd found within herself – the strength to move forward and live life fearlessly, despite the traumas of her past.

"All right," Michael announced, releasing Mia from his embrace. "Don't take long. The whole crew is waiting on us"

"I know. Ten minutes, top," Mia replied, excitement building within her.

Twenty minutes later, Mia walked out front to the driveway where everyone was gathered, playing with various kids in the front yard.

"Finally ready to head out?" Michael asked, his eyes shimmering with excitement.

"Absolutely," Mia replied, as she closed the door to their new lakefront home. Their friends' cheerful voices carried from the cars, where Danny and Megan were corralling their energetic kids, while Chloe and Kenny were fastening their little ones into car seats. Jen and John stood by Ryan and Lexie, laughing at something Kyle was saying, while Emma was checking out some of the flowers that Michael had planted.

As they all piled into their cars and headed toward The Big E, Mia leaned against Michael, feeling the steady rhythm of his heart beneath her hand. The anticipation of a day filled with joy and laughter warmed her soul, and she knew it would be a day to remember.

Upon arriving at the fairgrounds, the group was greeted by the enticing aroma of fried foods and the cheerful cacophony of carnival music. Bright lights illuminated the night sky, transforming the fair into an enchanting wonderland.

"Come on," Michael said, pulling Mia toward the Ferris wheel. "Let's start with a classic."

"Sounds perfect," she agreed, her heart swelling with happiness.

As they took their seats in the gently swaying carriage of the Ferris Wheel, Mia marveled at the beauty of the moment. She glanced down at her friends, who were scattered in their own carriages, all laughing and enjoying themselves.

Their laughter echoed across the fairgrounds as they ventured from ride to ride, their hands never leaving each other's grasp. They watched with amusement as Danny tried to win a giant stuffed animal for his kids, cheered Chloe on as she demolished her opponents in a game of ring toss, and snapped pictures of John and Ryan as they stuffed their faces with cotton candy and fried dough.

"Hey, did anyone try those deep-fried pickles yet?" Danny asked, eyes wide with curiosity.

"Best decision I've made today," John replied, patting his stomach with satisfaction.

"Better than riding the Ferris wheel with Jen?" Ryan teased, earning a playful nudge from Lexie.

"Of course not," John grinned, wrapping his arm around Jen's waist. "Nothing beats that."

Fucking voyeurs.

As they moved through the fair, they all did their best to avoid drawing attention to themselves. It wasn't easy; their fame had led to eager fans recognizing them from time to time. But for the most part, the fans respected the family atmosphere and let them enjoy it with their friends.

"Let's check out that haunted house!" Chloe suggested, pointing toward a dark, eerie-looking building.

"Only if you promise to protect me from the ghosts," Kenny joked, pulling her closer.

"Bullshit," she agreed, laughing as they headed toward the attraction.

As they approached the haunted house, Michael felt Mia shiver slightly beside him. He squeezed her hand gently, offering her a reassuring smile. "Really? A haunted house freaks you out?"

Mia rolled her eyes but smiled back at him. "I haven't been completely honest with you." She paused and looked around before lowering her voice. "I have a thing with clowns…"

Michael laughed and pulled her close. "Stick with me, and we'll be fine," he promised, leading her into the shadowy entrance.

They emerged minutes later, breathless with laughter and adrenaline. Their friends followed, buzzing with excitement over the unexpected twists and turns inside.

"Come on, there's one more thing I want to do before we head out," Michael said, leading the group toward a whimsical airplane-themed ride.

The sight of the colorful planes brought a smile to Mia's face. She turned and gave him a droll look. "Really dude?"

Michael threw his head back and roared his laughter into the sunset sky.

"Oh, a plane ride. What could go wrong?" Lexie asked, giving Michael an exhausted look.

"Count us in!" Danny replied, holding Megan's and the kids' hand as they jumped in line.

The warm glow of the setting sun cast long shadows over the fair, painting everything in hues of gold and orange. Michael turned to Mia, his eyes twinkling with mischief as they stood before the whimsical airplane-themed ride. The colorful planes swayed gently from their cables, inviting them to take a seat and let go of their worries.

"What do you think? Feel like taking a flight with me? I promise this one won't crash."

Mia looked up at him, her heart swelling with love as she took in the playful expression on his face. She couldn't help but smile, knowing that she'd follow him anywhere.

"You're a dork," she replied, her voice soft yet filled with warmth.

Their friends gathered around, each exchanging amused glances as they realized the absurdity of fitting into the child-sized planes. But it was the camaraderie and support among them all that brought them this far, and they wouldn't let something as trivial as size stop them from enjoying the moment together.

"All right, everyone, let's do this!" Jen announced with a grin, as she made her way to the nearest plane, tugging John along behind her.

"Bet I can fly higher than any of you!" Danny teased, hoisting himself and the kids into an orange plane while Megan laughed and climbed into the one beside him.

"Prepare for takeoff!" Chloe called out, securing herself and the kids in a green plane as Kenny tried to suppress a chuckle, squeezing into a neighboring blue one.

Ryan and Lexie shared a brief, competitive look before racing to try to squeeze into the same black plane with bright pink and blue highlights. They laughed good-naturedly as they pushed the other out of the way to vie for the driver's seat.

The others settled into their chosen planes with a much calmer level of energy albeit still passing the contagious enthusiasm.

With laughter and lighthearted banter filling the air, Michael helped Mia into a red plane and climbed in after her. They sat close together, practically pressed up against each other due to the limited space. Despite the tight squeeze, there was something undeniably intimate about their shared proximity, and Mia felt her cheeks growing warm.

"Ready?" Michael asked, his breath tickling her ear as he leaned in close.

"Always," she whispered back, her heart racing with excitement.

The ride operator gave them a thumbs-up, and with a sudden jolt, the airplanes lifted off the ground. They spun around, soaring through the air as laughter rang out from each of the planes. Even though they were clearly too big for the ride, none of them seemed to care – they were just happy to be enjoying the moment together, high above the fairgrounds.

As the wind whipped through Mia's hair and the vibrant colors of the fair blurred below them, she sighed and smiled into the breeze. Their friends' laughter carried out from the other planes, creating a symphony of joy that only served to heighten the magic of the moment.

"Thank you," she murmured, leaning into Michael's warm embrace as the ride continued to spin. "For everything."

"Anything for you, Angel," he replied, pressing a soft kiss to her temple. And as they clung to each other in the tiny airplane, Mia knew that together, they could conquer anything the world threw at them.

· · · ● · ● · ● · · ·

On the heels of an attack by a persistent stalker, Emma is forced to move in with her professional athlete ex-husband. Two hearts, a decade of secrets, and the second chance they never saw coming.

Click now to read the next book in the series – https://mybook.to/SSfs- **False Start** – A Steamy, Second Chance, Sports Romance

Discover More From Ella Haines

Springfield Spartans Standalone Romances:
Crystal Clear: A Steamy Springfield Stripper *Novella*
Offensive Holding: A Forbidden Friends-To-Lovers Stripper Romance *Novella*
Illegal Substitutions: A Friends-To-Lovers Steamy Sports Romance
Illegal Contact: A Steamy Sports Workplace Romance
Unsportsmanlike Conduct: A Steamy Single Mother Sports Romance
Intentional Grounding: A Steamy Opposites Attract Romance
False Start: A Steamy Second Chance Romance

Springfield Cyclones Standalone Hockey Romances:
Boarding: A Steamy Hockey Romance *Novelette*
Hooking: A Steamy Bachelor Auction Hockey Romance

Social Media Information - Ella Haines

Did you enjoy this book?

If so, please visit **www.EllaHaines.com** and sign up for the newsletter to receive additional scenes, freebies, and updates on future releases.

Newsletter signup here:
http://ellahaines.com/newsletter-for-freebies/

Also, if you have an eagle eye and caught any typos that slipped through the rounds and rounds of edits, take a moment and think if you'd like to be an ARC or beta reader for any future releases! If so, drop me an email! I'd love to have you on the team.

If you find any typos, you can let me know here: EllaHaines.author@gmail.com

About Author - Ella Haines

Ella Haines is a lover of all things love. Raised to know that she could be anything in the world, she made the wild and crazy decision to become a neurotic accountant. Balancing trial balances and filing taxes didn't quite fill her bucket, so she started dabbling in short stories. Those short stories evolved into complex storylines with empowered women, their families and friends, and the hunky men who adore them.

Request For Review

If this book brought you a smile, please review it on your purchasing platform (and copy it to Goodreads if you're willing and able).

This helps to spread the word about the book. Social proof to other readers is important.

It also makes the next book come out faster ;-)

Praise For Ella Haines

"It kept me hooked with the angst and sweet moments" - Nicole, book review

"All the feels from the frustration, anger, pain and hurt that came flowing out from the never ending angsty-ness truly hit hard many times throughout. Putting you through the ultimate wringer in what was a super emotionally charged ride." – Maddie, book blogger

"Is it friends to lovers? Women's lit? Humorous romance? A sports romance? In the end, it's a little bit of everything." – Cat, book review

"This is a well written emotional roller coaster, which is a friends / lover's sports romance, with angst, friendships, secrets, truths, drama, twists and turns, revelations, and love, which leads to an entertaining and compelling page turner. I look forward to reading more from this talented author whose work I highly recommend." - Wendy, book review

"I would definitely pick up another book or two by this author." – Reading In the Red Room, book blogger

Content/Trigger Warnings (may contain plot spoilers)

Warning:

This book will contain explicit language, PTSD, and sexy times. If these are upsetting for you – here is your warning to maybe avoid this book. Regardless, I promise there will be an HEA.

A note on PTSD: Remember, you're not alone. Seeking help is a sign of strength. Healing from trauma is a unique journey, recovery isn't always linear, and it can hit you when you least expect it. Reach out to professionals and support networks. Find hope in knowing that you can heal and grow. Reach out if you need any suggestions for resources or agencies that might be able to help.

This book was a work of my imagination, but I did consult with professionals when writing. Any mistakes are my own and a big thank you to the editors, proofreaders, and others who helped me craft this story.